NO TIME FOR
BROKEN MEN

A NOVEL

ISAIAH C ELLIOTT

No Time for Broken Men

Published in the United States by
Cyrus Elliott Communications
P.O. Box 122
East Dubuque, Illinois, 61025

ISBN-13: 978-0-9778592-1-4

ACKNOWLEDGMENTS

As this book evolved, my family, friends, and the strangers I've come to know as friends encourage me through troubled waters. With help gave me the opportunity to write *No Time for Broken Men*.

1

Erica Williams glanced with satisfaction around her impeccable house. Everything was big, fancy, and expensive, with vaulted ceilings higher than those in most museums and classic Victorian furniture. Why, she could entertain Clay's entire firm, branch offices and all, in the living room alone. It was a stark contrast to the dump she had grown up in—yet she felt no discomfort with its size or opulence. In fact, over the past few years, it had become her refuge. Erica sighed. If only her marriage were as perfect as her home.

She ran a careful hand along her jet-black hair, freshly pinned up into a sleek bun. The fleek edges sat neatly on her head. Her light mocha skin had a natural glow. At thirty-one, Erica was just as beautiful as she had been before she had gotten married and had two kids. With her curves and beauty queen smile that illuminated every room, every man imagined what they'd do with her if given the chance. But for reasons that remained a mystery, the man who counted the most didn't want to spend time with her.

As if on cue, the front door opened, then she heard Clay's heavy footsteps as he bounded across the foyer. Anger rushed through her as she braced herself for the fight she knew was coming.

A moment later, her husband appeared before her, with his short curly hair, hazel-brown eyes and lean frame. His pretty boy good looks had once made her heart flutter.

"Who were you with?" she asked in a quiet, strong voice.

He sighed. "Why would you think I was with anyone?"

She gestured to his loose tie and wrinkled shirt. "I can guess."

He pushed past her. "Don't start this shit, Erica, not tonight."

"Don't *start*?" she asked, her voice rising.

"You're going to wake up the kids."

"No, I won't," she said, fighting for control, "They're at Lashay's until morning."

He stalked into the kitchen, and she followed closely behind.

"You haven't been home for days, and I can smell her cheap perfume on you." Her voice cracked. "Am I supposed to be all smiles and sunshine when you stumble in here in the middle of the night? Why, Clay, when I've tried my best to make you happy? Well, I draw the line at being made a fool of."

Clay wandered from room to room, as if moving around could throw Erica off his trail, or at least make her lose interest in berating him. It wasn't working. At least he had left the kitchen, with its ready-made arsenal of plates, knives, and pots—Erica's weapons of choice during previous altercations. He considered stopping in the living room to fix himself a drink, then instead stormed down the hall to their bedroom and began throwing clothes in a suitcase.

"You still didn't answer my question. Where have you been?"

"I had some pertinent business I needed to attend to," he said, a light flush suffusing his face. "That's why I've been gone."

"Where are you going now?"

He sighed. "More business, Erica. The world doesn't stop just because you wish it were so."

"But what kind of business do you have at this time of night?"

"If you must know, I have arrangements to make before my business trip."

"A business trip to where?"

"To Chicago. I need to go there before the awards ceremony."

"Do you think I'm stupid, Clay? You don't need to be gone this much. Nobody does."

"Woman, I go out because you never shut your damn mouth. I work day and night making money so we can live in this nice big house. Last thing I want to do is come home and argue with you all the damn time." He shot her a seething look, then returned to his packing. "That's too much for one man to handle."

Erica stepped toward him. "Maybe if you stopped spending money like it grows on trees, you wouldn't have to work so much. And maybe"—she poked him with a perfectly manicured nail—"if you treated me right, you wouldn't have to deal with my bullshit."

"Don't poke me, woman," Clay growled. "I make that money for *us*. Respect your place."

Erica laughed. "Respect my place? How about you respect *your* place? A real man would spend time with his family. But you're not a real man, Clay. You're a fucking *boy*."

"Boy?" he raged. "I'll show you who the boy is, bitch." For a moment he looked as though he might strike her. Then he thought better of it and stormed into his office, slamming the door behind him.

Erica stood there for a minute, fists clenched, as she debated following him. Then a better idea came to her, bringing a small, twisted smile to her lips. She ran back to the kitchen, grabbed the pliers, and ran out to the circular drive, where Clay had parked his prized BMW. With the pliers, she squeezed the tire tube stems and let the air out. The wheezing of the air filled her with a sense of power and control. Clay always called the shots, but not tonight. After all four tires were flat as pancakes, she strolled back into the house, flopped down on the leather sofa and waited.

A few minutes later, she watched in quiet satisfaction as Clay stormed out of the house without a word or a backward glance.

3

Erica walked over to the window and peeked out. She watched as he got to his car and saw the flattened tires, then popped the truck and fumbled around inside. He grasped a dark, shiny object and stormed back into the house. He found her in the living room, a smug look on her face.

"Are you crazy? Do you have any idea how much it's going to cost to get that fixed?" He slammed the gun down on the coffee table.

Erica screamed. "I told you I don't like guns, you asshole."

"I bought this for protection for the business," he said.

"What dumb-ass business? You're a tax man." Her voice grew louder as her eyes slid to the gun. "What's that for?"

"I told you, it's for business."

"I told you I don't like guns." Erica shot him a look filled with rage.

"But you never told me why," he said.

"You wouldn't understand."

He paused. "It's imperative I have it for business."

"If it was for business, why did you bring it in the house?"

"Erica," he said, shaking his head. He sighed as he let go of her wrist and stooped down to pick up the gun. "I'll put this in a safe place."

"Listen to me, Clay. I'm tired of living like this."

He stopped to look at her. "What's that supposed to mean?"

"You know what it means. You're never here. It's so bad our own daughter wanted her birthday present to be a family breakfast together." Her head rocked side to side. "Our ten-year-old said that for her birthday, she wanted to have Sunday breakfast and play with her dolls with her daddy like he used to." She noted the slightly surprised look on his face. "Don't tell me you forgot?"

"No, of course not. I'll be here tomorrow morning, and you'll come to the awards ceremony Friday night with me."

"Are you trying to negotiate a deal with your daughter's birthday wishes?"

He shook his head. "No. I'm just saying we'll be together."

"We'll be together alright, but because you need me there for appearance's sake. Not because you actually want me there." She swallowed. "I'll go because I gave you my word."

"I appreciate that."

She nodded her head, her chin jutting out proudly. "Well, good. Bernice put blankets on the sofa in your office. I think you should stay there tonight."

Clay gritted his teeth, then nodded and walked down the long hallway to his office, while Erica retreated to the kitchen.

A few minutes later, she was about to turn in when she noticed the office door was slightly ajar. Quietly, she headed down the hall and peeked inside. Clay sat in the desk chair, his back to the door. He sniffed and wiped his nose before picking up a soft black briefcase and stuffing papers into it.

Something about the behavior was odd, even for Clay. Whatever was he up to?

Erica continued to watch as he reached into the top desk drawer, moving his hand like he was searching for something. He pulled out a key, then stuck his hand back in the drawer, this time pulling out a folder. Erica stared, wide-eyed, as he strode over to the file cabinet and used the key to open the top drawer.

"One of these days, Erica," he muttered as he placed the gun and the folder in the cabinet, "I may just end your bullshit for good."

This time, Erica could not stop the tiny, terrified squeak that escaped her lips. Clay's head whipped around, his eyes narrowing at the door. For a moment she thought he might get up, but then he shook his head and quietly closed the drawer, then returned to his desk.

Erica stood there for a long moment, then slipped down the hall, her husband's words still ringing in her ears.

One of these days, Erica...

2

"Erica, I love the way you have this room set up," Lashay remarked as she poured more syrup on her pancakes. "Antique-looking but with a modern feel."

"Thanks," Erica replied, eyeing her sister across the dining room table. "We like it too. Don't we, Clay?"

Clay grunted from behind his newspaper, his half-eaten plate of food in front of him.

Frowning, Erica returned to her own meal, almost wishing she hadn't asked her sister to stay for breakfast when she'd dropped the children off. She had wanted things to feel normal, if only for them, but even the delicious smell of bacon wafting through the house did little to hide the tension. If anyone could pick up on tension, it was Lashay. A petite woman with short natural curls, Lashay had a feistiness that more than made up for her stature. Her short, curvy body made her the desire of many men. In fact, aside from her chocolate complexion and loud mouth, Lashay reminded Erica of herself. She loved her sister almost as much as she loved her children, but Lashay thrived on conflict, and Erica had had enough of it to last her ten lifetimes. Erica knew Lashay gave her opinion on any subject, whether she was an expert on it or not. If you wanted peace of mind, like it or not, she would give you a piece of hers. Everyone knew it, and everyone had the same thing to say about it: "That's just Lashay."

"Anybody want more French toast?" Bernice, the housekeeper, asked as she walked around the table with a steaming plate.

Lashay reached for the plate. "Bernice, old biddy, you really have outdone yourself this time."

"I'm sure any food tastes better than what they serve you at the psycho ward," Bernice quipped, but she was smiling.

"Bernie, I'm surprised you can see through those Coke bottles you call glasses," Lashay said, and they laughed together. She then turned to her brother-in-law, who still had his nose buried in the financial pages.

"So, Clay, I hear you get a big award Friday night. How many people did you cheat out of their money to get it?"

He glared at her. "It's an award from the Chamber of Commerce for building the largest tax franchise in the state, and a pretty big deal, though the best part about the evening will be your absence."

"You never know. I might show up and take the award myself." She laughed.

"And you wonder why you don't have any friends."

She stabbed at a piece of French toast. "Just because you never met any of them don't mean I don't have any."

He scowled at her, but the desired effect was lost when he started sniffing and wiping at his nose.

"What's wrong with you? You back on that stuff?" Lashay said.

He ground his teeth together. "Erica, please tell your sister not to come to my awards ceremony."

Erica shook her head at her sister. "Lashay, not right now."

"Mommy, I'm done and so is CJ. I'm ready to play house," Chloe said.

7

Erica smiled at her daughter, who had long, thick hair with hazel-green eyes.

"Okay, baby. Go clean up and I'll be right in," Erica said, smiling at her.

"Auntie Lashay, you can come to my room too."

Lashay glanced at Clay, then back at her niece. "Oh, baby, I'm sorry, but Auntie has to run a few errands. Then I have to rest up for my singing gig tonight. I hope you like my gift."

Chloe picked up the new doll and squeezed it. "I love it, Auntie Lashay. Daddy, time to play."

Clay laid the paper down, then pushed his chair back from the table. "Baby, I'll be in there soon. I have to go check on the men fixing my tires."

Erica ignored his comment or didn't hear it. She just kept eating her French toast.

"'Bye, Auntie Lashay," Chloe said, giving her a hug before running down the hallway.

"Bernice, can you take CJ to his room and keep him occupied for a couple hours?" Erica asked.

"Of course. Enjoy your time with your little birthday girl."

CJ jumped up and started clapping. Bernice put her hand on CJ's shoulder to calm him down. He relaxed and began to tiptoe down the hallway.

Clay followed after Bernice and CJ. "I'll go check my car."

Lashay watched Clay until he was out of sight. "Damn. What the hell is going on in this house? This felt more like a funeral than a relaxed birthday breakfast."

"Lashay, you just don't know…"

"Yo, fo' real. I know one damn thing. I should've just taken Chloe out to eat."

"She enjoyed herself, so stop tripping."

Lashay rolled her eyes and took a bite of her breakfast. "Please, slow yo' roll and come clean."

"I don't feel like it right now, but I'll explain everything to you later."

Lashay nodded. "Later, huh? Later might be too late."

"Too late for what?" Erica said.

"I don't trust him, sis. Not one damn bit."

"What do you mean?"

"I can feel it. Why is he always trying to keep you from your family?"

"When you say family, you mean you?"

"You know what I mean. Daddy did that same shit, keeping Mom from Grandma and Grandpa."

Erica's mind circled the comment and compared it with Clay's recent actions.

"Actually, I do know what you mean," she said quietly.

"Right now I'm feeling like Grandma was right when she told you not to marry young."

Erica shot her an indignant look. "I was twenty-one—"

"Yeah, and he was thirty-one. That's a big gap."

"My age isn't the problem, and neither is Clay's. The issue is he no longer wants to spend time with his family."

Lashay shook her head. "That's that shit Dad started doing. Remember? He used to love being with us whenever he could and doting on us. Being a good husband and family man. But then he lost his job and couldn't find a new one. He started spending more time drinking and less time at home. The alcohol messed with his mind and made him paranoid. He became obsessed and so jealous that he didn't even want Mom talking to another man. If he thought she was looking at another guy, he would hit her in the stomach or the back of the head, places that wouldn't leave visible marks or bruises, so Grandma and Grandpa wouldn't know."

"Clay has never hit me!"

"Not yet, but he is doing that other shit that leads up to it. You guys just in the argument stage, about him spending money without your knowledge and him staying out all the time."

Erica paused and thought about what she'd heard him mumble the night before.

"You know how this cycle works, Erica. Remember that night

9

Mom found out Dad was spending our singing lessons money? That night was beginning of Dad taking shit to the next level."

"Why you always bringing up those horrible things?"

"Because if I can't save you, at least maybe I can save my niece and nephew."

Erica got quiet and turned her head to wipe away the moisture building up in her eyes before Lashay could see it.

"See, sis, I only brought that up because you don't want your kids going through the same shit we did."

"I know, and I miss Mom so much. Every time I think about that night, I get sad."

"That's the problem. You need to be getting pissed off. That's why Clay better watch his step."

"You're right, and if he keeps messing up, trust me, sis, it is over."

"You give me the word, and me and my crew will make sure he sleeps with the fishes." Lashay paused, eyes flashing. "You know I'll fuck your husband up if he's messing with my family."

Erica rolled her eyes. "Bernice is right. You crazy."

"Crazy is as crazy does." Lashay responded, then burst into laughter.

Erica laughed too, but her eyes were weary. "Okay, okay, enough depressing shit. My head hurts and I need to go and check on my kids. Chat later?"

"You sure you don't want to sing with me tonight? It will take your mind off things," Lashay asked.

"You know better than that, Shay. I'm retired from the mic. I knew you had a reason going down memory lane. You know them Mom thoughts always make me want to sing."

"That is what she wanted, for us to sing together."

"That's your thing now."

"One day I'm going to be doing a duet with Kem. Then you going to wish you were singing again."

"If you make it to that level, then you won't need me to sing with you."

Lashay took one last bite from her plate before pushing away from the table. "I'm out. Tell Bernie she put her old wrinkled foot into that food."

"Girl." Erica laughed as her sister kissed her forehead.

Lashay grinned. "I'll see you at the awards show Friday night."

Erica's eyes went round. "Please don't come to the awards ceremony. That's his night. He'll be furious."

"I don't care about his awards. I want to talk to the DJ doing the after-party. G Money is a big record producer with contacts."

"Lashay! Clay is serious about you not coming."

"Okay, okay, sis. I won't let Clay see me there, but I'll see you Friday."

The two hugged, then Lashay let herself out while Erica carried her plate into the kitchen. As she set it in the sink, she felt a sharp pain in her side. She put her hand on her stomach and grimaced. It wasn't the first time she'd felt the sharp pain. It had come and gone with some frequency the last few days, but she worried it could be a problem with the new baby. She already had an appointment to visit her doctor in two days, and she'd let him know about it then. She thought more and more about Lashay's words. They were penetrating the wall she had built up since that awful night—the night their lives had changed forever.

3

Erica woke up to hear her parents fighting again. Then it got quiet, and Erica heard the shower, soon followed by the familiar creak of the water closet. Her mom had drained the hot water. She'd done it before. Even at eight years old, Erica knew this would prompt an argument.

Her mom's footsteps came rushing toward her room. She leapt back into bed and pretended she was sleeping as her mom tiptoed in. With one eye cracked open, she watched her mother grab the superglue from her school supplies and dash back out. The front door opened about the same time as her father stormed out of the bathroom and headed for the water heater closet. He mumbled angrily as he turned the water heater back on and returned to his shower.

When the bathroom door closed, her mom came rushing back into her room. "Wake up, baby. We're going for a drive."

"What happened to your face, Momma? Are you okay?"

"Don't worry. Get up and go wait out by the car."

Still wearing her pajamas, Erica rushed down the hallway. Her mother followed quickly behind with little Lashay in her arms. They had just made it to the car when they saw their father, Keith, come running from the house. He rushed up to the car and tugged on the door, but her mom had locked all the doors.

Erica could barely see the shadow of his twelve-inch Afro through the foggy, steamed-up windows. He stood next to the window, hollering, "Get out of the car, Debra. You ain't taking my kids anywhere!"

The car roared to life, and the dashboard glowed an eerie green. Erica could see Lashay seating in her car seat, her little eyes wide, with her head swiveling from one sound to the other, but she didn't seem afraid. Her mom fumbled with the gearshift.

"I'll take my kids anywhere I want, motherfucker," Debra yelled at the closed window, then they screeched out of the driveway.

Erica turned around to see her father rummaging through the grass. Finally, he picked something—it looked to be a set of keys—up from the ground.

She watched, terrified, as he tried to get into his car. But the key wouldn't go in the lock, so he yanked off his shirt, wrapped it around his fist, and punched in the car window. In the dim light, shards of glass scattered across the lawn.

Erica clutched her seatbelt when they hit a pothole. She wondered if they'd make it to wherever they were headed. She prayed they would. It wasn't until they reached a stoplight that her mother finally spoke.

"We're going to spend the night at my friend's place, but don't say anything about tonight. Understand?"

"I'll lie to your friend, but won't they see your black eye?"

"It's not lying," her mother replied. When they reached a red stop light a few blocks from the house, she slammed the gearshift into park, hit the trunk button and jumped out of the car. A moment later, she returned to the driver's seat wearing dark shades just as the light turned green. Erica glanced sideways at her, wondering how she could see the road with sunglasses on.

They rode in silence. Every so often Erica looked behind them, but she didn't see her father. They pulled up to another stoplight, and suddenly a car barreled out of nowhere and swerved right in front of them.

"Oh, shit."

It was her father's Cadillac.

Her mother tried to put the car in reverse as her father jumped out and rushed over to the car. His face was full of rage. Her mother had forgotten to lock the door when she'd climbed back inside. With one quick movement, her father snatched the door open and yanked her from the car. The car jerked as her foot left the accelerator. Her father pinned her mother against the open door and slid inside the car, jamming his foot on the brake.

"Now, see, Debra, you choose to act a fool," he muttered as he put the car back in drive and began to drag her alongside the car.

Her screams filled the quiet midnight air, but no one was around to hear her. She stumbled over the rough-edged potholes in the asphalt as she struggled to keep up with the car. Finally, when Erica was sure her mom was going to die, her dad pulled over to the side of the road. When they stopped, her mother tried to break away, but he lunged after her. He wrapped his massive hand around her throat, picked her up, and slammed her against the hood. Erica's eyes widened in terror. She felt completely helpless. She couldn't do anything to protect her mother.

Her mother frantically slapped and clawed at her father face's until he could no longer keep her against the car. Letting her go, he turned away. Her mother didn't hesitate. She leaped onto his back and dug her nails deep into the back of his head. He grabbed her by her hair and flung her over his shoulders like a rag doll, tossing her onto the hood of the car. The sound of her body connecting with metal broke little Lashay's horror-induced trance.

As she began crying, Erica watched their father pick up their mother's one-hundred-twenty-pound body and drag her over to his Cadillac. He threw her into the car and drove it to the side of the road. Then he dragged her back to the Celica. "Erica, get in the backseat with your sister," he said.

Too scared to argue, she did as she was told. He threw her

mother into the passenger seat and climbed in.

Crying filled the car. Her mom and Lashay couldn't stop sobbing. She could see her father's bruised face steadily swelling. He wasn't crying, though.

Finally, looking meaner than all hell, he screamed angrily at her sobbing mother, "Why the hell you put superglue in my car door locks? I had to break my fucking window to get into my car."

"Because you were going to go out and spend the money for the girls' singing lessons."

Sitting in the back, watching the whole scene, Erica was left feeling paralyzed.

"You put glue in my locks, again. I'm going to kill you."

Suddenly, her mother started swinging at him. While he dodged the blows, the car swerved from side to side, barely missing a streetlight pole. He pulled over to the side of the road and turned off the car, snatching the keys from the ignition in one horrifyingly quick movement. He leapt out of the car, walked to the passenger side, reached in, and yanked her mother out by her neck, her feet kicking in the air. She wouldn't stop screaming, and all Erica could do was listen and be scared. She held Lashay's little hand and watched through the window as he dragged her to the back of the car, opened the trunk, and put her inside.

Erica could hear banging on the inside of the trunk, then her mother's muffled voice coming through the backseat of the car.

"*Let me out of here, motherfucker...*"

4

The nightmare always hit Lashay when she least expected, and tonight, it hit with a vengeance. She woke up twisted in her sheets, screaming for Shorty. He was the only one who could calm her down once the terrors from her childhood came for a visit. He banged on the door, trying to get in.

"Baby girl, unlock the door," he yelled, but she was so caught up in her nightmare, she didn't hear him. She just kept screaming his name over and over.

Desperate to help her, he kicked in the cheap luan plywood door. His Timberland boots smashed through the wood, ripping the door right off the hinges. When it swung open, suffocating heat blasted at him as he rushed over to her.

"I got you babe," he said, unwinding the soaked sheets from her body. He scooped her up and carried her out of their room that felt like a sauna. "I got you."

She nestled her head into his chest. Shorty was a tiny man who was so ugly he was famous for it. Many times, when people tried to describe him, they would say, "You mean that short ugly cat?" There were even rumors that the police had his fingerprints in a file marked "Ugly Cat." But he wasn't ugly, not really, at least she didn't think so. Besides, she was pretty enough for both of them.

He carried her into their office-den and laid her down on the loveseat against the wall. He draped a blanket over her, then asked, "Can I get you anything?"

Her man always took care of her. She loved that about him. She smiled at him. "Babe, I'm okay now."

"Let me get you something to drink." He hurried over to the sink to pour her a glass of water.

"Baby, really I'm okay now," she said weakly from the sofa, but he knew what she needed, and it was about time she let him take care of her.

He sat down next to her, handing her the water. "You serious? I thought something was wrong with you?"

Sweat dripped down her forehead. After the nightmares, she always felt helpless and afraid, just like when she was a little girl and her big sister tried to shield her from their fighting parents. She drained half the glass. She guessed Shorty did know what she needed. She wiped her sleeve across her wet lips. "I'm fine now."

Shorty hated seeing her like this, but it also made him feel like her man when she let him take care of her. He didn't believe for one minute that she was fine. "Why the hell were you in there with the door locked?"

"I don't know. I just needed some time on my own and must have fallen asleep."

He laced his fingers in hers. "Were you thinking about your childhood stuff again?"

She pushed herself up. "I don't know. Maybe. I was thinking about how Erica and I used to sing together, and how together we always killed it on stage, but then I guess, I got to thinking about what happened with our parents, and how Erica always shielded me from everything."

"Babe, you have to let that stuff go. Where the meds the doctor gave you?"

17

She reached her hands behind his neck and pulled him closer to her, preparing to kiss him. "I don't need those meds."

He pulled away from her. "Why?"

She grinded her teeth. She hated explaining stuff to Shorty or anyone else for that matter. She did what she did, and no one could stop her or tell her what to do. "Because one, they don't work and two, they make my hair fallout."

"But babe, the doctor said those meds will help you cope with everything when you start feeling anxious."

"I just have a lot of stuff on my mind.

His forehead furrowed as he looked at her. "Like what? The trunk incident?"

She shook her head. "You see why I don't tell you the whole story… You keep throwing that shit up in my face."

He reached for her, but she wouldn't have any of it. He kept trying to touch her anyway. "No babe, I'm just saying I don't like to see you suffer and that stuff makes you…."

Now he did it. He really knew how to push her buttons, and anytime he brought up the past or the pills, she came out swinging. "Make me what?

He realized his mistake too late, so he played it dumb. "I don't know."

His reply seemed to satisfy her for the time being. "Listen, at work tonight, G Money's boys were in the club, and one of them told me G Money's going to DJ Clay's after-party. I'm going to talk to him about making a record."

Shorty paused. "Didn't you tell me Erica and Clay didn't want you there?"

She waved her hand back and forth. "Yes—at least, Clay doesn't. But this is the chance I need."

He rubbed her leg up and down. "Maybe it isn't the right time to see that nigga. Besides, he thinks he's a big-time street hood, trying to get street cred. Plus, those fuddy-duddy people won't be playing hip hop."

"I'm not asking you to go with me."

He stopped moving his hand. "Oh... Good... 'Cause I've got to do something with Moe."

She didn't notice his reaction. She just kept right on talking. "I know my sister. She needs me to be there. She hates being there by herself."

"Babe, did she invite you?"

He tried cradling her in his arms, but she kept swatting him away, getting more and more excited about the award party and what she had planned. "Well, no, but I seen it her eyes. She knows Clay's lying about taking a business trip to Chicago. The ceremony's been planned for months, and now all sudden three days before it, he's going to Chicago for business? No one believes that shit."

"I know that your sister is important to you, but you have to let her live her life."

"You just don't understand. I know when my sister needs me." Of course, her mind shifted back to her reoccurring nightmare and what happened that night all those years ago. If she knew anyone, she knew her sister.

"What I don't understand is, here I am the man, who wants to live the rest of my life with you, and you can't even tell me the whole story that makes you go crazy every time you think about it."

Lashay turned her head to look at him. She could smell his cologne, and damn, he smelled good. She thought about telling him the whole story, but she and Erica had promised never to tell anyone what happened after they got home, and their father took their mother out of the trunk. She might tell her future husband, but that ceremony would be a long way off. "I'll tell you the whole story, one day. I promise you. I'm just not up to it now."

He shrugged his shoulders. "Babe, you can tell me when you're ready, but that's not why I brought that up. I didn't mean to upset you."

"It's okay," she said, wiping the sweat off her forehead with a napkin.

19

He took the dirty napkin and the empty glass and set them on the table, before returning to her. "We don't need to talk about that now. You look sexy as hell when you're upset." He held her chin in his hand. "You know I'll support whatever decision you make on that, right?"

She inched closer to him, resting her head on his chest. He reached down and rubbed her thigh. She didn't protest. In fact, it felt good. Her nipples grew hard, and she hoped he would soon follow.

"Damn," Lashay said to herself. As she looked into his eyes, all she could focus on was how much he cared about her. She noticed the bulge coming from his jeans and reached down to grab it.

He began playing with her nipples, watching as they grew firmer with his touch.

"Okay, okay, bae," she said, suddenly Silly Putty in his arms.

"Shorty," she groaned as he began sliding his hand between her legs. Her panties were already soaked with her love juices.

Shorty always took care of her. Now, she was going to take care of him. She stood up and stepped in front of him. She placed one hand on his crotch and unzipped his jeans with the other. When she reached inside, she found he was ready. She dropped to her knees, eye level with his penis. She put it to her watering mouth and sucked it. He moaned. It only encouraged her to keep going. She licked the split, while her hands pumped the base. While she was getting busy with everything that made him a man, he unhooked her bra and let it drop to the floor. Her breasts pointed like gumdrops against his thighs as she continued massaging his member using her tongue. Her mouth. Her lips…The woman knew how to work him. He pushed deeper reaching the back of her throat. He might be short in height, but he was extra-large where it counted. She gagged at first, but then relaxed allowing to ease in. When she pulled off him, a popping noise filled the space between them, and damn if that didn't turn him on too.

She led him over to the desk, pushing her ass into him, as she cleared the desk. Then she began kissing him. Nice, slow, and sexy as hell. They were both ready for the next act. He flipped her around and bent her over. She lifted up her skirt. He ripped off her panties and rammed into her so quickly she let out a whimper. He slammed into her again and again. She moaned as he went deeper with every stroke. The faster he moved, the more she moaned. When he was almost at his peak, he flipped her over and laid her on her back, stroking her until she came. Then he rammed into her, and they came together and fell to the floor, too weak to stand.

They laid side by side panting for breath. Eventually, when they returned to their senses, Shorty helped her up, then gathered his clothes and walked over to his desk. "I'm going to take a shower and clean up. You're welcome to join me."

"Damn, I love you," she giggled.

As matter of fact, she was ready for round two.

5

Clay's plane landed at the Philip S.W. Goldson International Airport, about eighteen miles from Belize City. Belize was off the eastern coast of Central America, bordering Mexico. The population was over three hundred thousand. He walked to the baggage area and claimed his bags, then headed outside the airport. He stood on the curb. The sunshine and fresh air made him feel relaxed.

A young man picked up his bags, and Clay got into the back of a Honda Accord. The driver played Punta music on the radio on the drive into the city. Clay reached into one of the bags and pulled out some pictures of a house on the Caribbean island of San Pedro, Belize. He'd been to Belize several times, but not since buying the house. The smell of sea intensified as he glanced at the ocean that ran alongside the road. Men were fishing along the shoreline. There were people everywhere. They walked on the sidewalks or rode bikes. Many of them were of dark complexion, and they dressed and looked like regular black people back in the States.

The Honda pulled up to the Fort Robert Hotel and Marina. Clay paid his cab fare and walked inside to check in. When he finally entered his room, he began to really relax. The five-hour plane ride had worn him out. He spread out on the bed and stared at the ceiling.

Twenty minutes later, a knock at the door brought a smile to Clay's face. He opened it to find a short, curvy woman with long dark hair and green eyes, a thin gold chain around her neck that complemented her caramel complexion. She threw down her bags and jumped into his arms.

"Hey, baby, I missed you so much," she said, covering his face with kisses. He tried to stop her, but she was relentless.

"I missed you, too, Leslie. Six months is too long to be away from you," he said.

But she didn't care what he had to say. She just pushed him to the bed as she undressed him, and for the next hour they attacked each other. Clay took in her body as he took off her clothes. He ran his hand down her thick, toned thighs. She ripped off his shirt and threw it on the floor. Then she tore off his pants. He pushed her on her back on the bed, and she took off her panties and spread her legs open to reveal her pleasure zone. He took off his underwear. He lay on top of her and entered her, moving in the rhythm of an island dancer. She moaned and gripped his arms tightly. Her body squirmed as she was soaked with her juices.

They went at it until he finally came and they both went limp on the bed, lying there and breathing hard as they stared up at the ceiling. Then they turned toward each other and Clay smiled and went into deep thought. *I love this woman—her positive energy— the way I feel like my old self when I'm with her.* Clay loved how she was always down for anything and not afraid to take chances, unlike Erica, who wanted to be by the book when it came to doing business.

He remembered the day when she'd walked into his small office to get her taxes done. She was nineteen then and had only been in the States two years.

After he'd finished her taxes, she'd started sending all her siblings and friends to him, helping to build his business before he'd started working for the Unit. They'd begun a relationship. By the time Leslie found out he was married, with just one child at the time, it was too late. She was already pregnant, and her green card was about to run out. Clay had supported her through the pregnancy with financial help and promised to leave Erica when the time was right.

Clay showed her some bogus separation papers to prove he really was going to leave his wife, and she thought they were going to be a family once his divorce was final. But he didn't want to get a divorce at the time and knew she would be a problem here. So he took it to another level. She never found out that he was the one who'd called INS and told them she was breaking the law, so she got deported.

"I'm only here for a few days, so we can't miss the boat," he mumbled as he snatched up the keys. "We need to get dressed and go."

On their way to the dock, the smell of seafood filled the air. As they walked along the boardwalk, Clay watched fishermen get on boats and sail off into the sea. Other people gathered on their boats, sitting around, talking and drinking beers, as they continued to walk to the boat at the end of the dock. As the deckhand eased the boat out of the pier, Clay watched the horizon. Behind him there were other boats and people snorkeling and customers enjoying seafood, but he was only concerned with what was always just out of reach. Out on the water, he admired the wonderful shades of aqua, turquoise and cobalt blue. It reminded him of his favorite marbles when he was a little kid. He reached into his bag and handed Leslie some papers.

She looked at the papers. "What? You are getting divorced? I'm so happy." She hugged him. "Now, we can get married and you can bring your daughter and she can meet her brother and your mom can meet her grandson. We'll be so happy."

After a forty-five-minute ride, the boat docked on the island key of San Pedro, an island about thirty-five miles east of Belize City. The small island was surrounded by blue waters. The shops were filled with tourists. Clay was excited to see the new house he had purchased. Leslie approached the old Mercedes 190 on the right side and got in.

"That's right, I keep forgetting it's the opposite of the States," he said. Before he could close the door, Leslie floored the gas pedal. Clay looked up at her, eyes wide. "Are you mad or just crazy?"

She giggled. "I'm just excited."

Most of the houses were English colonial architecture. Gift shops, boutiques, bars, cafes, and restaurants adorned the side of the streets.

"I wish I was going to be here for more than three days. I have to be back for awards show on Friday."

"Love, I wish I could be with you when you get your award."

"There will be plenty of other awards, and when I move here, and you'll be right by my side when I get them."

"I know. We're doing so well here. I don't see why you just don't move now."

"I have to finish setting things up in the States. I should be done in three or four months, then I'll start the process."

Her face brightened with excitement. "I can't wait, love."

Clay was proud of himself. In the next three days, he would put the final touches on his Belize setup; he had businesses and bank accounts in different names, and no one would ever find him. He'd originally set everything up to hide money and access from Erica. She had threatened him with divorce too many times already, and he didn't want her to get a single dime. He was also ready if something went wrong with his business partners. Once back in the States, he had three months to move his entire family to Belize. Well, except Erica. He had other plans for her. Also, he needed to figure out how and when he would tell Leslie about CJ.

Twenty minutes later, she pulled the Mercedes into the driveway of a luxury house. It was beautiful. A two-story oceanfront house located directly on the beach, with a large outdoor balcony located just off the master suite. He knew he could spend the rest of his life here.

25

As they walked up, the door opened. An older woman stood while a little boy ran out of the house behind her. He was around the same age as CJ and looked like him.

"Daddy." He jumped into Clay's arms, and all three of them walked into the house.

6

The ballroom's giant crystal chandeliers illuminated the tables with hundreds of bright lights. Each round table held an exploding floral centerpiece. The radiant colors contrasted with the cream-colored tablecloths adorned with gold charger plates. The crowd packed the room, everyone dressed as elegantly as the white-gloved servers greeting guests at the door.

The waitstaff, dressed in black jackets, scanned the room, ready to pour wine for anybody who wanted it. After social hour and an extensive meet-and-greet time, the four hundred guests were signaled to take their seats by a faint clink from a crystal glass. The women sparkled in the light against the black-tuxedoed men as they seated themselves.

Erica's sequined mermaid cocktail dress swept the floor as she walked. She sat at a table near the front and looked around the room to see the city's most powerful people, there to honor her husband. Seated around her table were Clay, his mother and Aunt Mena, then Mayor Berry Caldwell and his wife Sarah. Next were State Senator Wally Braggs and his wife Brenda, and Police Chief Sean MacKay and his wife, Margaret.

Erica noticed Clay's close friend Officer Frank Carter towering over the crowd at the side entrance, eyeing everyone who walked into the ballroom. Clay had probably hired him to ensure the invitation-only code was enforced. His six-foot frame filled his black Armani suit. His hair and goatee were neatly trimmed, with grey around the edges. He was always by his long-time friend, hobnobbing with the money crowd.

A tall, well-built man came from behind a curtain in front of a makeshift stage. Cheers erupted from the crowd. The man walked to the podium and grabbed the microphone.

"Hello, everyone," his voice boomed, "We all know why we are gathered here today." He paused for effect. "This is a very special occasion." He waited until the applause died down. "The Business Summit would like to honor a man who pretty much does everybody's taxes in this city." He laughed, and the crowd laughed with him. Erica had butterflies in her stomach, which intensified as he continued. Clay held her hand tight across his lap with one hand and had his other arm behind her chair. He played his role well.

"Without further ado, this year's Tax Board State Public Service Award goes to…" He held the card out for dramatic effect. "Clay Williams."

The entire room exploded with applause. The audience turned to watch him pull his jacket together and walk toward the stage. He approached the podium and shook the announcer's hand, leaned in for a quick shoulder bump, and grabbed the microphone. More applause followed. Once it subsided and everyone returned to their seats, Clay began to speak.

"Hello to you all. I don't know what to say, except that I am thankful. As many of you know, I'm rarely speechless." Everyone in the audience laughed. "I want to acknowledge the great introduction by a man whom I respect." Everyone clapped again. "He's a hard act to follow."

Erica glanced around the table. His mom, his aunt, and the other people were focused on Clay's speech. None of them seemed to care that he'd left his phone on the table, and it kept flashing new messages. She picked it up and read the newest message.

Good luck, baby, wish I could be there. I'll see you soon. I love you.

The message was from someone named Lee. A large lump formed in Erica's throat. The applauding and cheering was in slow motion. Her rage was mounting.

Clay came forward from behind the podium, putting one hand in his pocket.

"Mom, we did it. I don't know how to thank you. You've always believed in me," he said, putting his hand over his heart. His mom put her hand over her heart too as she watched her son. "And I'd like to thank my kids, who better be in bed right now," he said, and the crowd chuckled.

"I want to thank all my business partners as well. We accomplished a lot in a short amount of time. The late nights were worth it." He turned with a serious expression on his face. "I want to thank the Business Summit. When I opened my first tax office, I wasn't sure what to expect. I just knew I wanted to do taxes, and I wanted to have ten offices all over the city one day. Today is that day, and our potential is unlimited thanks to you, and thanks to the people of the city of Rockton. You all helped make this possible. I accept this award on behalf of all of you."

He continued above the roar of applause. "I'm still a businessman, so I would be remiss if I sat down without a plug. We will be opening offices up all over the state, then nationally. So stay tuned, as I will represent the city the best I can." He paused again. "This honor would not have been possible without the long nights and all the sacrifices we've made as a family, and that's why I'd like to thank the most important person in my life, my wife. I would be nowhere without her. I'd like to let her say a few words and accept this award with me."

He glanced at the expressionless Erica. He stepped towards her, holding the microphone out. She made her way up to the podium, and he handed her the microphone.

"It's true. Clay is a great businessman. And, yes, there have been a lot of sacrifices, there have been a lot of long nights. But unfortunately, the long nights Clay spoke of weren't with me." A collective gasp went up from the crowd, mixed with anxious giggles from people who thought she was joking. "That's probably why he's putting men's names in his phone so I won't know it's really women. So, Clay, is Lee a code name for Lilly? Lena? Leah? Because I know you're not on the down-low." She choked out a sob, but her blood boiled with rage. Her eyes zoomed in on Clay's mother, but she didn't look at Erica. She was too busy staring at her son in shock. Goose bumps covered Erica's arms as she looked out into the now-silent crowd.

Frank approached a few people who had their phones out, filming. They immediately put them down. Clay reached to take the mic, but Erica wasn't done speaking. "I can't any more. Not one more day. I am done with you, Clay." She let the mic drop.

The sound system echoed through the room as the audience watched in stunned silence. Clay watched her stalk off the stage, but he didn't follow after her. He returned to his position of guest of honor. "I'm so sorry for all that. Sometimes alcohol gets the best of my wife. But, hey, the night isn't over. On the next floor, we have live music and dancing for all. Enjoy, and thank you."

Erica walked out of the ballroom. The frigid frosty wind hit her delicate body. Her eye makeup was smeared on her face. The moonlight hit her face as she headed to her car. Lashay, her gaze fixed on her sister, walked up ready to explain what she was doing there. Instead, Erica stood frozen with a look of shock plastered across her face. She had clearly been crying.

"What's wrong, sis? What did he do?"

"Nothing. I just want to go home."

"I'll take you home."

"No, I want to be by myself."

"Why, what happened?"

"Clay. I'm done. I'm leaving him." She started crying again. "Never mind. I'm just going to go home." Erica headed for her car.

"I'll be back. I need to go to the DJ inside," Lashay snapped.

* * *

Once inside the building, Lashay paced up and down the staircases and through several ballrooms. The wide-open rooms were filled with small groups of people, staring as she bolted through the hallways until she reached the main hallway. It had a long burgundy, gold, and navy-blue Persian rug running the length of the hallway. On the left side of the hallway was a mirrored mahogany cabinet, sandwiched in between two elevator doors. And on the right were rows of blue velvet Queen Anne chairs that sat up against the wall. She got to the end of the hallway and looked up at a picture of a giant buffalo head, mounted on the wall above an entrance to another part of the building.

As she entered the different section, she peeked behind closed doors. She saw people standing around talking and rooms packed with lots of smoke. There were so many rooms, and she couldn't find Clay in any of them. She ended up back in the main hallway, yelling his name. People stared at her. She glanced up and spotted Clay getting into the elevator. She kicked off her high heels and charged right in his direction. He stepped in the elevator, and she reached in and grabbed him by the collar, catching him off guard.

"You better watch your back, Clay. You keep messing with my sister, I'm going to kill you," Lashay shouted.

"Whatever. You better watch your back."

7

Erica waited impatiently outside their gate. She stared at the small guardhouse to the left. She wondered why Clay had bothered to have a guardhouse built; they never had a guard there anyway. Once the gate slid to the side, she sped up the long driveway, gazing out of her car window to the yard, where the kids had been playing that afternoon. Toys were strewn everywhere. She pulled the Rover in front of the house and jumped out, clutching her Coach purse in one hand and her cell phone in the other. She ran up to the front door and realized she'd left the keys in the ignition.

The moment she reached inside the car for the keys, a sharp pain penetrated the side of her abdomen. She dropped the phone on the ground and doubled over in pain, hugging her sides. The pain was getting worse.

Once the pain subsided, she turned off the car and grabbed her keys. She heard Lashay's familiar ringtone from under her car. Lashay's song guided her beneath it in search of her phone, but she couldn't quite reach it. She knelt down and stuck her head under the car for a better angle. That's when she noticed the shiny fluorescent-green device attached to the underside of the car. At first it startled her, but she was more curious than worried. She cautiously touched it, in case it was hot. When she discovered it wasn't, she grabbed it and pulled it off. She scooted back out, sat up, and grabbed her phone. Her sister was calling again. She ignored the call, grabbed her things, and walked toward the house, not taking her eyes off the device.

Once inside, she wasted no time. She sprinted to the computer room and sat down at the desk. Another pain shot through her stomach. She gripped her stomach as she examined the device. Bernice walked in the room.

"Are you okay, Erica?" Bernice asked.

"Yes, Bernice, everything is fine."

"The kids are already asleep, but I thought you were going to be out later."

"I didn't feel like staying for the whole thing."

"Where's Mr. Williams?"

"He wanted to stay."

"Honey, are you sure you're okay?" she asked, her eyes watching Erica's hand on her stomach.

Erica quickly moved it. "I'm fine. Really. Let me show a few things you can do tonight or tomorrow."

Erica rushed through the house, reviewing tasks: the clothes needed folding, a wall in the hallway needed wiping down. As they walked down the hallway past a closed door and back toward the living room, there was one last door that Erica hadn't mentioned.

"You didn't mention anything about that room," Bernice said, pointing at the door.

"Mr. Williams's office. We don't go in there," Erica said with a mischievous grin.

"Yeah, I know. I think he is building a bomb," Bernice said, laughing.

"If he wants it cleaned, he can either make the arrangements or do it himself." Erica guided Bernice back down the hallway. "Bernice, I need to get on the computer. Can you check on the kids and do as much as you can tonight, before you go to your quarters?"

"Yes, ma'am," Bernice said and headed back down the hallway.

Erica hurried into Clay's office and headed for the desk. She reached into the top drawer, felt around for the key, and found it stuck to the top. She rushed over to the filing cabinet. Inside she found the gun, a folder with documents inside and a SanDisk flash drive. She grabbed the flash drive and the folder, rushed over to the couch, and sprinted down the hallway to the computer room.

Erica analyzed the device from under the car first. She googled the name Linxup. When the website popped up, she mumbled, "What the fuck." A vehicle-tracking device on her car? Who'd put it there and how long had it been there? Why had it been on her car? She looked for it on YouTube to see how it operated and discovered there was a USB port.

Her phone rang again. She answered. "Lashay, I am okay. Please don't come, I want to be by myself. Okay, come by the shop when you get a chance. Okay." She hung up the phone.

She connected the device to the computer and clicked the mouse, and a map popped up showing highlighted streets. She realized it was showing all the places she'd been over the last month. When she clicked on the dates, it showed her whereabouts on each day. She clicked on the menu and saw contact info for the device: Quality Enterprise.

She stuck in the flash drive and opened documents. Most of the files were stored in folders labeled "Evans File" and "Quality Enterprise." She clicked on Quality Enterprise, but the files included spreadsheets and charts. She didn't want to waste time reading everything tonight and have Clay walk in on her. She decided to print out as much as she could.

While she waited for the printer, she looked inside the folder at the documents. The first one was a legal separation document with her signature on it. She made a quick copy of it.

Through the windows, she noticed headlights coming up the driveway. She moved swiftly and hurried to return the flash drive and folder to Clay's cabinet. When the time was right, she'd put the GPS device back, then act like she didn't know. She closed the computer screen and rushed out of the room.

8

Erica maneuvered her Range Rover like an expert, navigating traffic without effort while her mind wandered. *Clay, how could you?* she thought, over and over on a loop. *How could you?* Her cell phone rang, echoing over the car audio system, interrupting her thoughts. It was her sister, Lashay, again. After everything that had happened the night before and all that she'd discovered, Erica had forgotten to call her back. She touched her mounted screen to answer the call, and Lashay's voice came loud through the car system.

"Hello, Lashay," Erica answered. "I'm in the car. Only have a few minutes. I'm going to meet someone."

"Who?"

"It's nothing, just business," she said, not wanting to get Lashay involved. She wasn't ready to tell her the truth. Not yet. For the next few minutes, she listened to her sister about having a singing audition for a big club. Whenever a big audition came up, Lashay was a hot mess.

"I know you're nervous, but you'll do well. I'll see you at the wig shop tomorrow."

Erica hung up the phone. She jumped on the freeway ramp and headed north toward the city. Erica pulled up to a small restaurant called Park's Café and put the Rover in park. She was twenty minutes early.

It was dark inside, and a few patrons made enough conversational buzz to complement the soft music. The faint sound of glasses clinking and people drinking sounded routine and comforting. Three couples sat inside the booths, talking quietly, and two men perched at the long bar. Erica picked a booth in the back, far away from prying eyes.

Within minutes, Will Jones joined her. Erica had known Will since childhood, having grown up with him down the street on the same block. He'd practically lived at Erica's grandparents' house every summer. He always knew how to make Erica feel better, especially after the deaths of her grandparents. A lanky caramel-colored man with broad shoulders and a small potbelly, he smiled over at her.

"Hey, Will," Erica greeted him as cheerfully as she could muster. "Wasn't sure if you were gonna show."

"You know I'd do anything for you."

"Thank you for seeing me so soon. I couldn't wait too long. I didn't want to leave any of the information I copied in the house," she whispered.

"No problem. Once you called, you knew I'd come running." They started laughing.

"Well, you're the only person I knew who could help, and that I trust," Erica said.

"I'm not the only private investigator in the city, but I am the best." He laughed. "On the phone, you sounded like you were in pain. Are you going to tell me what's going on?"

She searched through her big purse and pulled out all the information she had printed out, pictures of the GPS device, and the legal separation paper. After she handed them over to Will, she fell silent. Tears began to well in her eyes.

37

Will reached over and squeezed her hand. "It's okay, Erica. I'm here for you. Whatever you need."

"Thank you. What I need now is a good lawyer. I'm leaving Clay, and I want what's mine. And I don't want to lose my kids."

"Is it that bad between the two of you?" Will asked as he rubbed her hand. "Do you think he had anything to do with the GPS on your car?"

She nodded her head.

"Who knows? I don't care. He is not the man I married."

Will stiffened. "That selfish, arrogant prick. He's never appreciated you. But could he stoop so low? Be so ruthless?"

"My marriage hasn't been right for years. Hell, I don't know if it was ever right. I found a document, a legal separation document that I never signed. But it had my signature," she said. "I haven't been able to tell anyone. It would be like admitting I failed at one of the things most important to me . . ." She trailed off.

"None of this is your fault. You're not a failure, Erica. Do me a favor. When you get a chance, come by my firm, and I'll introduce you to Bob, our lead attorney. I also have some friends at the police station. I'll ask them some questions to see if I can figure out what's going on. If Clay put the device on your car without your permission that is a serious crime."

Erica had tears in her eyes. "I hate to say it, but I'm pretty sure Clay is up to something no good. He brought a gun home," she said.

Will looked at her in disbelief, at a loss for words. "I have more questions, Erica, but they can wait. You get some rest, and then I'll call you when I have something for you. I want to get on this right away."

9

Officer Frank Thompson walked around the room with a scanner, checking for listening devices in a hotel conference room. When he was done, he sat down at the circular table and hit the spoon against the glass on the table. When he had everyone's attention, he straightened his tie and began to speak.

"For the last five years, the Southside Unit has controlled everything on the streets of this city, and I am proud of the fact that we have never been penetrated since forming our organization ten years ago. We have made a lot of money with no hiccups," Frank said.

"On the streets they call us the Blafia," said Delo Brown, a middle-aged black man who loved dressing in suits with big lapels like he had just stepped out of a '70s-era blaxploitation movie. He ran the entertainment businesses, strip clubs, high-end clubs, and a record label.

"No one says that to our faces," Marvin Brown said. He was Delo's brother, and he ran the street-level dealers, the soldiers, and the drug houses. He was ten years younger than everybody and was quick to show his thug side. He wore street clothes that represented him being from the hood. He secretly laughed at his brother.

"We have controlled most of the drug distribution in the city. Everything had been running like a well-oiled machine since Clay became our accountant and started laundering our finances five years ago. Everybody has a job: Delo does his job, Marvin does his job. My job is to deal with security and police and to have all the political connections. Clay, your job is not just to deal with all the paperwork, but also to stay low-key, since everything is in your name. This is how we set everything up."

Marvin jumped up. "Yeah, Clay, you're not playing by the rules we set up."

Frank glanced at Marvin and a hint of humor crossed his face. "Listen, this shit is getting out of hand," Marvin said.

"Yes, it is," others responded in unison. If Clay was surprised Marvin took the floor, he didn't show it. Usually the three men in higher positions spoke first, and then Marvin spoke. "We—well, you guys—always said the key is to be low-key. Well, this motherfucker right here just had a public embarrassment." Marvin pointed at Clay, glaring.

Marvin let that first sentence hang in the air for a few seconds, then looked around the table. "So, because of this man, the one man who has to always appear as a family man is not keeping his house in order." He shifted back to Frank. "When we first started this thing, we vowed not to let the money get to us, or the drugs, or the pussy, and Clay's done all those. He didn't start with us, and now it seems your friend is fucking everything up, Delo, Frank."

No one said anything as they waited for Frank, who had known Clay the longest, to speak. "Clay, I'm obligated to tell you that your wife met a private investigator. He's from the old neighborhood."

Clay spoke up. "And why do I care about some black private dick from the Southside?"

"Because your wife found the GPS, and some of your documents. Please tell me you didn't mix your personal papers with your business papers?"

"What are you talking about?"

"Yesterday around seven, she went to a bar on the west side of town. I have access to her GPS, and I heard her talking on the phone in the car. You do remember you asked me to put a camera and microphone in her car."

"Yeah."

"You must have left the flash drive out somewhere. She printed out some documents and put the GPS back, so you wouldn't know she knows."

Clay ran his hand over his face. "I'll go get everything, then move it to my other, more secure spot."

"This PI works for a law firm. Your wife is thinking about divorcing you and taking the kids. Your appetite for young women is making you sloppy," Frank said.

"Divorce *me*?" Clay said, sucking his teeth.

Frank began to speak. "I heard her on the phone in the car, speaking to the PI."

"What are you going to do now, Clay?" Delo asked. "Do you have a plan to get yourself out of this mess? We can't take a chance on your wife having any information about what we do, and getting a divorce will allow the courts to go through all your business. You've gotten sloppy before and that business audit almost got us caught. If you keep slipping, the *feds* will be back."

Clay folded his hands together, as if he had all the answers. "First, no need to worry. None of the businesses are connected to us, so my wife will not be able to hurt us on the financial side of the game."

"You've already been hurt twice. The investigation and the public embarrassment at the awards show, and now she's given your documents to a PI," Delo said.

"That's two too many times, motherfucker," Marvin blurted.

"First off, let's tone it down and watch the language," Frank said. "Marvin, you may sit down. I don't think that carrying on like this is the most productive way to conduct this conversation right now." Marvin glared at Frank and then slammed back down into his chair.

"I just want to make sure he doesn't jeopardize our investment," Marvin said.

"Clay, is the sale of your tax firms to the major conglomerate on track?" Frank asked as he stared at the windows that sat high up around the room.

"Yes, and I will hold on to a certain percentage. And when they go public with IPO, we all will be rich," Clay shot back.

"Clay, you need to stay clean for a few more months to make sure the negotiation doesn't affect anything."

Delo's eyes were fixed on his nice shiny Ferragamo shoes, his arms wrapped tight atop his chest. "I think it's come time that we take things into our own hands for the so-called accountant. We are the silent partners."

Clay put his hand in the air. Frank gestured to him, giving his permission to speak. "Listen, I know I've made many mistakes in my personal life. I been driving myself crazy trying to figure out what went wrong."

"You lost control of your marriage a long time ago. You bring your girlfriends to Delo's clubs all the time. He had to kick you out of one of his strip clubs the other day," Marvin stated.

"We all have girlfriends on the side. No one's marriage is perfect in here," Clay said.

"That's true," Delo said. "My marriage isn't the best. Marvin's has issues with his girl, and we all know Frank's wife left him years ago, but nobody's personal situation affected the business like yours will. Do you get it, Clay, or do I need to draw you a picture?" Delo cleared his throat and raised an eyebrow.

Marvin nodded his head, and one of his shoes started to tap the floor. He took another deep breath. "I'm the one dealing with the street-level shit. Some of you sit safe in nice cushy offices and live worry-free in your suburban homes." Marvin looked around the room. "You don't have to worry about all the shit that goes on in the gutter on the Southside and this city. Every day, some young punk wants our territories, and I'm the one who handles it. My life's at risk every day, and for this chump to fuck every young broad he sees and hang out at strip clubs all day isn't right."

Clay looked at Marvin. "Okay," he said. "When we started this thing, we said we would have rules and regulations. Has everybody in the room always followed all the rules?" He held up his hand, palm out. "Let's first start with a simple rule. We're supposed to wear suits to all meetings, but look at Marvin."

"This is an emergency meeting, and I'm going to my nephew's basketball game after this," Marvin shot back at Clay. "Some of us value spending time with our families."

"I'll take care of everything," Clay said in his most reassuring voice.

"How are you going to get control of this situation, Clay?" Frank said.

"I'll tell you about control." Clay straightened up as if getting poised to recite a poem. "Nothing is controlled by the people. People are controlled by the laws. Laws are controlled by the politicians. Politicians are controlled by the rich. The rich are controlled by greed. Greed is controlled by nothing. In the end, you get nothing from nothing. It's all part of the game to me. That's from the great philosopher Cyrus."

"What does that have to with the predicament you're in now?" Delo blurted out.

"It means, we have friends everywhere, and my wife has no power. Once I'm done with her, this will be behind us."

Frank sat up and leaned forward. "The sooner you get this resolved, the sooner we can feel safe."

"Well, we could just get rid of the bitch and her sister," Clay said.

"You stupid motherfucker, you know how much attention that would bring after what your wife did at the awards show? They would know it was you," Delo said.

"Tell us why you want the mother of your kids to expire, Clay?" Frank asked.

"Because she is a terrible mother, and she knew I didn't want any more kids with her. The bitch tricked me and got pregnant."

"We have never seen or heard about her being a bad mother," Delo said.

"You guys don't know, but now she may compromise us with the information in a divorce."

"Motherfucker, you want her gone because she embarrassed you at the awards ceremony in front of everybody and your mommy," Marvin blurted out.

"One of our rules was we would never give the green light on family, because that's too close to home and brings a lot of attention. However, in this situation, we need to do something just in case she decides to divorce him. We need to dirty her up and buy us some time until the sale is done. You'll just have to give her some money in a divorce," Frank said.

Delo gave a cautious nod.

Marvin cleared his throat. "How do you feel about that, college boy?"

"I don't answer to you, Marvin," Clay responded.

"I'd like to add something," Delo said. "Clay, you are a valuable piece in the unit. I understand that she's the mother of your children, but if she becomes a problem, we're going to blame you. We helped finance your business. Your empire is because of us."

"If we didn't help you, you'd have one office, college boy. We've been a great organization for you, but nobody in this room thinks it'll be hard to find another money man to wash our money," Marvin added.

Frank shifted his seat and spoke. "The private investigator with information on our business is a high priority. All who say 'yeah' raise your hands." He stopped and scanned the room. "Okay, that's four to nothing. An expiration date will be set for him, but first, we need to see what he knows."

"Let's take a vote on my wife, too," Clay added.

Frank glared at Clay. "Okay, even though we've made arrangements to make sure the wife is neutralized, let me see hands for her expiration date." He scanned the room again.

"That's three to one, so that's a no on the wife and the sister. I am sorry, Clay. Both of these situations have been resolved. We dirty up the wife and help you with the elimination of the pregnancy. However, if she knows more than we think, then we will take another vote later and maybe it will go in your favor, Clay. This meeting is over."

Clay shook his head. "So you guys are going to vote against me to keep my wife alive? If she divorces me, they will open up my books and that could expose me. And I have a lot of information on the unit."

"Are you threatening us? If we get your files on us, then we'll take a vote on you," Marvin said.

"See, Clay? This is why you should have just stayed behind the scenes and put everything in corporate names, and kept everything separated. But you wanted to be Mister Big Shot businessman, and now we can't get rid of your wife. After the public scene at the awards show, people will look at you more closely. Now we have to set something up to buy us time and put us in a better situation to help you deal with her," Frank said.

10

Lashay searched for the perfect wig inside Erica's shop. She was excited. G Money was coming to watch her sing. She needed a wig with a style that matched her stage personality, and after the third wig, she'd found it.

"You in a hurry, Lashay?" Erica asked from her perch behind the counter.

"You know I've got that big audition today." She spun around the three-way mirror. The wig went perfectly with her skinny jeans, her off-the-shoulder flowered pastel blouse, and her favorite Miu Miu black leather stilettos. She had dressed that morning with a mind to slay, and the wig added to her confidence.

"I know you don't want to talk about what happen at the awards ceremony, but I gave Clay a piece of my mind."

"Shay, not now, but come over to the house tomorrow and I'll tell you everything that's going on. And you can tell me how the audition went."

"Is everything okay?"

"I'll tell you when I see you. So you go break a leg."

Lashay pulled a stocking cap over her head, placed the wig on snug, and pinned it with bobby pins. "You sure you don't want to come?"

"Shay, we've talked about this. I'm done with singing. But look at you, all professional with your portfolio," Erica said, paging through the binder.

"Erica, come on. Mom always wanted us to sing together. I know you want to come. Get Bernie to watch the kids and sing with me."

Erica hesitated. She was tempted but shook her head. "Hey, we have those new colors and styles coming in that you wanted Wednesday."

"Come on, Erica. Sing with me. It will take your mind off of everything."

"You better get going. Don't want you to be late for your audition," Erica said, writing some new orders down.

Lashay glanced at her phone. "Oh shoot, I gotta hurry. The next bus is coming."

"Where's your car?" Erica said.

"In the shop. Meeka went to pick up my outfit, and she's going to meet me there before she goes to work."

"How is she doing now?"

"A lot better. Okay, I gotta head to the bus stop."

"A bus? Why not an Uber or Lyft?"

Lashay scowled at her sister. "Come on, now, I'm not about to pay ten dollars just to go a few miles down the street. The bus costs a dollar and goes to Main Street. It will get me there in twenty minutes."

"Love you, girl. You'll kill it," Erica said, reaching over the counter to give her sister a hug.

"Good luck, Lashay. Don't forget us when you a big-time star and doing duets with Kem," one of the customers said as she walked out the door.

"You know it," she said, strutting out of the store. Lashay enjoyed the local love.

The store was about half a mile from the bus stop and sat above street level, giving the staff and customers a good view of the street. Lashay made her way to the bus stop.

A loud, boisterous laugh rang out near the window of the shop. Erica jumped.

"Oh, shit," a customer shouted through her laughter. "Lashay's runnin'."

"Look at her go," chimed in another.

Curious, everyone flocked to the window. The bus was plowing down the street at full speed, and Lashay was doing her best to get to the corner in time and in one piece, running as fast as her high heels would carry her. She had a tight grip on her singing portfolio. Inside, she also had her headshots, resume, and other important documents. A few people at the bus stop waved at her to hurry up. Erica had never seen Lashay run so fast.

The customers near the window seemed to be amused and concerned at the same time. A few of them seemed worried for Lashay, but the loud woman from earlier kept laughing.

"Go, girl," she cried through her laughter.

"Don't break a heel," the other woman added, also laughing.

The bus had stopped and the passengers had all boarded, but Lashay was about a hundred feet away, huffing and puffing, still trying to get there. She yelled for the bus to wait, while the shoppers cheered her on.

Lashay was almost there. The people cheered louder. Erica found herself cheering too. After all, Lashay was her sister and best customer. When Lashay was about twenty feet away, disaster struck. The combination of her sprint in stilettos and the uneven, rocky asphalt caused her to fall flat on her face. Her wig flew right off her head. There Lashay lay, in a stocking cap on the ground, showered in humiliation and trying to decide whether to catch the bus or chase after her wig that was blowing away. Lashay decided to go after the wig and dropped her portfolio in the process. All the contents blew into the street and scattered to the four winds.

The loud woman laughed again, louder than before.

"This bitch," yelled the other woman, to the other customers' delight. "You gotta be kiddin' me."

"Look, Erica." One of the customers laughed. "Her hair is blowing down the street."

Everybody laughed; everybody but Erica. Lashay took off her stilettos, jumped off the sidewalk, and started a wig pursuit against traffic. Showing no concern for her personal safety, Lashay ran through traffic, screaming at every car. People on the bus were pointing, cars were honking, and time was running out. None of this attention distracted Lashay from her mission. Each time Lashay attempted to reach down and grab the wig, the wind blew it farther away. Lashay didn't give up. She kept reaching for it, against all odds. It was clear that nothing would prevent her from recovering her wig, even if it meant getting hit by a truck. When Lashay caught up to the wig, the customers gave a thunderous cheer as if she had just made a touchdown.

"She did it," screamed the two women between gales of laughter.

Lashay did her best to get the wig back on, though it was wildly disarrayed. People on the bus were clapping, patrons were cheering, and people who were rubber-necking jumped out of their cars and started helping her pick up her papers.

It all seemed like an eternity, but minutes later, Lashay had her portfolio in hand and her wig resting lopsided on her head, with still enough time to reach her destination.

People were still clapping, and some of them were giving her hugs as she entered the bus.

11

Lashay and Meeka sat in a private corner of the posh, upscale club, illuminated only by candles and low lighting. The doormen wore slim-fit tuxedos, but at two o'clock in the afternoon, the need for bouncers was nonexistent. Behind the empty dance floor hung a large screen that streamed R&B music videos. The women, now in their midtwenties, had been best friends since high school. There was a time when they had done a lot of things together, not all of them legal. However, in the last six months, they hadn't hung out like they used to, with Lashay trying to work her way up in the music industry and Meeka doing volunteer work at a nonprofit organization for women.

"I'll have one drink with you, then I have to go work," Meeka said.

"Ever since you started working for that nonprofit, we don't spend time together like we used to."

"They helped me, and I want to help other girls. But I have regular hours, and I have a lot of free time now, unless they give me a special assignment, like tonight."

"Okay, that's good."

"Shit, I don't know what hot messes are going on nowadays, but you know if you ever need me for anything, I'm here for you straight up."

"I know, and thanks for the ride," Lashay said as her voice started to fade out.

"Are you nervous?"

"No, I think I hurt my voice."

"Oh, shit."

"Yeah, I was yelling at cars and shit."

"Why?"

"I'll tell you later. Right now, let me see if some water will help me."

She grabbed the glass of ice water she had ordered earlier in the afternoon and took a sip, swishing it around in her mouth. The soft sound of jazz music played in the background of their conversation.

"At least they're not playing any of that mumble rap or autotuned singing videos. We would need closed captions to understand what they were saying." Meeka laughed.

"Or we'd need an interpreter. Damn shame. Can't even understand what your own people rapping or singing about," Lashay said. They both laughed. The place catered to the downtown professionals, and it was not the type of place they usually hung out. When they ordered, they didn't know exactly what type of drink they were getting. A Manhattan or a highball or something.

Meeka took a sip of her drink and winced. "Oh man, that stuff's nasty." Lashay took a sip of hers and winced too. They laughed again. Meeka twirled her drink. "A toast, to nasty drinks and mumble rap."

Lashay shook her head. "Meeka, you're a few French fries short of a Happy Meal."

Meeka glanced at her phone. "Oh man, I've got to get to work, but I know you're going to knock 'em dead."

Meeka took one last swig of her drink. "I'll catch up with you later, somewhere more our speed." They hugged and Meeka headed toward the entrance.

Lashay's gaze followed Meeka out of the club as she walked past two striking middle-aged men coming in. They were tall, dark, and very handsome, with rich cocoa skin. One was dressed in a well-tailored suit, and the other wore an Adidas sweat suit. She knew one of them must be the famous Earl "G Money" Thomas, the main record producer at the biggest urban record label in the area.

She began to sweat. Would they like her? She had a terrible itch under the wig. She tried to scratch it through the layers and hoped it wouldn't keep bothering her. She watched as a young, short, full-figured woman walked over to the men. G Money straightened his tie as he talked to her. She took them over to a corner table with a perfect view of the stage. People in the surrounding area watched the two men make their way through the club. The man dressed in the Adidas suit knew how to radiate a "don't mess with me" message, and people quickly looked away from him. He pointed to Lashay as he said something to the hostess. She nodded. He said something more and handed her something. She came over to tell Lashay she could take the stage.

Lashay made her way to the stage as the music changed to a more upbeat R&B rhythm.

She introduced herself to the small crowd, then walked over to the musicians to let them know what key she planned to sing in. She knew all she had to do was hit that first note, and she would be all right. She squared herself in front of the microphone and leaned in as she opened her mouth to reach the first note.

As she began to sing her own rendition of "At Last" by Etta James, the chatter in the room hushed. Even the waitress stopped to watch. Halfway through the song, a couple of the bartenders on break came out to listen too. When she delivered the last note, her voice was hoarse. The whole place went silent. She tried again and her voice was the same. Lashay placed the mic back on its stand

and made her way back to her seat. She glanced in the direction of the two men in the suits. One of them motioned her to come over.

She strolled to their table as soft beats penetrated the air. The dance floor was perfectly lit as she made her way across the room. She held her breath, like when she was a little girl blowing out the candles on her birthday cake. All her wishes were coming true.

"Hello, I'm so sorry for my voice," Lashay said, trying to contain the enthusiasm boiling inside her.

"Have a seat," he said to her. She sat across from them. "I'm G Money. You can call me Money, and this is Bull," G Money said as he straightened out his tie again.

Bull nodded at her. "What's up?"

"Hi. That has never happened to me," she said.

"Don't worry about it. I heard you before it went out. That happens."

"But not to me."

"Lashay, you can sing. I heard it and heard about it."

"Okay, thank you."

"What are you drinking?" he asked.

"I'm not drinking. It's too early for me."

"So, you all about that business, then?" Money said, sounding impressed.

"Sho', you right," Lashay said as they both laughed.

"I like that," Money said as he got up and sat next to her. He didn't even try to hide that he was trying to get a better view of her legs.

"I think we can do a lot of business together," he said, not taking his eyes off her lower body.

"Right now, I need some studio time, Money, so if you can help a sista out with a recording, then we can discuss business."

"Well, you can check my record. I am not above helping those who want to help themselves, provided they have the talent. And you have the talent," he said, moving closer to her.

"Not to get off topic here, but, uh..." she said, trying to redirect Money's attention, "my boyfriend and I want to put all our efforts into the music thing. He is a rapper and we could use your help. We don't have to go into details right now, but I have big dreams."

"Hey, baby, come on. Let's dance," Money said. He grabbed her hand and asserted himself as the music street tycoon he was.

She grabbed his hand and placed it on her hip. They swayed back and forth to the beat. He guided her hips when she lifted her arms and twisted her middle. She turned around, bumping her backside up and down against him. As they moved, she felt on top of the world. She faced him and their eyes locked. He was in control now. He embraced her like he never planned to let go. She submitted to his advances. Her body melted into his, and she allowed him to lead. It seemed like forever, but it was just one song.

"Okay. I thought about it," he said, speaking over the music as they continued to move around the dance floor. "Come by the studio and we'll start recording. If things go right, we'll talk business and begin the paperwork."

"Great," she said. "Do you need my portfolio? I brought it."

"I'll take a look at it," he said with a slow, sexy smile.

"I'm glad I came today. I've been singing my entire life, and it's all my mother ever wanted for me and my sister. Oh, can I bring my sister? You should hear her sing. We sound great together." Lashay knew she was rambling, but she could not stop herself.

"Bring whoever you want."

While they danced, Lashay noticed the silhouette of a man in the distance, staring at her. He seemed vaguely familiar, but before she could get a better look, Money twirled her. When she came back around, the man was gone. She glanced around the club and located him at a table, grabbing the arm of a young woman. She squinted to get a better look. She stopped dancing and asked Money to hold up a minute. As she walked toward the couple, the man and the young woman got up quickly and headed toward the exit. She followed them, but they left out the side door.

Lashay exited the club just in time to see Clay and the woman laughing in front of his car. He reached down to kiss her. Lashay burned with rage. She took a deep breath as they unwrapped from each other and the woman slipped into the passenger side.

Clay pulled out his keys and pressed the button to unlock the doors. Lashay glared at him, but he still didn't see her. Her head shook side to side, and she picked up speed with every step she took toward the car. Lashay jumped in his face, but before she could start her tirade, Clay pushed her away and turned to get into the car.

"You motherfucker, I'm going to kill you." Her dress ripped, but she grabbed his neck and rode his back.

"Bitch, get off of me," he yelled.

He flipped her off and her body slammed to the ground, hard. The fall sent stabs of pain through her ribs. She jumped up and went after him again, grabbing him by the collar and yanking him to the ground. He fell hard. The top button of his white shirt popped off and struck her in the face. The smacking of her fists against his skin drowned out his cries of protest.

"Help," he cried, as if he were in danger. She felt his cheeks and his chin crash against her forceful fists.

"Stop," the young woman yelled.

Lashay snapped out of her rage. She pulled herself back and composed herself. She stood, pulling her damaged dress back into place. She tried to catch her breath as her hands trembled. She felt weak from the adrenaline rush and worried that her legs would give out on her. She flexed her raw, swollen fingers to make sure they weren't broken.

A few men in the crowd yelled at Clay, taunting him for getting his ass beat by a woman. He tried to defend himself, but before he could say anything, Money grabbed him. Clay yanked his arm away.

"Get in," Clay yelled to the woman, and they drove off as if nothing happened.

Money rested his hand on Lashay's arm. "Are you okay?"

"Yeah, sure. Sometimes you just have to release some tension. I am sorry about this happening."

"Don't worry about that."

"Did I ruin my chance to get a record deal?"

"No, but since you lost your voice, let it rest, and I want to hear it in the studio."

"Awesome sauce," Lashay said.

"And you can bring your sister too," he said, trying not to laugh.

12

Clay drove the silver Benz frantically. He shouted at every slow car he passed, zigzagging the sedan through traffic as if being chased, running every yellow light. He looked from his watch to the road to the clock on the dash and back to the road again. He had already dropped off his new girl, and now he used alleys to cut across streets and drove through gas stations to avoid stoplights until he reached his destination. When he saw the Corporate Car Storage sign, he breathed a sigh of relief. He stopped in front of the gate, and when it rose, he drove the Benz up to the security keypad and entered the gate code. He parked the car and hurried to his storage unit. He pulled the lock off and raised the steel door. His white 3 Series BMW sat there waiting for him. He pulled the Beamer out, and then he backed the Benz in. Before he closed the door, he gave his new pride and joy one last look.

"What the fuck?" he yelled.

He looked closer. A little smear on the front grille of his baby, from something caught midflight. He took a handkerchief out of his back pocket and bent over to wipe it off. He cursed Lashay. It was her fault his new baby had a blemish. Erica had forbidden him to purchase the silver Mercedes with dark-tinted windows. Her ultimatum had made him want it more. It sat in the storage unit, beaming at him. His wife had no idea he'd bought this for himself.

Cars switched, Clay pulled onto the freeway, wiping his face. He wasn't worried about what had happened earlier with his wife's sister. He could do without that woman. She caused him more trouble than a mad viper, but he'd deal with her soon. The headlights came on as the sun started to fade. He wanted to turn the radio on to help him relax but decided he'd rather stay focused. He raced northbound on the freeway for another thirty minutes, the late-afternoon sun shining in his face.

Within minutes of pulling off the freeway, he entered the upper-class neighborhood of Morada Estates. He turned left at the corner and pulled up to the security booth. A guard stepped forward in front of the iron gate that separated them from the community within.

"Hello, Mr. Johnson," Clay said to the older guard sitting in the booth. The guard squinted. It took him a moment to recognize Clay.

"Hello, Mr. Thomas. How are you doing this evening?"

Clay paused, then he realized the guard was talking to him. He had forgotten everything was under his mother's maiden name. "Good," he said.

The community was exquisite. It was a gated Beverly Hills–style neighborhood. The luxurious mansions were each separated by a couple of acres and skirted a large, manicured golf course.

As the sun slanted across the lawns near dusk, every cut green blade stood perfectly in its place, and the many flowers danced in clusters on their beds. Clay pulled the car up to the grand house. He grabbed his briefcase and got out of the car.

He stood by the closet for a minute, looking out onto the balcony. The full view of the golf course always made him feel as if he had made it. Inside the closet, he tripped over some clothes on the floor. He caught his balance and continued to the back wall. He pulled some clothes out of the way to expose a file cabinet with a key. He placed the black briefcase down on the floor, took out its contents, and placed it in the file cabinet, relocking it with the small key. He put all the contents from the briefcase into the safe. This was where he kept the flash drive with James Evans file, which held all the financial records on the unit, including the dirt he had on each member. No one knew about this house, and he planned to keep it that way.

He went downstairs and sat on the padded bench in the wide hallway outside his mother's bedroom door. At 4 a.m. it was still dark, but that was okay by him. He admired the photos on the wall: his prom, his business promotions, his kids. He took a sip from a glass of scotch. No one would have ever figured that a kid from the Southside would buy a big house in Morada Estates.

At first his mom had thought the house was too big, but he'd thought it was perfect for her. There were two master bedrooms downstairs. His mom had one, and his Auntie Mena had the other. As they both got older, they wouldn't need to go up and down the stairs. Clay had the entire second floor to himself. It had four bedrooms, one for him and another he'd turned into an office, where he kept more documents for his eyes only. The last two would be for his kids, once they moved in.

He'd told his mother he didn't want Erica to know about the house. It was his personal retreat from a life he no longer wanted. His mother loved walking the trails. She enjoyed being able to get out into the sunshine, and Mena seemed to settle in to fancy living too. Clay liked that he could play golf anytime he wanted. He was a member of the community golf club under one of his aliases.

A ray of light peeked from under the door of his mother's room. He tiptoed to her bedroom and opened it a crack.

"Mama?" Clay poked his head inside.

The old caramel-skinned woman looked over her glasses. Her thinning gray hair was matted down on one side. She opened her mouth, and he could see her yellowed teeth. "Clay, baby," she exclaimed.

"I wanted to say good morning," he said.

"Then come in here, son." His mother's steady voice comforted him, more than he'd expected it would. He stepped into the room as she got out of bed. She held her arms out to him, and he fell into them, just as any son seeking comfort would.

"What happened to your face?" she asked. He didn't say anything. "What's wrong, baby?"

"Nothing, Mama," he said.

"Clay, I know my son. Something is bothering you. Is it this thing with Erica? How dare she embarrass you like that on your special night?" He breathed deeply. "Clay?" his mother pressed.

"I kind of got into it with Erica's sister earlier."

"About what?" she asked.

"She has some major issues, and she's crazy like Erica."

His mother stroked his arm. "You have to allow her to come to her own reality, baby. Erica is a young woman, and she wasn't ready to be married at such a young age. What did you expect? I have faith that you will make the right decisions."

"I think she wants to leave me and take the kids."

"Where would she go, and how is she going to take the kids? You make all the money, don't you? You bought the house and the cars."

Clay nodded his head in agreement. "Well, she bought her Rover, but that's the only thing. What is she thinking? I'm not going to let her take my kids. She's not getting anything."

"Do what you have to do, baby. I'm here for you, no matter what you decide," she said.

"Okay, Mama." He fell back into her arms.

"Baby, everything will be all right, and whatever you do, remember what I've always told you—you are better than them."

"Thank you, Mama."

"Now, go clean up so I can feed you some food."

"Okay, Mama." He hugged her.

Clay went upstairs to his room to get cleaned up. Fifteen minutes later, he found his mother already seated at the dining room table, coffee in hand. Clay strolled in without a care in the world.

"Come on, son," his mother said. "I've got your favorite leftovers. Chicken and rice, just the way you like them."

His mother always had his favorite ready for him. He got a home-cooked meal like this whenever he came over. Erica had stopped cooking for him years ago. He didn't know what he would do without his mother.

Aunt Mena walked in with her pajamas on and a scarf wrapped around her head. She scowled at Clay, hesitating to take her seat. She had always hated how her sister babied her only son.

"Don't you have your own home, with your own family, Mr. Important Taxman?" Clay didn't respond, as he had a mouth full of food. Mena glanced at his face. "Finally, somebody got you back."

"Leave my baby alone. He can come and eat anytime he wants," his mother said.

Mena put her hands on her hips. "Baby, huh. Is that right?"

13

Lashay scratched her head, glancing at her watch. How could it be a few minutes past nine o'clock? She was worn out from singing and dancing with Money, but the fight with Clay had gotten her adrenaline flowing.

She took an Uber to Erica's house, feeling both excited and fearful. She walked through the open guard gate and continued to the front door. Finding it unlocked, she let herself in. Total silence greeted her. No sounds of children laughing and playing. No television buzzing. She walked through the foyer and the hallway, then into the living room. She looked at her sister, who sat staring at a piece of paper.

"Hey, Erica," she exclaimed. "What's up? Girl, you missed it."

"Hi, Lashay. I thought you were coming tomorrow?" Erica asked, but there was no life to her.

"I wanted to talk tonight."

"I just put the kids to bed." She folded the paper so as not to bring attention to it and then set it down. "How was the audition?"

"Well, it started off not all great, then my voice went hoarse, but because he knew I could sing, he wanted to give me another chance and wants to hear how my voice sounds in the studio. So they booked me for some recording time at the studio."

"That's awesome, Lashay. You always wanted to be a big-time singer." Erica put her drink down on the coffee table and looked at her sister, who sat down on the couch.

"You can be a big-time singer too, Erica. It's what Mom always wanted for us, both of us singing together. I miss Mom so much and—"

Erica stopped her. "I understand that, but that was a long time ago. We've moved on and live very different lives now, and we each do the best we can to honor her." She put her hand on Lashay's thigh. "I'm happy for you, but you know my singing days are over. I want to focus on my family."

"I called you hours ago. How come you didn't answer your phone?"

"I was busy with the kids."

"Look, Erica, I wanted to talk to you about something that happened after the audition."

"Okay," Erica said, concern creeping into her eyes.

"Did Clay buy a new car? A new sports car?"

"Hell, no. I stopped him from spending money like that last year after he bought the Beamer."

"I saw Clay at the club with another woman, and when he saw me, he took off."

"To be honest with you, Lashay. I don't care."

"Well, we sort of got into a fight."

Erica reached for her sister's hand and her face stiffened. "Look, Lashay, I don't want to relive the memory of the many arguments we've had over the years about Clay. I can take care of myself. I have my kids to worry about, and you know CJ needs special attention, so right now is not the time. I have a lot on my mind." She blinked to compose herself. "To be honest with you, it's not the perfect situation right now. It is very hard being married to a man like Clay."

"Fuck that shit, it's not hard. You shouldn't be married to a man like that. You deserve fucking better."

"Keep it down. You might wake my kids."

"They're asleep on the other side of the damn house, and maybe they need to know their dad is a shit husband."

"It's not that simple. You don't have kids. When you get some, come talk to me."

Lashay clenched her fists. They stared at each other in a battle of wills. She noticed her sister's wistful eyes, realizing Erica was starting to get emotional. A tear rolled down her face.

"Listen, Lashay…" Erica paused, as if unsure. "I'm gonna tell you something I haven't told anybody." Her face twisted in pain. "I'm pregnant. I didn't want to say anything at first because I know how you feel about Clay."

"True, but are you happy?"

"Yes."

"Then I'm happy for you. Is it another niece or another nephew?" Lashay put her hand on her sister's stomach.

"I'm happy about being pregnant, but I'm leaving him."

"Good, you deserve much better than that scumbag. I felt something wasn't right for a while," Lashay said.

"You've felt something wasn't right ever since I started dating him. Looking back, I should have listened. I'm okay now. I cry a lot, but that's also probably because of the pregnancy. I didn't want to bother you. You have your own relationship to deal with."

"Never mind about me," Lashay said. "I'm your sister, so I'm here for you. I will always have your back. I want us to be close like we used to be—"

Erica cut her off. "Lashay. It's not like I'm the easiest person to get along with. I'm sorry for not being straight with you. I was trying to be strong, but we're stronger when we're honest with each other."

Lashay could feel her eyes tearing up. "I'm sorry, too, sis. I shouldn't have been so hard on you. I understand what it's like to depend on a man that's not available for you. We can work on that together."

Erica wiped the tears from her face and wrapped her sister in a tight hug. "We can start by forgiving each other and beginning with a clean slate."

"We can start with you coming with me to the studio. You don't have to sing, unless of course you want to," Lashay added, winking.

"You know what, I'll go to the studio with you, but I'm not singing."

"It's a sister date," Lashay said. Both of them laughed, then grabbed one another in a tight embrace.

Lashay freed herself from Erica's hug. "Are you going to be okay?"

"Yes, I'm fine now. There's more to tell you, but I'll do that later, okay?"

"I love you, sis. I will help you get outta that toxic marriage," Lashay said, and they hugged again.

14

Lashay drove her car through the business district downtown. The massive warehouses dwarfed them. She had never realized how intimidating the immense concrete-and-steel buildings could be. She rolled down the window, stuck her head out, and inhaled the air. She pulled into the underground parking garage of the five-story Benton building and went inside.

The elevator opened to a large office with an open floor plan and glass walls. A nicely dressed woman sat behind a looming ebony desk. "Hello, Mr. Harper is waiting for you. The studio is at the end of the hall."

As Lashay and Erica went down the quiet hallway, goose bumps rose on Erica's arms the closer they got. The long walls were covered with awards, plaques, and pictures from successful records. Some were gold and some platinum. Famous faces beamed at them through black metal frames.

As soon as they entered the studio, they smelled a stench, like something woodsy. Burning leaves, maybe, and something else Erica couldn't quite place. She had never been in the building before, but something seemed familiar about it. She was surprised to see how the office space had been transformed into a fully operational recording studio. The large room was divided into two different workstations, each with its own unique equipment. One room was closed off, but they could see three microphones with stools placed underneath them. The other room held computers and soundboards with a lot of flashing buttons. The expansive glass walls separating the stations created the feeling of being in a large but private space. A wide rectangular electronic clock spanned the room, displaying the time in six different time zones. Flat-screen TVs were plastered all over the walls, showing music videos.

They entered a smaller adjacent room where two black velvet couches sat atop the wall-to-wall carpet, with muscular guards sitting on both of them. One guard rose and retrieved a can of soda from the stainless-steel refrigerator, but he didn't offer to get one for anyone else. A small bar sat in the corner, and a chair was pushed against the wall next to the couch, with a large circular coffee table in the middle of the room.

G Money wore a shiny green suit. With his back to them, he talked to a short young black man dressed in sagging pants and a waist-length fur jacket. While the rapper listened, they observed he didn't quite close his mouth all the way, and when he spoke, a bright reflection on his teeth shined like a brand-new dime.

"I want to rap about my real life," he was saying. "Some of it's good and some of it's bad. It doesn't matter. I have to get this cheese. I have a wife and daughters, G Money." The young man gave G Money a nervous grin that resembled the front grille of a Chevy. The rapper had diamonds in his teeth.

"I don't give a fuck if you have a wife and kids. You'll come to my studio and rap about being a player and a pimp, or you'll lie in the alley and rap about being broke and bloody. I mean, let's get real, partna, cats like you come a dime a dozen. If you don't do it, I'll find the next little rapping hoe to do it. Capisce? Now get the fuck out of here," he said, not the least bit deterred by the fact that Lashay and Erica were standing there.

When the rapper left, G Money spun around on his heel to face them. "Lashay, my number one recruit," he said, without missing a beat. "C'mere, baby girl. How you doin'?" He glanced at Erica. "I'm G Money. Call me Money. And you are?" Then he winked, shooting her a knowing grin as he bit down on a stinky cigar.

"Hi, I'm Erica, Lashay's sister," she said, with a fabricated sense of excitement.

"Erica, your sister has something going on here," he said, pointing to Lashay's throat and rotating his finger in circles. "We can make her into a real star, as long she doesn't lose her voice. She would be known all over the world. They'll be dressing like her, walking like her, and talking like her. I love that shit. This girl is so bad she has people all over the city talking about that voice, and I do mean some very powerful people." He wrapped an arm around Lashay's shoulders. "You ready?"

"G Money, thank you for giving me another chance. I'm ready and I won't disappoint," she said. "You're the man."

He put his hand on her face. "Yes, I am. Your job is to sing. My job is to make us money. We can talk contract after a few demos, and you will have creative freedom. Would you like a drink?"

Erica shook her head.

"Please," said Lashay.

G Money nodded to one of the guards. He got up went to the fridge and grabbed a bottle of water. As the guard bent over, Lashay saw he had a gun holstered under his arm. He handed Lashay the water and she took a drink.

"Now," G Money said. "Lashay, you go into the booth and let's get started. I wanna hear some songs about love and relationships. I'm even thinking about changing your name…maybe to 'Shay Day.'"

"What does it matter what my name is?" Lashay said.

G Money laughed. "Let me worry about the business end. We need something with a ring to it. That's the way it is. We're going to make money." He turned to Erica. "After she's done, we want to hear you sing, too."

"No, I'm sorry, I don't sing anymore," Erica said.

"What do you have to lose, Erica?" Lashay said.

"Yeah, don't you want the opportunity to make some money? Doing what your sister tells me you used to love doing?" G Money said.

"What the hell," Erica said. "I'll sing a little, but I haven't sung in a long time."

"That's what I'm talking about. Okay, Lashay, you do a couple of songs, then Erica will do a few, then you both will do some numbers together. Sister duets are becoming a big thing right now, and you both have the look."

"Works for me," Lashay said, feeling less sure of herself as she stood face-to-face with G Money, who was inches away from her with his burning cigar. He was a beast. All the courage that had welled up in her chest dropped into the pit of her stomach. She thought she might pass out if it got any worse.

"You can do it," Erica said. Lashay mustered the strength from deep within as she walked into the booth.

G Money walked over to the big computer board, sat on the edge of the chair, and put out his cigar in a large crystal ashtray. After a few minutes of instructions, Erica heard a clear female voice coming over the mounted speakers on either side of the room. Lashay sounded fantastic, and her voice was flawless. She sang three songs without any retakes. Erica could tell she'd nailed it. G Money nodded in her direction. Erica took a deep breath and decided to go with it. Lashay gave Erica a hug before Erica continued into the booth. At first, she felt a little off her game, but after singing a few notes and following G Money's lead, she was all right. G Money had a great sense of humor, and he was able to help her relax. She sang as if she had never taken a break from it. When she finished singing her set, she came out of the booth.

"Let's take a break, then both of you go in and sing together," G Money said and then continued, "Erica, would you like a drink?"

"No, thank you, I'm not thirsty," Erica said.

The sisters discussed what songs they had enjoyed doing together and which ones would highlight their voices the best. It had been many years since she'd sung with Lashay, and it gave her a great sense of satisfaction. She wished she had not waited so long to do so.

When G Money told them he was ready, the girls went back into the booth. Lashay gave Erica a slight push into the middle, and she found herself standing next to one microphone, with Lashay in front of the other. Music began to play, and they started to sing.

One of the bodyguards, at a signal from G Money, made sure the studio door was closed shut. The girls could see what was going on, but they were focused on their voices. As they sang, G Money started playing with the buttons on the board.

After the song ended, they saw G Money peeking up at a spot on the wall, and although Lashay glanced up, she thought nothing of it until she noticed that the inconspicuous hole in the ceiling behind the mounted speakers began to emit a misty air that showered down on them. The more he turned the knob, the more the mist came out. Lashay began to lose her balance. Her knees buckled, and she lost her balance. Erica stopped singing, reached for her and laid her down on the floor. She raised her head, looking for one of the bodyguards to come in and help. No one came. Dizzy now, she tried to get up but stumbled toward the door and dropped. Inside the booth, they both lay on the floor, unmoving.

G Money picked up his cell phone and called someone. "They're ready, boss," he said.

15

The old black man who ran the pool hall on the Southside sat behind the bar, staring with his bloodshot eyes at the lifelong buddies. Shorty was next to the pool table, measuring out his next shot, while his best friend, Crazy Moe, lay on the couch with his feet up on the wall, twirling his pool stick in the air.

Maurice, the one they called Crazy Moe, was a hardhead. He had a muscular build and a square chin and was not as ugly as Shorty. It only took minutes to realize that what Crazy Moe lacked in ugly, he more than made up for in stupid. He talked slow and began most sentences with "word." He also ended most sentences with "word," and his most-asked question was, of course, "word?"

"I was watching my favorite cartoon this morning, *The Flintstones,* and I started wondering how Fred Flintstone's car could run on foot power. It was easier for him to just walk, without carrying the heavy car frame, and besides, he was using his feet anyway. Word," Crazy Moe said.

Shorty shook his head and passed a blunt over to him. He picked up his cell phone and dialed Lashay. Still no answer.

"Dammit, Moe. She still hasn't answered her phone. Dawg, I done called her three times without no answer." Crazy Moe took a

71

big hit from the blunt and tried to speak while holding the smoke in.

"Maybe she still mad at you, word?" Moe said as he started coughing.

Shorty looked down at his phone. "Man, you know Lashay, she is not the type to just ignore my calls. She would answer and curse me out if she was mad."

"Oh, word, man. Slim is here," Moe said, sitting up. A tall skinny black man walked in, dressed in a nice shirt and pants. "Now it's time to go get the money. Word," Moe said.

"Man, where you going tonight dressed like Uncle Tom? I thought we were going to rob people, not go to have church wit' 'em," Shorty said.

"Shorty, I didn't know you had an uncle named Tom, hell. I didn't know you two were related," Moe said.

Slim shook his head. "Naw, man, I'm going to work, and y'all gonna do the robbin'."

"We can make this money fast and easy," Slim said.

"We ready. I want to do something special for my lady," Shorty said.

"Which one?" Crazy Moe said. Shorty glanced at him.

"Lashay, fool."

"Oh. Word," Moe said.

Slim walked around the pool table. "My boss down at the factory sponsors Halloween parties for his wealthy associates. A lot of old rich white people."

"And what, we dress up like you and say, 'yes massa' and they'll just give us poor little dark colored boys money?" Shorty said.

"No, he lets some guys at the factory work the doors and park some cars for a little extra cash for private events out by the lake. It's after hours."

"But it's not Halloween for another four days. Word," Moe said.

"You do know you don't have to wait till the day of Halloween to have a Halloween party?" Slim asked.

"Word, I didn't know that." He laughed.

"I suppose I could work the door, check coats, or park cars," Shorty said, getting excited.

"They already have enough people doing that," Slim said. "At the party, off the back patio, some gambling goes on. It's an enclosed patio. Your job be to rob them while they get liquored up at the poker tables."

"Now you talking, my nigga," Shorty said.

"It's across town, so I'll ride with you guys. Then once we get there, I'll go in and make sure everything is cool," Slim said.

They walked out to the parking lot. Slim stared at Shorty's ride. It was an old classic 1970-model car. A Caprice Classic. The car was painted bright yellow, with brown trim. It looked like a big yellow M&M, with shiny rims. They called it a donk. The tires were bigger than the car, and it sat so high up that it was at least three feet off the ground. It looked ridiculous.

Slim walked to the passenger side and then heard an odd noise coming from the other side of the car. Shorty, being very short, was trying to get in it. He backed up and hopped around like he was a track star about to run hurdles. He ran toward the car and jumped. His knee hit the bottom of the doorjamb right before his chin did, and he fell onto his back. Slim struggled not to laugh.

"Moe," Shorty hollered.

Moe walked over to the driver's side of the car. Shorty backed up a few feet and, with a running start, stepped onto Moe's hands. Moe was waiting for him with his hands clutched together and launched him headfirst into the car. The rest of his body was still hanging out. His legs were scrambling as he tried to get in, so Moe gave him another boost and Shorty made it into the car. He acted as though he hadn't just made a scene. Moe walked back over to the passenger side and jumped in with no problem at all.

"Where is that little step stool you use?" Moe said.

"In the back. It broke earlier."

Slim looked at the broken stool on the backseat floor. "You two like two peas in a ghetto-ass pod that don't nobody want."

As ridiculous as the car looked, it felt even more ridiculous to ride in it. The way he slouched down in the seat, Shorty could tell Slim hoped no one would see him. The seats were torn, and there were areas of yellow foam peeking through the cracked pleather. Slim tried to find a seat belt, without any luck. Moe turned the music up so loud that the car rattled and vibrated as the bass boomed out of the subwoofers. The music system and the rims were worth more than the car itself. Slim yelled at Moe to turn the music down, but it took several attempts before Moe spun his head around. Slim motioned thumbs down, and Moe turned it down.

"What?" Moe said, irritated.

"I said we should turn down the music, so we don't draw attention to ourselves," Slim said.

"Word," Moe said, looking confused. Shorty laughed.

They drove across town, following Slim's directions. He navigated using the GPS on his phone. They passed several nice houses before reaching a big three-story house sitting on about three acres. The house was decorated for Halloween. It looked haunted, but the only ghosts going in and out were living and breathing. They were all pale and not much more than privileged bones, with purple-white hair and varicose veins. This place said old money, right down to the elm trees in the front yard and the gazebo off to the side. The front of the house looked like an upscale car lot. Mercedes, limos, and Jaguars were parked out front, and elderly people milled around everywhere. They were all dressed in elaborate costumes, chatting and making their way into the house.

"Drop me off in the front. After I go inside, park down the street around the corner," Slim said as Shorty came to a stop. Slim jumped out of the car.

"I'll be right back," he said, and within minutes he was back, dressed in a business suit and a President Nixon mask. "Here are some masks for you guys. They always keep extra ones. In about

74

two hours, I'll open the back door." Shorty looked at Slim like he was crazy.

"You're kidding, right?" Shorty asked, waiting for the punch line. "I mean, this ain't the fuckin' eighteen hundreds and shit. We ain't like *Dead Presidents*," Shorty said.

Slim had a straight face and cold eyes. Shorty's grin disappeared. "Okay, I get the masks, but why we have to wait like that?"

"It don't make sense that we hafta wear those stupid masks. We have ski masks," Moe said.

"Look, it's all a big game. This is a low-key setup for some very important people. It's no big deal. If we wait, all the money will be in one place at one time, and everyone will be drunk as hell. On top of it all, they won't even be able to remember what we look like because we will be in costume like them. Just trust me."

"What are we supposed to do for two hours?" Shorty whined as Slim headed back toward the house.

"Word," Moe replied.

An hour passed slowly, and they were bored as hell. When Moe got out of the car and took a piss, Shorty's phone rang. He pulled his phone out of his pocket. He didn't recognize the number, and he didn't make a habit of accepting calls from private numbers, so he ignored the call. Moe got back in the car.

"Man, I'm ready to make this money, word," he said. Shorty nodded in agreement. His phone rang again. He saw that the phone number was the same. This time he answered.

"Hello?" he said, unsure who would be on the other end of the line. "What?" he said, pointing to the phone. "What tha fuck. Serious?" Shorty mouthed Lashay's name at Moe as he listened. "Are y'all okay?" he said. "Okay, give me the address. Moe, hand me a pen out of the glove box." Moe reached in and pulled out a gun and set it on top of the dashboard, then reached back in again and pulled out a pen and handed it to Shorty. Shorty wrote the address on his hand.

"Okay, I'll be right there. Okay … okay, got it. We're on our way." He hung up the phone. "Man, you won't believe this shit."

"What?" Moe said.

"That was Lashay. She and her sister need a ride. They stuck. They need us to come get them, and check this out, she said they need some clothes."

"Word? What happened?"

"She didn't say. She said it's a long story and that it's an emergency," Shorty said. "You think she cheating on me?"

"So, we are going to go after we rob this joint, word?" Moe said.

Shorty shot him an evil glare. "Man, is you stupid? She said it's an emergency and we need to hurry. They need clothes. These white folks can wait. Fuck that. Fuck Slim. This was stupid anyway."

Shorty looked at the address on his hand. "I know where this area is, but if we go back to my pad to get clothes, then come back again, that would be way out of the way. I don't have gas like that. We gotta figure something else out."

Moe sat there thinking. "Look, there goes an old white couple getting out of their car." They were dressed up like Superman and Wonder Woman. Shorty started the car up and drove toward the couple.

16

The first-floor hall of Dameron Hospital was empty except for a doctor who was writing on a clipboard. He walked down the hall while reading the patient file. He looked at the name posted on the door of Room 222 and stopped. He tapped on the door and peeked in.

"It's okay," a female voice said. As he walked in, he saw a male standing beside the bed and a female sitting near the patient. A nurse trailed in behind him.

"So," the doctor began. "My name is Dr. Putnam. Are you her family?" he said as he pointed to Erica.

"Yes," Lashay said before Shorty said anything.

"Well, we ran some tests," Dr. Putnam said.

"The nurses said everything checked out negative with her kit, but that isn't the last of it," the doctor said. "When we pumped her stomach and ran blood tests to see what other toxins might be in her blood, we found high levels of an unknown chemical and CHC."

"She has been under a lot of stress, and my rape kit came back clean, too. They told me I had the unknown chemical in my system as well," Lashay said.

"Like I said, although her rape kit didn't show any trauma or anything," Dr. Putnam explained, "the CHC hormone is usually present when someone undergoes a great deal of stress."

"But I feel fine, other than a headache," Lashay added. "I just don't understand why my sister seems to be taking it harder than me."

"Well, miss." Dr. Putnam cleared his throat. "I don't know if you knew this, and if you didn't, I'm sorry. But your sister was pregnant."

"You said 'was,'" Lashay whispered as she looked at Shorty, then Erica.

"Yes. She suffered a miscarriage within the last twenty-four hours. Our best guess is that the stress and the chemicals contributed to it."

"You're mistaken," Lashay said as her shoulders began shaking.

"I'm sorry, miss. I understand this is difficult. She will need a lot of rest, and I am also going to suggest some counseling."

Lashay turned her back to the doctor and turned to Shorty.

"What is he talking about, Shorty?" She began to break down. "My name is not miss." The doctor handed the orders to Shorty and gave him brief instructions on the way out, then made a quick exit. Shorty grabbed Lashay and held her close.

"Come on, baby, anger ain't gonna help," Shorty said and then he walked out of the room chasing the doctor.

Lashay buried her face and sobbed. Erica's fluttered her eyes open.

"How do you feel?" Lashay asked, walking closer to her bed.

"Fine . . .," she responded.

"Okay, and your body?" Lashay continued. "Do you have a headache?"

"I'm okay."

"Well, we were both affected, but in different ways. Dr. Putnam just came by."

"Where's Shorty?" Erica said.

"Erica, I'm trying to talk to you," Lashay pleaded. She looked at her while trying not to blame her. "The doctor said you were under some sort of stress and there was a hormone on the test and something."

Erica stopped her. "I'll be fine once we get out of the hospital."

"Fine? You're not fine, Erica," Lashay said. "I'm trying to tell you what the doctor said while you were asleep."

"It's simple," Erica said. "I lost the baby. End of story."

"You were awake?" Lashay said. Erica nodded. "Please, sis, let's talk. We need to figure this out. I don't want this to eat at you. I'm going to get to the bottom of it myself," her sister said.

"Stop. You've done enough." Erica closed her eyes. Lashay slumped down, defeated. When she pulled back, she realized Shorty had returned.

"Erica, what really happen?" Shorty asked.

"I told you," Lashay said.

"I want Erica's side, babe. You guys were a little woozy last night."

"It's a long story, but Lashay and I were at some guy name G Money's studio, recording a few songs. Lashay sang first. She was drinking, I was not. I noticed she was kinda loopy," Erica explained. "Not normal loopy. Then they kept insisting that I relax and offered me a drink, but I said no. They didn't seem to like that."

"I don't remember that," Lashay said.

"After Lashay sang, then I sang, then they insisted that we sing together. There were bodyguards everywhere, and at least one of them had a gun," Erica said.

"I don't remember any guns," Lashay said.

"We got in the booth together and began singing, and it sounded beautiful. Lashay lost her balance and I tried to help her, then I felt this mist and she fell."

"I fell?" Lashay asked.

Erica sighed. "The bodyguards and the producer were all just standing there staring. I called to them to help, but they didn't move. It was so strange. One moment we were singing, then we woke up out in an open field about twenty-five minutes outside of the city with no clothes."

"That's the part I remember. Damn," Lashay said as Erica finished.

"Lashay waved a car down, and this guy pulled over and let us use his cell phone. He gave us the shirt off his back and an emergency blanket he had."

"Why didn't you call the police?" Shorty asked.

"We didn't really think. Lashay just kept saying she needed you, and that's who she called. I started cramping, and between the drugs and the pain I couldn't figure out where we were and didn't connect everything at first."

"The man offered to call the police, but we said no," Lashay said. "I don't really know why we said no, but it made sense at the time."

"Once we talked to you and realized that we were missing for hours, we started putting two and two together. We had you take us to the police station and tried to explain to them what happened, but they insisted we go to the hospital for testing first. I was in bad shape, and I don't think they took us very serious because of the way we were dressed."

"Shorty, I don't know where you got that shit," Lashay chimed in.

"Yeah. Why was I was wearing a Wonder Woman outfit and Lashay was another superhero? Plus, we pulled up in a car that looked like a damn ghetto fantasy," Erica said.

"Well, it is Halloween time, and I bet anythang that's not the first ghetto-fabulous car from the hood they laid their eyes on," Shorty said.

"They did rape kits on both of us and found nothing. Strange, right? Why go through all that trouble in the first place? Nothing physical happened to us, but they found some unknown chemical in my system. They sent it to a lab, and we're waiting for the results. They won't be back for a few weeks," Erica said.

"That makes no sense. We need to find out what's going on," Lashay added.

"I wonder why the officers said they went back to that studio and didn't find anything. No evidence of anything at all," Shorty said.

"Said the place wasn't even a studio," Lashay said.

"I'm so upset and confused. I need to get out of here," Erica stated.

"You need to rest right now," Lashay said.

"I have to find out what is going on. Why would somebody to that to us?"

"Maybe it's nothing but a prank," Shorty added.

Erica ignored the comment. "I'm supposed to meet Will in a couple days. I hope he has some information on the papers I gave him, and maybe he can talk to some his police contacts and look into this."

17

Will drove his Ford Taurus toward the first address on his list. He had on his favorite jogging suit and his most comfortable running shoes. He had not worn either in years, not since the last time he'd worked out. He felt like a prime-time track star.

He pulled the car into a spot in front of the minimart store. When he got out, he noticed a beautiful woman. An exotic beauty, maybe Asian, Indian or Hispanic. He didn't know, but she had dark, pretty hair, and the little droplets from the fog coated her hair, making it shine like jewels when the sun peeked through. They smiled at each other. He walked into the store and purchased two prepaid credit cards. He got back in the car, pulled up to another minimart, went inside and purchased two more prepaid credit cards. He drove down the main street toward the downtown business district. It had a suite number address, and the sign out in front read, "Bank of Rockton." The bank was in a nice, busy neighborhood.

He parallel-parked on the side street. The ATM at this bank was one of the few that were inside the first door area, out of the view of bank personnel. A tall, slim lady with blonde hair, wearing shades, waited to use the ATM. He walked past her into the bank.

He glanced around to make sure no one was looking before slipping into the back offices.

A woman in a business suit approached him. "May I help you, sir?"

"Yes, I have an appointment with Mrs. Jenkins."

She pointed to the other end of the room. "Have a seat over there."

As he waited, he considered grabbing some of the business magazines on the coffee table but decided against it. He needed to stay focused on the meeting.

A striking black female dressed in business attire came up to him. "Mr. Brown?" Will nodded. "Follow me."

Mrs. Jenkins led the way into her office. She sat down behind the desk and motioned Will to sit in the other chair.

"Now," Mrs. Jenkins said, "do you have something for me?" He set the large envelope on the table. She fingered through the cash and the prepaid credit cards. "That looks like everything." She pressed a button on the machine on her desk. "I'll be right back." She walked out holding the folder. Mrs. Jenkins returned five minutes later. "I just confirmed the account numbers, so you should find everything in order," she said, handing him a different envelope.

"Thank you, Mrs. Jenkins. Our agency appreciates your bank's cooperation in this investigation."

"Will, stop being so formal," she said. He walked over to give her a hug.

"Deneh, you are the best."

"Now, you know we can't run those accounts again. The bank can't risk getting caught."

"I understand. Thanks again for all your help," he said before the door closed behind him.

Will walked out of the bank and headed toward his car. Out of nowhere, someone bumped into him with such force that he hit the ground. As he was falling, she snatched the folder out of his hands. He jumped up and chased after her. From the back, she looked just like the woman standing at the ATM when he walked into the bank. She ran like she had a motor stuck up her ass. As she sprinted out of the newly paved parking lot, the blonde wig flew off her head.

She crossed the street, maneuvering between passing cars. He chased her down an alley and saw her jump into a gold Camry. As the tinted window on the driver's side went up, he saw the driver of the car. It was the exotic woman he had seen earlier.

The Camry sped off. Across the street, a white guy with a crew cut was watching everything from his parked car. A blue-haired elderly lady sat in the passenger seat. Will rushed across the street and showed the man his private investigator badge. "Can you follow that car? I've been robbed. I'll give you five hundred dollars."

"Sure," the young man said.

Will jumped into the backseat of the car. The man punched the pedal of his Dodge Dart. The car made a screeching U-turn. As he came around, they could see the taillights of the car ahead.

"Son, don't drive my car like that," said the old woman in the passenger seat. She was oblivious to what was going on. Will didn't think she'd even noticed him in the backseat.

"Okay, Grandma," the man said, smiling. He pushed down the accelerator.

The old lady flew back in her seat. "Why are you driving so crazy?"

The Camry turned onto a narrow street, and they weren't far behind it now.

"Fuck man, I ain't never done nothing like this," the driver said excited.

"Watch your mouth," the old woman said.

"Okay, Grandma."

They turned onto the little-used street, going at least fifty. Grandma held on to the sides of the car, but in spite of that, she slid against the driver. As the young man held tight to the steering wheel with one hand, he used the other one to push his grandmother back over to the passenger side. When Will saw how close they were to the Camry, he breathed a little easier.

The Camry turned right into an alley. They approached the alley, but before they could get there, the gold Camry came flying out, followed by another Camry: same color, same everything. They sped off in opposite directions.

"Which way?" asked the driver.

"Forget it," Will said. "If you can get back to my car as fast as you can, I'll give you the money for your trouble."

The man drove him back. Will jumped out and rushed up to his car. He unlocked the door and was relieved to find that nothing had been disturbed. He pulled five one-hundred dollar bills from the money bag. When he handed the money to the guy, the guy thanked him. The grandma continued to look confused.

Will sat still in his car for a few minutes to calm himself down. He cruised down the road, his eyes flitting from the road to the rearview mirror, making sure no one was behind them. He had just begun to believe that his worst fears were unfounded when at the next stoplight, a car barreled at him out of nowhere. Shocked, he still managed to hit the gas as the other Camry swerved in front of them.

"Oh shit," Will said, at the same time realizing he couldn't go forward. He shifted the car into reverse as a woman jumped out and rushed the car, her face full of rage.

In a quick, fluid movement, the woman snatched the door open with one hand, her other hand holding a small gun. Will grabbed the gun, then pushed her backward, yanking the gun from her. The car jerked as his foot hit the accelerator in an effort to get away from the crazed woman, but it must have slipped. He grabbed a handful of the woman's blouse and wrapped it around his hand. The woman's eyes grew wide. She tried to wriggle from his grasp, but he held on.

"What do you want?" he demanded. He put the car back in drive and began to drag her alongside the car as it moved forward. Her screams filled the quiet air. Will screamed at her to shut up.

The woman stumbled backward over the rough-edged potholes in the asphalt as she struggled to keep up with the car. His grip was like a steel claw. He stopped the car and got out, and his massive hand encircled her throat. He picked her up and slammed her against the car with such force that the entire car shook. He slammed her to the ground. He picked her up like it was nothing and dragged her to the side of the road and threw her to the ground. Bullets flew past him as the other Camry chased toward him. He sprinted back to the car, jumped in the driver's side and sped off.

18

The hum of the car's engine was so quiet Erica could barely hear it. It lulled her into a calmness she hadn't felt for the last few days. She had been careless and willing to accept lies over truth. The truth had slapped her in the face and put her in the hospital. She wondered how much pain was required to make a blind woman see. She had trouble getting dressed and acting normal, but she had to keep putting one foot in front of the other. Her children had kept her going since she'd been out of the hospital.

CJ played in his booster seat, and joy filled her. CJ represented the best part of her. If someone were to ask her if she was happy, she already knew the answer. She had forgotten what happy was until recently. Now Will and his team had given her hope.

Erica turned into the Costco parking lot and began the difficult task of finding a parking space. She finally found one and parked. She put CJ in the front of the basket and dug in her purse for her Costco card.

Inside, CJ started humming out loud, clapping his hands together. People stared as they passed by. Erica didn't stop until they reached the back of the store, where the electronics and flat-screen TVs were. There were about twenty smart TVs on display, all on the same channel. She reached up to change the channel on one of them, but it wouldn't budge.

"Can I help you?" asked a Howdy Doody–looking white guy dressed in Dickies and a white Costco polo shirt.

"No, sir, I'm waiting for somebody," she said.

"Okay, miss, let me know if you need any help."

The man walked away.

"Hi, Erica, thanks for meeting me," Will said. She jumped, then turned to face him. Will had a baseball cap on and some shades, and he wouldn't look directly at her.

"Let's walk," he said.

They walked to a more secluded section.

"Hey, guy. Clayton Junior is a big boy now," Will said, trying to interact with her son.

CJ began jumping with excitement. Will paused. CJ bounced as his excitement kept escalating, and he was having trouble self-regulating. Erica grabbed his hand, and CJ calmed down. She reached in her pocket, pulled out his favorite Lego block and handed it to him.

Will glanced at his watch. "Erica, please don't panic when I tell you this … I was attacked, and I think I'm being followed."

"What?"

"Yes, I was attacked earlier today."

"Oh no. Will, I'm sorry. What happened?"

"No need to go into it right now."

"Well, I'm glad you're okay and here. I had a rough last few days myself."

"What happen?"

Erica filled him in on the events of what happen.

"Wow, I'll check with my police contacts. Did you file a police report?"

"Yes, but they're saying the place is clean and not even a studio."

"That's crazy. Maybe it's something to do with Lashay."

"My sister—you know my sister. Every time, it's something with her."

"Yeah, we know your sister. She's always been a risk taker, to her own detriment. No disrespect."

"None taken. Anyway, so what happened with you?"

"No need to go into that right now. I got some information about the things we discussed before. You need to hear it," Will said.

"Oh goody."

"It was hard to find people who would talk about your husband and his associates. But your husband was under FBI investigation a few years ago. I think it went away, but I'm not sure."

"That bad, huh?" Erica asked.

"Yes, it was some pretty serious stuff. I almost lost my life over some financial information I got this morning. I wanted to show you some proof about all your accounts. I'm so sorry." They walked past washers and dryers and stopped in front of some outdoor furniture facing away from the aisles.

"So, what about the finances, the house, and my businesses?"

"Have a seat," he said. "Listen, Erica, I'm sorry to tell you this, but we couldn't find anything in your husband's name or yours. No businesses. No properties, not even the house. The only thing that came up is that he works for some company called Quality Enterprises. Under this business, his salary is eighty thousand a year. The worst part is that we have been unable to find that business, and the financial information on the business got away."

"What do you mean you couldn't find anything in my name? I own three wig shops," she said.

"Erica, nothing has your name on it. Even the house you live in is owned by the company. The only thing in your name is your Range Rover."

"What the hell? I own that house, plus fifty percent of all the businesses. I showed you the papers," she insisted.

"Yes, you did, but remember the forged legal separation papers you showed us?" He paused.

She pinched her lips together. "Yes."

"We believe he fabricated documents for all of the assets, transferring ownership to corporations and/or enterprises several times over. The paper trail is buried deep. So deep we don't even have a lead right now. I even visited the county clerk's office. There are zero records that match the paperwork you gave us. Also, most likely Clay used the fabricated separation papers to demonstrate to other women that he was legally separated."

"Shit," Erica said under her breath.

"We went over everything, and nothing is in your name. I mean nothing. But we haven't given up. We know we're onto something big, we just have to find out where he's hiding everything."

Erica put her head down and wrapped her arms across her middle. Her hands grabbed her sides. She didn't know what to feel. She couldn't cry or scream. She felt empty, angry, and full of despair all at the same time. She began to rock herself. Will put his hand on her back.

"Erica, I know this is a lot to take in all at once, but you must stay strong."

Will's voice became a distant whisper. Erica realized she had been a fool and gotten played. This whole time, she had been a pawn in Clay's demented chess game. She had helped him build the business into something major, only to find out it didn't exist for her. The home she'd lived in for the past seven years with her kids wasn't hers. *What the fuck?* She flashed in rage. How could it be that *she* had been written out of the company as if she wasn't the reason the business was thriving today?

She was the one who'd balanced the books every year in the beginning. She was the one with the level head. She was the one that had budgeted their expenses down to the penny. She was the one that had saved the firm from bankruptcy. She was the one that had sacrificed her career for their children, so he didn't have to.

She was the one that had taken her life savings to get Clay's ass out of a hole.

She'd used the money she and Lashay had received from their grandmother's small house after she'd passed. She wanted to scream. *Now who'll get it?* Erica heard her name and CJ began to cry. She grabbed CJ's hand and lifted her head.

"I'm so sorry about this. We believe this is the tip of the iceberg. We're committed to this case, and we'll get to the bottom of this. I'm dropping all of my other cases just to focus on this one."

"Will, I don't know what to say." Erica grabbed CJ out of the basket and perched him on her lap. She kissed him on the cheek and held him close. Her eyes began to fill with tears.

"Erica, don't worry. I'm here for you. Everything will be okay, trust me. We'll get him," he said, pleading with her to hold it together. She could see his deep concern for her. It appeared he was about to take her in his arms. She could feel it, but she also knew he wouldn't.

"Thanks," she said through her tears. "And thank you for meeting me like this." She tried to regain control of her emotions.

"Do you know where Clay may keep his documents? We need as much information as you can get so the lawyers can have some leverage in your divorce."

"The only place I would know is his home office, but he moved stuff out of there. I checked when I got out of the hospital."

"The way everything is set up, Clay has some silent partners somewhere, and knowing him, he probably has information on them that he keeps for himself," Will said.

"Will, I need to go home and talk to him." Erica pulled out her phone and walked away. When she returned to him, she said, "I'm going to drop off my son at my sister's."

"What are you going to do, Erica?"

"I'm going to find out what's going on, from the horse's mouth."

"Maybe you should wait till you see the lawyer."

"Let me talk to him before we do anything."

"You think that's the right thing to do?"

"Will, I have to give the father of my children one last chance to come clean, no matter how disgusted I am with him."

"I understand. I need to go see a lady who may be able to help us. I'll call you so we can meet later."

"Okay, that will be great."

19

Erica stood at the window of the big Brookside Manor. The house was empty except for her. She knew Clay would be home, at least to get a change of clothes if nothing else. She tried calling Bernice to tell her she'd dropped the kids off at Lashay's for the evening. Bernice had never called her back. Regardless of how Will felt, this was something she had to do to for her own peace of mind. She couldn't operate like Clay. All she wanted was her kids.

From inside the living room, she could hear Clay talking on the phone as he walked up to the door. He walked into the house and jumped when he saw her standing there.

"Clay, please sit," said Erica.

"Why?"

"Please, Clay, have a seat."

Clay sat in a chair, but he didn't relax. His light brown complexion took on an angry reddish tint. "What's this all about?"

"This is about everything that's been going on. I know you're behind the studio situation," she said.

He jumped up. "I don't know what you're talking about."

"Clay, just listen," she said to him. Then she walked over to him and handed him the information Will had given her.

"I know it's not everything, but it's enough for us to negotiate." He didn't say anything. "What do you think of that, Clay?"

"I don't know anything about any of that nonsense," he answered.

"How could you do this to me? I know about everything—the business, the forged documents. You even forged my name on separation papers just so you could date other women." Clay didn't say a word, and it was making Erica angry. She stood with her fists clenched. "You're going to tell me the truth. I know you set up everything. Start talking. You need to come clean."

"I have no idea what you're talking about."

"Please, Clay, I want the truth. I believed in you, I supported you, I loved you. Now, I want the truth—the whole truth."

"Erica, you're wrong. I am a businessman and that's it. I do taxes," he said.

"Clay, have it your way. We're getting a divorce. I just want my kids. I don't care about anything else." Erica's eyes narrowed. She began to breathe heavily. "I said, all I want is my kids?"

"They're my kids too," Clay said.

"You never spend any time with them. You're never there for them. You don't want them."

"It's up to a judge to decide, and you might be going to jail," he responded.

"What are you talking about?"

"I've heard things."

"You and I are done for real this time," she said.

"If I was you, I would watch what you say," he warned.

"What the hell are you talking about?" she said. Clay reached into his black briefcase, pulled a piece a paper out and handed it to Erica. "What the hell is this?" she asked, confused.

"This is a PPO I will be requesting for the safety of the kids," Clay said.

"What?"

"Yeah, Erica. I heard there are pictures and videos of you naked with minors. How could you be so stupid?" Clay said.

"Clay, how could you do this to me? After everything I've sacrificed for you. You know I love my kids. You know you set that all up."

"I haven't done anything. You did this to yourself, Erica. The law is the law. This paper says you have to stay away from the kids. You better hope for your own sake that this mess gets resolved. I think you have fourteen days to respond. You could lose them forever," he said with a laugh in his voice.

Erica walked up to him, never taking her glare off him.

"I had no idea you were doing child pornography," he said. "I knew you liked money, but damn, Erica. Porn with kids? That could ruin you forever if it got out." Clay caught his refection in the wall mirror and admired himself. He flexed and admired his physique. "I look damn good for a man almost forty, don't I?"

"You're not a man. You're a monster. I know you're behind the studio, and me losing my baby somehow—everything. I never want to see you again," she said.

"What, you were pregnant and lost it?"

"Yes, you knew I was. You had a GPS device on my car. You knew I was going to the doctor."

"Erica, I'm so sorry about all that had to happen to you. You're lucky that you had the opportunity to be the wife of the great Clay Williams. I gave you a chance, and you changed on me. So, it is what it is."

"You weren't great, Clay. I bailed your ass out, remember? We built that company together, with my money. I was there when you had nothing. I balanced the books. I hosted the parties. I kept your bad decisions from making the business go belly-up. Not you."

"Erica, there was no 'together.' I built everything myself," he said. "Who's gonna testify to what you say, Erica? Your family? Oops, they're all gone and your sister is in trouble too."

"How could you?" she shouted back. "You never did love anyone but yourself, Clay. I'm sorry it took this long for me to realize that. I will win in court. Whatever you have, they'll know it's not real, and I will have the kids!"

"Don't worry about all of that, Erica. I'll take care of them now. They'll be in good hands. I love them too. They were always *my* kids, not yours," he said.

"You're a sorry excuse for a father."

"Well, if you must know, I never wanted to marry you in the first place, but you got pregnant and then I had no choice in the matter. I did love you at one time. But your poor choices caused you to get here, and now you'll never get anything from me," he said.

"I don't want anything from you, just my kids," she said. "Clay, you'll get what's coming to you one day."

"A new mother for my children, perhaps?" he said.

"After I show them this information, you'll be arrested. I wanted to give you a chance to come clean."

"You think so? You do child porn. What judge is going to give you the kids? The information you have won't help you now. You're the one going to jail. You'll need someone to bail you out. Do you know anyone with that kind of money, besides me? If I was you, I'd be worried about not breaking the law anymore."

"Clay, you're so useless. I have proof of what happened at the hospital and other information."

"You'll soon see how useless I am. That information will be of no use to you."

"It might be useless in a court of law, but in a divorce and custody battle, it will show a pattern."

"You better have a great lawyer, because my lawyer is the best. I do his taxes and get him great refunds. As a matter of fact, I do most of the lawyers' taxes in the city. You may have to leave the city for a lawyer who isn't a friend of mine."

"I already have a lawyer and will see him tomorrow. I will see you in court."

"Enjoy your time with the kids, because it'll be the last," Clay said.

"Fuck you, Clay, you fucking lowlife!"

"What did you say?"

"I said, 'fuck you'!"

In one swift movement, his hands wrapped around her arms. His body pressed against hers. Clay grunted and said, "Yeah, I should kill you right now, bitch!" He grabbed a handful of her hair at the base of her neck. She howled in pain, and Clay laughed. Her body flooded with heat like lava running through an empty riverbed. She could barely see, then he came into focus and she zeroed in on Clay. He pushed her away and turned his back.

She kicked off her loafers and sprinted after him. She grabbed him by the collar, yanked. He twisted in the air and crashed to the ground. His top button broke loose and popped her in my face. A blister of heat surfaced there and spread throughout her body. Her fists flew through the air, one after the other. He was a drum set. The smacking of her fists against his skin drowned out his cries.

"Awww!" he cried like a two-year-old. She felt his cheeks, his chin, and his eye sockets crash against her fists. Her knees locked on his rib cage. Her fists throbbed. The only thing that made them feel better was every delicious hit.

When she thought he might be dead, she pulled herself together. Her hands trembled. Her legs weak, she brought her hand to the nape of her neck, where Clay had pulled her hair. Her skin throbbed from Clay's cruelty. Her hands ached, too.

She looked around, stretching her fingers to make sure they would still move. They were all there—puffy, red, and blue, but there. Then her hearing returned as she watched him get up. He rushed her, pushing her up against the wall and pinning her there while he choked her. She slid down the wall, her eyes the color of hot liquid chocolate, brimming over with tears. The salty sweat from her forehead caused her to blink hard as the light from the ceiling shined in and out. She was losing her breath. When she thought she might be dead, she pulled herself to a standing position. She was empty of the will to fight but mustered one strong knee to his groin section, and he hit the floor in pain.

She got up and ran to his office. She felt under the desk, grabbed the key, and rushed over to the file cabinet. Opening it, she reached in and got the gun. She quickly ran back down the hallway and saw Clay stumbling into the dining room. "Freeze, motherfucker."

Erica had the gun pointed on Clay.

Then she heard Bernice's voice. "Erica, *please*! Oh, Erica, no! Please!"

Bernice was standing in the middle of the dining room doorway, with the light from the kitchen enveloping her eerily. She was wearing a terry-cloth robe that used to be white. She had rollers in her hair, no shoes on her feet, and pure fear on her face.

Erica's hands shook. The gun she held looked like a small cannon in her tiny hands. About seven feet from her stood Clay, grimacing and holding his side. Erica's lips quivered and she bared her teeth like a wild animal. Her eyes were full of hate and fear.

Bernice stared at Erica. "Baby, *please*!" she cried. "This just ain't the way. He is not worth it!"

Erica turned her head toward Bernice, and through her tears, you could see pure daggers coming from her eyes. But she never turned her body or that gun from Clay.

Bernice continued to plead with Erica. "Listen, Erica, he is not worth it."

There was complete silence. Bernice stood there frozen, watching Erica stand there shaking. "Fuck him, he's trying to take my kids from me!" Erica screamed into the air. Bernice's eyes never left the scene.

"Erica. I will get you. You better listen, 'cause you will end up in jail. Do what you have to do, Erica," Clay said.

"You will not get my kids!"

Clay snuck up closer to Erica, who let her guard down as the tears rolled down her face. She turned back and forth between Bernice and Clay. She let the gun fall every time she turned towards Bernice and had to re-aim whenever she turned back to Clay. And every time she turned, he was a few feet closer.

By the time Erica looked again, Clay had moved closer and leaped towards her, overpowering her with one arm around her torso, his hand grasping her neck. Her feet kicked violently as he lifted her off the floor by her throat. His other hand enveloped hers and pried the gun from her hand.

Bernice appeared behind Clay and hit him on the back of his head with an iron skillet. Clay fell to his knees, and the gun slid a few feet away from him, right in front of Bernice's feet. Bernice picked it up and hit Clay in the head with the butt of the gun, and blood gushed out. Clay hit the floor hard and fast. When he tried to get up, Bernice hit him again.

"Stay down."

Clay got up on his knees and raised his hands. Erica grabbed the gun from Bernice.

"Get out. Don't fucking come back to this house ever again. I will see you in court."

Clay slowly got up and limped out the door.

20

Will pulled up to the front door of a building in the industrial district. The sign out front read "WAVES," and beneath that, "Women Against Violence Emergency Shelter." He parked around the side of the building and walked to the double doors in front. The wall near the entrance had poster-sized pictures of famous women who had suffered domestic violence and had escaped from abusive relationships. On another wall hung published newspaper articles about notable women who had been awarded big divorce settlements. He approached the receptionist.

"May I help you, sir?" she said, no uplift in her voice. Another woman walked in. She peered at Will as if he were a suspect in a crime.

"Yes. My name is Will Jones. I called earlier. I'm here to see Ms. Porter."

The receptionist picked up the phone and dialed. "Mr. Jones is here. Very well." She hung up, then looked up at him. "She'll be right out, sir."

"Thanks," he said.

"You may have a seat."

He sat down on a chair up against the far wall and watched as the woman gave her donations to the receptionist. Along the wall were pamphlets for anger management and classes for couples. Francine, a woman he knew from his work, came from the back and walked over to Will.

"Follow me, please," she said. She led Will down a long hallway with many doors. Will glanced into one room that had its door cracked open and saw a group of women sitting in a circle. They were speaking in hushed tones. As he walked by, the silence broke, and they all shouted, "I am worth it." In another room, the door was wide open. He peeked until a woman noticed him and closed the door. Another large room held a group of women dressed in sweats and practicing what looked like kickboxing and other self-defense moves.

"This is it," she said, pointing inside. He walked in and recognized the small woman with the stern face in the business suit who sat behind the desk. It was Joy Porter, the founder of WAVES. She'd received a big settlement years ago from her husband. According to the papers, he had died mysteriously, but she'd won the case and had a fortune to show for it. The rumor was she had killed her husband for money. She used her new platform to help other women. She'd dedicated her life to making sure women got treated fairly in the courts, and the media.

"Hello, Ms. P–Porter," he stammered.

She instructed him to have a seat. "How can I help you, Will?"

"Well . . .," he began, a bit uncertain. "I'm here because I'm helping a woman I love who is in a bad predicament right now. She believes her husband has hired people to destroy her. She woke up in a field naked."

"Are you referring to Erica Williams's husband?" she asked.

"Yes, I am. I believe he's behind everything going on," he said.

"Oh, yes. We here at WAVES are following that situation closely. It was brought to my attention after what happened at the awards ceremony."

"So, you're already familiar with Erica's situation?"

"Yes, we know about many things pertaining to women in this city. You of all people should know that, Mr. Jones," she said.

Will was thinking she sounded like the female version of the Godfather with her slow, deep cadence.

"Okay, it's good you're already aware."

"We are aware of many things."

"What do you mean?"

"Meaning you're a PI who's helped a lot of our women in their divorce cases. You know, we tried to hire you full-time here, and you turned me down. Now, you're coming to me for help."

Will didn't know what to say, so he didn't say anything.

"Tell me what we can do for you, Mr. Jones."

"Like I said over the phone, I just want to find out who's trying to hurt me and what happened to Erica at the studio, and I want her to get custody of her kids. She doesn't care about his money."

"Sorry to hear that," she said, examining her fingernails.

"I know I made a mistake by not taking the job with your organization, but right now, I'm in a big bind. Nobody's perfect, but I am a good man."

"Sure, you are, Mr. Jones." Mrs. Porter paused. "But you're not on trial here."

"I'm here for Erica."

"Please understand, I just need you to know where we stand as an organization, and that we don't play. I know why you came to us. You know we'll fight just as dirty as they will."

He blinked. He hadn't expected her to be so blunt about their methods, but he needed to tell her the truth. "Yes, that's why I came here."

"Okay, so what happened at the studio?"

"Erica and her sister were singing in this studio. Next thing they know, they're naked in a field. There was no evidence of rape."

"Sound to me like she's being set up for the okeydokey."

"Okeydokey?"

"My first husband had a friend that used to hit on me all the time. I always turned him down. One day, I gave him a kiss on the cheek. All of a sudden, there were pictures being circulated around my community, and the narrative was that I was cheating on my husband."

"That's what I was thinking it was—a ploy."

"Did her husband know she was going to file for divorce?"

"I don't think so. Not at the time."

"She needs to get those pictures. Even if they're bogus, they could ruin her reputation, and it could take years to be cleared if they're really compromising."

"So why attack me?"

"The husband works for some powerful people. Maybe they think she told you something about their business."

"So can you help me, Ms. Porter?"

"You know there's a fee for everything."

"I'll see what I can come up with."

"In the meantime, I'll put someone close to the situation on the case and see if we can find out where they're keeping those pictures."

"Thank you so much."

"This isn't about you. This is about a woman being treated badly by her husband."

"I understand."

"Go to the front desk and leave the folder, and they'll give you the information. We'll stay in touch as much as possible," she said.

21

Marvin rolled down the avenue at a steady pace with his moonroof open. The night was perfect, with a warm summer breeze and a light, sweet scent in the air that enveloped the senses. Marvin pulled in front of the building; the sign read "The Strip Mall," with the suite number and address below. The building was etched with Victorian-style art around the crown and sat in the middle of the block across from a few empty run-down office buildings. He turned off his engine, grabbed the manila envelope off the passenger seat, and stepped out of the SUV.

As he walked, he glanced up at the dark, inconspicuous building. Faint music and laughter emanated from inside. This was one of the most glamorous strip clubs in town, known for its high-end clientele, headlining musicians, and luxurious setups, including living art and crystal chandeliers.

It was increasingly difficult for him to resist mixing business with pleasure, but he knew that any consequences for a stupid slipup far outweighed any quick temporary pleasure he might have wanted. He stopped in front of the side entrance, took a deep breath, and then tilted his head back to gaze at the midnight sky. The stars dotted the inky blackness like bright, shiny diamonds.

The side door swung open, flooding the darkness with soft club lights.

A tall, muscular guy with smooth, dark skin opened the side door. His full lips parted to reveal straight white teeth. "Aye, Marvin," the doorman said.

"Where's your boss man?" Marvin asked.

"Your brother is in there." The doorman motioned behind him. "In that back room," he said.

The club was full of smoke. Everything moved to the beat of the music, and the lights kept the room in perpetual motion. All the men appeared as though they spent most of their time in the gym: lean, sculpted bodies wrapped in tuxedoes and black suits. The women oozed movie star glamour, their hourglass figures draped in brightly colored floor-length gowns. They swayed their hips as they moved. Against the far wall sat a marble fireplace, its surface silky smooth, in bronze and ivory. Living art models lay on dark mink rugs, covered in nothing more than shimmering gold body paint. Their bodies were intertwined in erotic poses mimicking intimate acts of pleasure for all the patrons to enjoy. A giant white circular couch was placed in the center of the room beneath a crystal chandelier that sparkled like diamonds. The chandelier reflected a kaleidoscope of beautiful half-naked bodies against the ceiling. The music changed to a pulsing beat, and Marvin felt it vibrate through his body.

He took a detour to the bar, not convinced that he would get a drink. He felt a tap on his shoulder. "Marvin?" Delo said. He wore black Hugo Boss slacks, a white shirt, a tie, and no smile. Tonight, he wore his "I mean business" wire-rimmed glasses.

"Man, I was just about to be in your office," Marvin said over the music.

"The whole place is my office," Delo said with pride. "Any word on the streets where the PI might be?"

"No, I got everybody searching for him. Nina wants his ass, since their fight in the car."

"The Ghetto Pocahontas."

"She's the best."

"At least we got the information we needed from him anyway," Delo said.

He pointed at the envelope. "Is that them?"

"Yes."

Delo grabbed the envelope. "Have you seen them yet?"

Marvin looked around. "No, boss man, you said no one was allowed to rip that shit open. It still has the seal on it."

"Follow me." Delo walked down a long hallway and through a small crowd toward the back area. Marvin followed. They entered the office, and Delo closed the door.

Marvin looked around the room. Delo had a setup like a little one-bedroom apartment. A mahogany desk and a couch took up the front, and in the room next door was a bedroom with a shower.

Delo tore open the envelope.

"Wait, won't college boy be upset?" Marvin said.

Delo glared at Marvin. "How is he gonna know?" Delo pulled the eight-by-ten photos out, drooling over each one. "This is professional work here." He seemed unable to take his eyes off of them. Marvin grabbed one. The photos were of Erica and Lashay naked, with young men in compromising positions.

"Them are two fine women. When this is all over, I'm fucking Lashay," Marvin said. Delo placed his arm around Marvin's shoulder.

"See, now you acting like that college boy. These printouts are for him, but we have the original digital ones too. I think we should make more copies, for insurance purposes." Delo grabbed the photo from Marvin and stuffed them all back in the envelope.

"Maybe he right; we should get rid of her."

"In due time, my brother. She high-profile. You can't just get rid of her like some street thug. We have to dirty her up first, create her some enemies, or put her in jail."

"Yeah, nobody ever cares when someone dies in jail."

"See? You learning. I need you to be here for the auction on Friday. Tyson has a basketball game."

106

"I want to see my nephew play in his basketball game."

"One of us needs to be here for that big night, and I'm going to watch Tyson play."

"Will Clay be here? You know I don't want to be in the same building with him."

"I'm sure he'll be here to bid, but don't give him the photos yet. We need to make copies," Delo said as Marvin shook his head.

"See? Why we doing all the dirty work while his punk ass is having all the fun?" Marvin tugged at his tight collar and then grabbed a peppermint from the glass bowl on Delo's desk.

Delo nodded his head in agreement. "You need to understand, we need him, and we need him clean; he has all the files on us, and you think if he gets busted he won't break?"

Marvin played with the candy wrapper. "Why not just give him an expiration date instead of all this wasted energy?"

"We're getting paid big-time for all this. Plus, once college boy finishes the sale to the corporation, we won't need him," Delo said.

"We don't need him now."

"Do you know where he's keeping the organization files?"

"No."

"Then we need him."

"If I find them, then I'm going to fuck him up."

Delo walked over to the wall. He pulled a picture off and revealed a safe; he opened it and put the envelope in it. "Do you remember the combination?"

"Yes, I do."

"Remember to get the money after every round of bidding."

"I know; I worked the auction before," Marvin answered.

"I gotta go get Nina and look for the PI."

Marvin left the office. As he passed through the dance floor, a slim white female snaked down the front of him. Another woman squeezed him from behind while the first female worked her way back up. He went to grab that drink he'd missed earlier and wondered what he needed to do to get this type of action. He took a quick swallow before he decided to bounce.

* * *

Marvin pulled up his Benz SUV in front of a small beat-up flat at a project housing community. He put his vehicle in park, took the keys out of the ignition and opened his door. Nina came out of the house.

"Hey, Marvin. Where we going today?" she asked as she climbed into the car.

"We need to drop some stuff off at the main house. Hopefully by then, one of the boys will call me and have some information on the PI."

"We just want to talk to him, right? You better tell me straight up if we're doing otherwise."

"Yeah, we need to find out what he knows. Then we go from there."

His eyes drifted to her face. Mix with Spanish and black. She usually wore her long natural hair in a sophisticated bun. When her hair was down, she really did look like the Ghetto Pocahontas. He observed a gold tooth with a little diamond chip peeking from behind her "I'm happy to see you" smile. Marvin also noticed she had a matching stud in her nose. She had so many gold chains on that Mr. T would have been jealous. Her tight zebra-print tank top was tucked into a wide copper-colored belt with a large square buckle with a smooth, flat surface. Her exotic beauty was striking. At a stoplight, he saw that the buckle was a small digital screen. The word "Nina" flashed across the front of it. Her leotard leggings stretched thinly across her legs, and a tight black leather skirt held it all together.

"Whatchoo lookin' at?" she asked.

"Nothin'. When we get to the house, you going to need to change and get ready for some work," he said.

"Change, huh?" she said. "Why? I can do my job dressed any way."

"You crazy."

"Wait a minute, did you just call me crazy, Marvin?"

"No, no," he said.

She grabbed his hand and put it on her leg. He yanked his hand back. "'Scuse me? You straight up trippin."

"Hey, it's time for business right now. We have time for that later," he said.

She settled back into the passenger seat. "You know, I know you don't like mixing business and pleasure. It's cool and shit, but you love this shit, and don't you eva forget that."

He glared at her. "Why we doin this again, Nina? We was done wit' that."

"Well, I just want make sure you know I'm all you need, and I'll do anything for you." Her eyes shined. "See, my philo…philosofay…however you say it, is if you hang with nine broke people, sooner or later you be the tenth one, and you ain't broke."

"Girl, stop."

"That's all you got to say?"

"I'm just sayin'…I got a lot on my mind with Clay and shit. We doing all this shit, and all this motherfucker had to do was divorce his wife. Oh yeah, we have to be at the club on auction night."

"We?"

"Yeah, babe, I want you there with me."

"Nip, you just don't want to be in the office by yourself."

"To be honest with you, I'm tired of dealing with all this shit, Nina. I love this life, the street part of the game. My brother and his friends trying to be on that mafia-type shit—that ain't me."

She laughed as she reached over and rubbed his arm. She shook her head, took a deep breath and leaned back in her seat. "Can I smoke in Delo's office?"

"You know you can't, but the back door is right there into the alley."

"I don't wanna be outside smoking while them hoe dancing bitches walking in."

"Not that damn door. The one that leads to the alley. Nobody using that door except me and Delo."

"Okay, then I'll be there with you, babe."

She turned on the radio. Before he could say anything else, loud music thumped from the speakers of the car. The words were offensive: "*Bitch, brang yo ass home, and take care of my itch.*" He turned it down before he pulled up in front of a beat-up house. The closest neighboring houses were three hundred yards away. They used houses like this around the city to stash money and drugs, often in holes they dug out in the backyards of the houses. They called them the ghetto banks. Nobody would ever expect that this house was home to a lot more than cockroaches and termites.

He jumped out of the car and pulled out one big duffle bag after another. They took in bag after bag. They were careful to avoid the trash strewn all over the yard. Nina got distracted by a dirty glow that escaped through the layer of dust on the front window. The front screen hung slanted, with only two of its three hinges attached.

As she approached the living room, she glanced around. The place was a dump by anyone's standards. Everything in it was either outdated, torn up, or both. The paint was peeling, the carpet was dingy, and the kitchen was just plain scary. A beat-up table and a ripped-up couch completed the picture of squalor, unless one included the drug scales and bags of marijuana on the table.

Nina dropped the final bag on the floor. "That was a workout."

"That ain't nothing. In a few weeks, we have to go to the other place on B Street and dig a hole in backyard."

"Why we have to do it? Ain't that why we have flunkies?"

"We need to keep our circle tight. We can't trust just anyone with these ghetto banks."

His phone rang; he talked quickly, then hung up.

"It's time. They got a bead on the PI."
Nina grabbed her .45 semiautomatic handgun and kissed it.

22

Will stuffed his face with food. Erica didn't know how he could eat at a time like this. They sat in a booth in Park's Café with a view of the front door. Will had on an oversized baseball cap and dark sunglasses. He hated wearing the stupid hat. It made his head itch. On the other hand, after what had happened to him, he kind of liked being incognito.

"Where did you park?" Will asked.

"In front of a store on the other side of the parking lot."

"Good, nobody knows you parked here. Just in case, I parked in the back alley."

"This is crazy, all this covert stuff," Erica said.

"Yeah, I reached deep into my sources to get some help." He looked over at her.

"Clay and friends left no rock unturned. He probably has the judges on his payroll or does their taxes," Erica said, shaking her head. "Everything is happening so fast. It's as if Clay has someone in every agency, and always two steps ahead of everything we do."

"Why not just get a divorce and have one of his judges give him everything?" Will said.

"That's it, I don't think he wants a divorce. I think he wants his cake and eat it too. Once he found out I wanted a divorce, it became a game to him, like he couldn't let me win."

"The fucking ego on that guy. You'll need a gun for protection."

"I have never owned a gun. I hate guns."

"Why?" he asked.

Erica bit her lip. "No reason."

"But you will."

"Let it go, Will, okay? Just let it go." She held up her hand to stop him.

He wanted to say something but knew Erica was upset. "I understand."

She took a deep breath. "What I want to do is kill the bastard, Will," she said, and then she shook her head. "But I'm not sure what to do." Hot tears rolled down her cheeks.

"I feel so helpless too. I should have been able to do more."

"Did you get the information on Clay and all his associates? We need as much information as we can get."

"Yes, my source had some information, and she's willing to help us—thank God. She's a very powerful person," he said. He reached out and handed her a piece of paper. "These are some of the spots where Clay's business associates hide stuff."

"I'm not going to ask how she got it or if it's reliable," Erica said as she folded the paper and put it in her pocket.

"We'll find out everything," he said as he lifted a juicy rib to his mouth. "She believes that what happened the night of the studio was that compromising pictures were taken of you and Lashay. To use later, maybe in a custody battle, or maybe to get you locked up."

"That's what Clay was talking about. But it's not real. I didn't sleep with any boys."

"I know that, you know that, but if those pictures get out, you will be ruined. The time they take to track down the young men in those pictures will cost you time in a custody battle. We need to get them now."

Erica's face froze. "This is so surreal."

"The photos are in a safe at one of their clubs. Plus, she said there will be money there that night, so we can pay for the information. We need to find somebody to rob the place."

"Robbery? I can't do that."

"They know what I look like, but I'm working on something."

"Maybe my sister or her boyfriend knows somebody."

"Yeah, she has some hood friends, I'm sure. No disrespect."

"None taken."

Erica scooped up some mashed potatoes and brought them to her mouth. "This is very good."

Erica glanced out the window and took in the view. Her eyes followed a dark Camry with tinted windows as it pulled up. A tall, exotic woman and a stocky black man got out of the car. She went back to eating.

"I'll ask my sister."

"Okay. If she finds someone, bring her by the office, and we'll go over a game plan."

The man and the woman walked in, and the woman glanced around at all the restaurant's patrons. She spotted Will and made a beeline towards them.

"What the hell." Will looked up at the woman. "Fuck, that's the woman who attacked me."

"Hello, Mr. Jones. I'm Nina, and this is Marvin. We're not here to hurt you. We just want to talk to you," she said.

"There's nothing to talk about," he snapped.

"Excuse me?" Nina said.

Marvin noticed Erica. "You look familiar."

"Let's go, Will," Erica said and stood up.

"Wait a minute. Where you gonna go?" Nina asked, rolling her neck.

"None of your business. We just wanted to eat a nice quiet meal," Erica said.

114

"Don't be getting loud with me," Nina said while she chomped on gum.

The people at the nearest tables immediately started getting up and moving away from them. "Unless you have the information you took for me, then we have nothing to talk about. I know you work for the Unit," Will said.

"You don't know what you're talking about," Nina said.

Marvin put his hand on the gun in his pants.

"What do you want with him?" Erica said.

While Nina was trying to decide how to respond, she picked a brownie up off a plate and smashed it into Erica's face. "None of your business, so eat this shit."

Erica covered her mouth in disbelief. Nina slapped her so hard she stumbled. She grabbed her before she fell and yanked her back. Erica was within punching distance, and Nina landed one square punch on the side of her head. Erica's body flipped over one of the tables behind her and fell like a rag doll. Nina reached for her and was planning to punch her again, but Erica rushed her. She had used one of the chairs as a springboard and made a running jump for Nina. She landed on her back and reached around her head to dig her fingernails into Nina's eyes. Nina screamed while trying to get a grasp on Erica to pull her off.

Will saw Erica scrambling off to the side of the room, trying to recover. Marvin rushed him. Will grabbed a bottle off the table and with a full swing caught Marvin in the head. He fell to the floor. As he tried to get up, Will kicked him in the face. Blood and a few teeth splattered the floor. Will rushed over to him, stomped on his back, and pinned him to the ground. He grabbed Marvin's gun from his hip. Marvin struggled, and Will struck him in the head. Marvin's body was motionless.

Nina grabbed Erica's shirt and pulled as hard as she could. As she tried to throw her over her shoulder, Erica grabbed a chunk of her hair. When Nina tossed Erica forward, Erica had a giant fistful of Nina's hair wrapped around her hand. The force that Nina used to throw Erica was the same force that pushed her facefirst into the chairs. Erica took Nina down with her. Nina's body bounced off the table and landed on the floor on the opposite side. It took her a moment to recover. Erica grabbed an abandoned tray of food. The food was hot, and when the tray made contact with Nina's face, she let out a howling scream. She hit her face like a crazy woman, trying to get the food off while spinning in circles from the burn.

Erica picked up the same tray and smashed it on her face again, knocking her to the floor. Nina lay there floundering, trying to get back up. Erica found another tray and smashed more fresh, hot food into her face. Nina screamed, and Erica followed it up with a kick.

Erica's hair was matted with mashed potatoes and corn, and her shirt was ripped from her shoulder to her ribs. She limped over to where Will stood, breathing hard. Nina was beginning to come to.

"Let's get the hell out of here," Will said.

Marvin helped Nina up. "I'm going to get you, nigga."

Police sirens were closing in. Nina shook off the pain and pointed at Erica. "This ain't over, bitch."

Will led Erica through the kitchen and out the back door into the alley. They jumped in his car. "This is getting way too serious. We need to hurry up and get those pictures," Erica said.

Will nodded in agreement. "I'll drive you home. You'll be safe. They didn't know who you were. Hell, I didn't know who you were. Where did you learned to fight like that?

"My grandfather taught me and Lashay a thing or two."

"Well, I'll be dam. Go talk to your sister and then come by my office."

23

The three-story building was located in an industrial section of downtown, a couple of blocks north of the high-rises. Erica and Lashay took the elevator to the second floor. The doors opened, and the sign facing them across the hall contained the names of all the businesses. One of the names read, "McGrath, Attorneys at Law." Erica was anxious to hear Will's plan and see if his lawyers could help. Erica was more than ready to handle business and get what was owed to her. She had a scratch on her face, but she'd told Lashay that CJ had done it accidentally.

Inside the large law office, the tastefully dressed woman behind the reception desk greeted them. Soft cubicles divided the main part of the office into three different workstations, each with its own desk, chair, and flashing lights. The telephone lines were lit up and rang constantly.

Will walked toward them down the hallway. "Hello, ladies." He kissed Erica on the cheek and hugged Lashay.

"Hello, Willie. Long time no hear."

"Same to you."

"You really are a big-time private eye," Lashay said.

"Big-time? I don't know about that, but I get the job done. Can I offer you a cup of coffee?" he asked on their way to his office. Erica shook her head, too nervous to drink, but Lashay nodded. "I can have my secretary bring you some," he said. He pressed a button on his phone and asked for two coffees.

Lashay straightened her blouse and pulled on her jeans. She was uncomfortable in Erica's clothes. She looked closer at Will's face, noticing that he had a bruise. "What happened to your face?"

"Erica didn't tell you what happened?"

"What do you mean, 'what happened'?" She looked at Erica.

"It's nothing. We don't have time for that right now," Erica said and focused back on Will, then continued. "She has somebody who can do the job."

"Okay, great, here's the situation. The photos are in a safe in the back office at the strip club. The best time to hit the place is Friday. It's a special night. The guards will be real busy taking money to different spots. My source is working on getting somebody inside to tell us the layout," he said.

Erica glanced at him, hoping what he was saying would work out.

"Also, we have the documents you copied," he said as he dug through his leather satchel. He pulled out a bulging folder and laid it on the table. "In here," he said, placing his pointer finger on top of it, "are important legal records related to your business, along with paperwork relating to the estate and your marriage, including the false legal separation papers. This is enough information to file for divorce and maybe put enough fear in him that he'll just let you have the kids. But we still need a smoking gun to show his misdeeds. My source is working on that still."

"Why not you?" Lashay asked.

"Sometimes people with more resources can go deeper."

"What do you do?" Lashay asked again.

"I do a lot of sleazy work, gathering information to help people find out things they may have never known otherwise. But this is very sophisticated."

"So, Lashay, you think Shorty knows someone who will do the robbery?" Erica asked.

"Yes, it's a four-man job. In our case, a four-people job, two men and two women."

"I don't want you to do it."

"I'm going to do the driving, sis. They won't trust anybody else."

Erica began to panic. "I don't want you there."

"Listen, sis, I don't tell you everything that goes on in my life, but I've done worse. I'm in those pictures too. I can't have that kinda rep, trying to be a great star. That type of shit ruined Vanessa Williams's modeling career."

The door swung open, and Will's secretary entered, balancing two coffees on a tray.

"Oh, let me help you with that," Lashay said, jumping up to grab the coffees at the same time as Will.

He straightened his tie and sat back down at the table. "So, where were we?"

Lashay chimed back in. "I'm going to help you bring Clay down, sister, and this is just the first step. I think he is a wolf in sheep's clothing, but that's just me. I can be cynical, but I'm real."

Erica blushed. Will's phone rang, interrupting the awkward moment. "Excuse me, I have to take this." He listened to the phone. "Great, thanks," he said and put the phone back in his pocket. "They're ready to see you now. Don't mention anything about what we just discussed to them."

"Yeah, boy," Lashay exclaimed. "Let's do this." She jumped up so fast her chair fell back.

"Are you okay?" Will asked.

"I'm fantastic. Clay's finally gonna get what's coming to him, and I'll get to the bottom of what happened at the studio. Nobody gets away with doing that to me and my sister."

He guided them through the maze of cubicles and into another hallway. He knocked once. "Come in," someone yelled. Together, they entered a small office where a middle-aged man dressed in a dark suit greeted them. He had short spiked hair and a hard chin.

"Hello. I'm Tom McGrath. Nice to meet you."

"Hello, Mr. McGrath," Erica said. "Thank you for your time."

"Call me Tom. Have a seat so we can talk." She did as he requested.

"Will?"

"You'll do fine, Erica," Will said, and he and Lashay left the room, leaving Tom and her alone. Her hands began to sweat. She wasn't used to making big decisions, having important conversations or conducting business alone, especially with white-collar professionals. The door opened and a blonde woman wearing a red double-breasted suit with high heels walked in.

"Erica, this is Debbie. She's my top divorce attorney. She'll be handling your case. Of course, there's a fee, but I've already worked that out with Will, so don't worry. This is somewhat pro bono," Tom said. "Do you understand 'pro bono'?"

"Wow, thank you. I appreciate that, and, yes, I do," she said. Tom seemed genuine enough, but Erica was happy that she'd be working with a woman. She nodded slightly, approving the arrangement.

Tom walked around the big desk and sat on the corner with his arms crossed. He sighed. "Let me explain something to you, Mrs. Williams. This situation is serious for two reasons. One, these are serious allegations, which are punishable felonies; and two, the defendant will most likely do anything he possibly can to refute these allegations, including attacking your character. I hope you understand this."

She nodded her head. "I do. I know what he's done isn't right."

"Having said that, if you have anything in your past that could be used against you, you *must* tell us. That is the only way we can build an appropriate case for you. Make sure you tell Debbie everything when you talk with her, okay? In a case like this, if anything surfaces, anything claiming you did this or that, and we didn't have prior knowledge about it, that could mean the loss of the case. Judges don't like surprises, and if they award your kids to your husband, it can take a long time before you get another court date set. Understand?"

Erica nodded. "Yes, Mr. McGrath, I mean, Tom. I understand. Thanks again for everything."

"Will has explained to me that you need time to get some vital information. Once you get that information, come back in and we will start the process and catch your husband off guard. The information you provided us should make any judge rule in your favor."

"Here's my card," Debbie said. "Call me in a few days. This will give me time to finish going over the paperwork and prepare documents. This looks good for you. You did good."

24

Kendra was a new dancer at the Strip Mall. She took a deep breath and strutted around inside in a long black overcoat. She was curvaceous, with perfect, unblemished brown skin, and very aware that her body was tight and athletic without even trying. The club was packed with customers dressed in business attire. The dancers moved to the beat of the music.

Kendra stopped at one booth and started giving a man a lap dance. He grabbed at her to open her coat, but she stopped him. While she danced, she saw a middle-aged black man in a dark gray suit. She could tell that under the suit, he was lean with broad shoulders. He watched her while he took a sip of his drink. When she finished with the customer, he handed her a bill. She headed over the man.

"Hello to you. You're new, right?" he said.

"I'm not supposed to talk right now, but, yes, I've been here for about a week."

"I seen you in here few times. I like your vibe."

A short chubby bouncer walked up. He had on a lime-green Adidas tracksuit and a name tag that said "Jermaine." He looked at the man. "Hey, the festivities are getting ready to start in the main room, and you have to bid like everyone else." He gestured for Kendra to follow him.

As they walked to a big staging room at the back, adjacent to the main stage, she could hear the hum of voices all around her. Jermaine showed her outfits and said they had fifteen minutes to change, before leaving the room. A piece of wool draped across Kendra's hips. It barely covered her panties, and the straps that laced around her legs wound all the way up to her thighs. Ten or more young black women dressed similarly to Kendra were already there. Their bodies were a mix of muscular, slim, thick, black, shiny, and young. She doubted anyone in there was over twenty-five, but she had the feeling that she was the youngest one of them all at twenty-two years old.

Jermaine came in carrying white cardboard signs on strings. Each sign had a black number painted on it. He placed the number twelve around Kendra's neck.

"Stay in numbered order. Stay seated until called, and not a word from any of you." It was strange to hear such a stern, dry voice come out of such an unassuming man who had little authority. Kendra wanted to laugh, but she wasn't drunk enough yet. None of the other women were, either. She noticed a few of them making their way back over to a corner table for drinks, talking to one another in low voices. One of the girls came over to Kendra.

"Look, new girl, I know you think you're special 'cause you in college and shit, but these auctions is where I make my bread and butter. All the men have deep pockets, so play your role right."

Kendra didn't say anything. She just sat there focusing on what she had to do.

After ten minutes of waiting, she heard a loud female voice coming through a speaker on the other side of the wall. The crowd in the main room began to yell and cheer. Jermaine came to the door and called for numbers one and two. A tall slim woman bounced up, while a more compact woman stood and then crossed the room. The look she gave to Jermaine was like daggers. Kendra saw it and it killed her buzz, so she fixed another drink as they followed Jermaine out of the waiting room.

"All right, we are going to start the bidding at one thousand dollars," said the woman on the loudspeaker.

A low roar of voices spoke incoherent together. Every few seconds, one voice would get louder than the others and clearly blurt out a price.

"Two thousand in the corner, do we have twenty-five hundred?" A few moments of silence. "Three thousand, sold. To the man in the green suit."

Kendra listened as this routine repeated itself for another twenty minutes, with Jermaine coming back and forth to get more queens in numerical order. While they waited, she and the two other women drank as much alcohol as they could.

"Numbers eleven and twelve," he said.

A tall, muscular sister with dark mocha skin stood up with Kendra. She walked like Serena Williams, and Kendra felt clumsy as she followed them down to the end of the hallway, where numbers nine and ten were still waiting. Her heart started beating like crazy. She heard the woman call number nine, then ten and eleven.

"Twelve," the announcer shouted. Kendra felt as if her heart would burst out of her chest. She walked through the curtains and onto a stage. The woman she had been hearing over the loudspeaker all night was on the edge of the stage, leaning over a podium. She was white with a dark tan, dressed like an Egyptian belly dancer and wearing a mask that covered her eyes. As Kendra walked out onto the stage, the woman began describing her body. Kendra couldn't bring herself to look at the crowd. Instead, she focused on the woman. Her stomach was a bit flabby, and her mask made it impossible to identify her.

"Here's a strong young queen. She has the hips of a goddess and the strong legs of a gazelle. Her cocoa-cream skin is to die for. She's definitely a crowd-pleaser. If you don't start the bidding high on this one, I'll keep her for myself. So, who'll give me two thousand?"

She looked at the crowd and saw nothing but men—black, Asian, and white, many of them middle-aged, and all dressed in business suits. It was like looking at a sea of money. Kendra was flattered that she had been started out at two thousand instead of one. As soon as the bidding started, she saw one man scratch his nose. Another pointed a finger up, and another tugged on his tie.

"All right, who has twenty-five hundred?" the belly dancer asked.

She motioned for Kendra to walk. She walked to the end of the stage, and as she pivoted, one of the older patrons grabbed her ankle. She swatted his hand, careful not to lose her balance. When she looked down at him, she could see his yellow smile and she drew her hand back, not wanting to touch him again. The bidding had reached forty-five hundred.

"Sold. To the man in the dark gray suit for five thousand dollars," the announcer said. "I guess we saved the best for last, huh? Too bad for all of you who already spent your money." The minute she was sold, Jermaine led her off the stage.

"Pretty good, little lady," he said with a smirk. "People with money to waste have some crazy habits, sistah," he added.

He led her up the stairs to an empty bedroom lit with a low purple light and smelling of incense. There was a mini bar in the corner, a chair against the wall, and a large circular bed in the middle of the room. It looked just like what you'd see in a movie filmed in a cheap hotel for pimps.

As she waited, a surge of panic gripped her. She made herself a drink. Then she guzzled it down and fixed another. She began to relax. A bowl of condoms sat on the bar. They were candy-colored, as if that made them more attractive. She wondered what type of men paid for expensive lap dances in broad daylight.

There was a knock at the door. Kendra jumped. The man in the dark gray suit walked in. Jermaine's instructions were clear— no talking at all. She was waiting for the man to give her instructions. He guided her toward the circular bed and gave her a slight push in the middle. She lay on the bed while he made a drink. Jazz music began to play. He sat next to her on the bed.

"That's better," he said, smiling. "What's your name?" Kendra didn't say a word. "It's okay. I help with the finances here. You won't get fired. I promise you."

She stared at him, wondering why he wanted to talk. "I'm Kendra," she said.

"You're fired for talking," the stranger said.

Her face changed.

"I'm just playing," he said. She smiled. "Anyway, I'm celebrating tonight. My wife—I mean, my soon-to-be ex-wife—is going to jail, and I'm going to get full custody of my kids."

"So that's a good thing, your wife going to jail?" she asked, a frown creasing her brow.

"Well, that's a long story. She broke the law. Hopefully I can tell you all about it later."

"Wow, that's crazy," Kendra said, relaxing a bit more.

"Yes, it is. Now let's get this party started." He rubbed his hands together and smacked his lips. He lay down next to her. "Make me feel good, baby," he said.

She began to massage him, starting with his feet and working her way up to his inner thigh. Her hand moved across his manhood, then she grabbed it.

"Nice," she said, closing her eyes and smiling.

His phone started buzzing in his pocket. He pulled out one phone and looked at it, put it back, then pulled out another one. "Excuse me, I've got to take this." He walked away from the chair to the corner of the room. He spoke in hushed tones. "Okay, great." He paused to listen. "Are you serious? I didn't know. Okay, I'll call you tomorrow," he said. He hung up the phone and put it back in his pocket.

Kendra stared at him and shook her head. She was used to hearing all kinds of bullshit men told their wives and girlfriends, but she knew phone calls usually meant party over. She got up off the bed.

"Where are you going?" he asked.

"I thought you might not be in the mood for a lap dance."

"Come on, I need a lap dance."

"You're the boss of me for this hour," she said.

"Can I get your number?"

"No, that's against the rules," she said.

"Come on, I've seen you staring at me every time I came in here," he said.

"And I've seen you staring back. What's the big deal?"

"The big deal is, when Clay Williams sees something he wants, he gets it."

"Do you want a dance or not?"

He smiled. "No, I want more. I want to get to know you better, and I want you to know me. Come on. I'll walk you out of here."

25

Broken concrete and broken windows surrounded an old dilapidated building across the street from the Strip Mall. The old office building had been abandoned years ago. Most of the businesses around the strip club had closed. The second floor had a good view of the club, and that was where Lashay and her gang were holding their stakeout.

Lashay sat with Shorty at the main window, watching people coming and going at the club. Moe sat on the back stairs.

"Damn, Shay, isn't that your brother-in-law Clay over there?" Shorty said as he squinted to see better.

Lashay had already seen Clay. He was walking outside the club. "Yeah, I see him. I thought I asked you guys not to use his name," she said, a trace of venom in her voice.

"So, we get to hit the place and pound on Clay too?" Moe asked.

"Fuck, we can't do that, and didn't I just tell you not to use his name? If we hit this place now, he'll recognize us, and we don't want that." She got up and paced the floor. They sat watching her. "Once we hit them hard, they won't know what hit them or why, and they'll be scared. Nobody likes the feeling of being hunted."

"Can we at least put some fear in them? They'll never see us coming," Shorty said.

"No, we can't take any chances," Lashay said. She looked over at Moe. The smile on his face made her nervous. She knew he didn't care what they did, who they robbed, or what trouble they got into. Men like Moe and Shorty had nothing to lose. She appreciated the fact that they would do anything she asked, but she knew this wasn't the time. "We'll wait for Meeka," Lashay said.

Ten minutes later, Meeka rushed in. Lashay walked over to her. "Did you see the guy they call Delo?"

"No, but his brother Marvin is in the back room; I believe it's an office. There's one guard in the club area, one guard in the stage area, and one guard in the back office area, along with Marvin and a girl. Away from everything. The guard and the girl come out the back door to smoke a cigarette every so often. There's a trash can in the alley. We can wait right there until the time is right."

Lashay went back to the window and sat back down. "Okay, we wait until my sister's husband leaves." Shorty joined her at the window.

* * *

Moe and Meeka sat on the stairs on the same floor. Meeka wondered what type of man Moe was, and why they called him Crazy Moe. He seemed nice enough to her. After peeking for a few hours, Meeka tired of the surveillance. She wanted a distraction. She took a drink and scraped up the courage to talk to Moe. She walked over to him, not knowing what she was going to say, but she didn't care. He was busy rolling a blunt and didn't take much notice of her. She picked up her drink and took another swig.

"Can I take a hit?" she asked. If he was stingy, he wouldn't share.

"Almost done, word."

"Moe, you seem nice," Meeka said, smiling.

"Word?" he responded as he cocked his head sideways to look at her.

"Are you single?" she asked.

"Depends?" he said with a dopey grin.

She paused.

"Are you single?" Moe asked her.

"Yes."

"Why? A cute girl like you? You seem cool," he said.

"Thanks. I'm just focused on my goals right now."

"Goals?"

"Yeah, you know, things you want to focus on or accomplish. Ever since I was a girl, I've wanted to open a salon. Did you have any goals as a kid?"

"Okay, I get it. When I was little, I used to watch TV with my grandma. She stayed on one channel. It was TV Land all day. So, I would watch *Gilligan's Island*. One day, I decided to write letters to the US Air Force, the Navy, and the Coast Guard asking them to rescue Gilligan and the castaways from the island. I always wanted to save them. That was one of my goals. I got all the right addresses, but no one ever responded."

Meeka sat there staring at him. She wondered if he could even write. *First strike*, she tallied to herself.

"Okaaaay, what other goals did you have?" she asked.

"For a long time, I always wanted to travel to Hollywood, find the *Beverly Hillbillies* mansion, knock on their door, and ask for Jed and Granny. I thought that with the money they had, they could save Gilligan. I also wanted to buy Elly May some new clothes. My goodness. With all that money the Clampetts had, you think they could have bought her a belt, instead of letting her use an old string to hold up her pants," he said.

Meeka continued staring at Moe with a slight wrinkle on her brow. She shrugged her shoulders and looked over at Lashay and Shorty together, wondering how they made it work. They'd been together for years, and Lashay always smiled when she talked about him, even when he pissed her off, which happened on a daily basis.

"Was that your only goal, to have a salon?" Moe asked.

Meeka thought about changing the subject but decided to answer. "There was a time I wanted to go to college and study child psychology, then possibly get a master's, and maybe even a PhD, but that was a while back." She stared across the room and through the window. Moe looked at her and paused for a second.

"I have a PhD," he said, looking silly.

"You couldn't get a PhD if somebody paid you and gave you all the answers to every test," Shorty shouted.

"Wait, what do you think PhD stands for?" Meeka asked.

"Pretty huge dick," Moe yelled as he stood up, sticking his chest out. "You wanna see? I can prove it." He unbuttoned his pants. Lashay and Shortly were cracking up on the other side of the room.

"No, no, no. A demonstration isn't necessary. That wasn't what I was talking about," she said. She gave him a strange look. She got up and joined Lashay by the window.

"Meeka, duck down. We don't want anybody seeing us," Lashay said as Meeka squatted down.

In a low voice, Meeka said, "Okay, now I understand why I'm still single. Men like Moe can never be my equal, and all the men in this town are caught up, have zero ambition, or are just plain ol' dumb. The rest of them are in jail, and the good ones in their right minds wouldn't come down here. Lashay, are you even listening?"

"There he is over there," Lashay said as she squinted. Clay was walking outside the club.

"Oh, okay. We hit them hard and take all the money and drugs, whatever, but especially the safe. What we really want is in there," Lashay said.

"All right, girl. I can tell when your lightbulb is going off and you have an idea. Let's do this," Meeka said, ready to do anything but sit in that old building another minute.

131

"What lightbulb? I didn't see no light go off," Moe said as he looked all around and up at the ceiling.

"That sounds like a plan to me," Shorty said.

"Word. I'm ready to see some naked girls," Moe said. Everybody looked at him as he continued to stare out the window.

"Meeka, you drive," Lashay said.

26

Nina stepped from the bedroom, wondering when she would be allowed to announce her love for Marvin in public and take her rightful place beside him. He wouldn't even let her touch him in the car as they drove through town in case someone saw. She didn't know what he was so worried about. His brother and his friends ran around with different women. It wasn't like they tried to keep it a secret, so she didn't know why he had to.

Marvin sat at the table, surrounded by some weed and a brand-new forty. Music from a distance vibrated the walls. He motioned for her to sit down while he finished up. She sat on the couch as Marvin finished counting money and looking over some paperwork. He craved power just as much as she did, but right now, she craved something more.

"I'm glad I'm here with the future boss of the Blafia," she said.

"We don't use that word here. That's only used on the streets," he said. She walked over to him. Slow and sexy. "You know we can't do anything in here."

"Why not? Delo is gone for the night, and you in charge and the doors are locked."

"Because, I'm trying to conduct some business here."

She rubbed his shoulder and kissed the back of his neck. She didn't know why he was playing hard to get. She knew he wanted that hot, wet pussy.

"I love quickies in public places."

"This isn't public place, this is my brother's office."

She continued kissing him. After a few minutes, he couldn't take it anymore and grabbed her. He held her tight as he planted a kiss on her lips.

"So now you want to play," she asked, craving him so bad.

"Yes." He led her over to the couch.

She unzipped his pants. She reached in and found he was already ready. She said, "Marvin . . ." He lifted her up and began kissing her. He slipped off her blouse and pants but wasn't so patient with her panties.

He slammed into her. She moaned as he went deeper with every stroke. "Damn, papi, you feel so good." The faster he went, the louder she moaned until her body started shaking. Afterwards, she was spread out all over the couch, too weak to stand.

Marvin eventually got up and walked over and grabbed his bottle of beer and handed it to Nina. "Drink up. You need to replenish all that you just sweated out."

She picked up the bottle and took a long drink as Marvin watched her. "Let's go clean up."

* * *

The alley was still dark and quiet. Lashay heard a clicking sound. Crazy Moe and Shorty were cocking their guns. Lashay's heart was beating out of her chest. Shorty handed her a black ski mask and told her to put it on once they were there. She looked at the mask, and her stomach started to heave. "We're here for the pictures, the money, and to put fear in them," she whispered. "Nothing else."

"That's what we're going to do. Scare the hell out of them," Crazy Moe said with an all-too-eager grin, holding his gun. "Y'all ready?"

A short, husky man came out the door and started smoking a cigarette. His foot was placed in the door to keep it open, and his back was to them.

Shorty, Moe, and Lashay crept up on the guy, with Moe being the lead. He hit him in the back of his head with the butt of his gun, and the man fell out into the alley. Lashay stuck her foot in the door before it closed. Shorty jumped on the man and choked him out. They walked into the long, empty hallway. They could hear music and someone speaking over a microphone in the distant background. Lashay had her finger over her mouth, pointing down the hallway. They crept along until they got to a black door.

"I think this is it."

Moe walked up to the door, raised his foot, and kicked it in. His dramatic entrance made a loud boom, and the door fell in a cloud of dust. The three of them stood in the doorway in ski masks. Marvin was caught off guard as he lifted a forty to his mouth. He dropped it and jumped to his feet. Just then, Nina walked in from the back room. She was dressed in just a tee shirt. The sight of them made her yell, and she tried to run. Crazy Moe lunged at her and caught her arm, yanking her back. Shorty held a gun on Marvin. Nina began to whine, and Moe lost his patience.

"Quiet, bitch," he growled, dragging her back to the main room.

"Please, please ...don't hurt her," Marvin pleaded.

Lashay was shocked to hear him beg. Any other time, he was Mr. Big Shot Drug Dealer doing his damn thang, but now he whined shamelessly.

"Take this," Shorty barked at Lashay. He handed her the shotgun, and she held Marvin at gunpoint. Shorty reached into the duffle bag and pulled out duct tape. He tore off short and long pieces and taped up Marvin's arms and legs.

"What do you guys want? There's no money here."

135

Shorty finished binding Marvin and handed the tape to Crazy Moe, who taped Nina too. Back in the living room, Shorty had Marvin sit back on the couch. Nina was sitting on the floor. Lashay checked the house for weapons while Crazy Moe made sure there was no one else inside. Satisfied that they were alone, Moe locked all the doors.

Lashay came back into the room. "Motherfucker, I know you have some pictures of some innocent girls."

"I don't have anything and don't know what you're talking about." She raised her gun, pointing it at Marvin. "I don't know about any pictures."

"So, Mr. Badass, you going to give us what we want, or we going have to take your place apart?" Shorty said, standing over Marvin and waving his gun back and forth.

"I don't know what you're talking about. I don't have any money or pictures," Marvin said.

"Shut up," Shorty yelled. "I don't want to hear a word out of your mouth unless you're telling me where the money and the pictures are."

Marvin began to speak again. "I don't—"

Shorty punched him in the face. "I *said* quiet."

Crazy Moe chimed in. "Where's the cheese, I mean the money, word?"

"Man, think where would they keep the safe," Lashay mumbled, looking around the room.

Marvin heard her and his eyes got big. "Yeah, I don't have any money here," he repeated as if relieved. Crazy Moe laughed. Nina tried speaking through her gag.

"Word," he said and laughed some more. "You better tell us where the safe is before we hurt your girl, word." He swayed back and forth.

Lashay left the room, returning five minutes later. "Nothing. I searched every place I could think. This office is better than my condo, bedroom, shower, yeah they big time."

"Where is the safe, punk?" Shorty said.

"Man, this is my boss's place. I don't know anything about a safe."

"Oh, word? *Now* you want to act dumb?" Crazy Moe said. He hit Marvin with the butt of the gun, leaving a large gash in his forehead. Marvin grunted as blood squirted from his head. Moe struck him again. He didn't respond this time. Then Shorty slapped him. "Where's your boss keeping the safe? Where's the money? If you don't give us some information, your ass is going to get fucked up tonight," Shorty said. "We will turn this place upside down until we find something."

Lashay saw Moe screwing something onto the end of his gun. Her eyes opened wide with fear.

"Watch them while we go look around," Shorty said. Shorty and Moe headed for the bedroom. Nina didn't move or mumble a word while Lashay pointed the gun at her.

Shorty and Moe returned with a duffle bag each. "Let's go hurry up and get the hell out of here. We got some money and the weed. It's over," Shorty said, and before Crazy Moe could protest, Shorty cut him off. "I *said* let's go, before somebody comes."

Moe grabbed the gun from Lashay and poked it into Marvin's rib cage.

"I'm going to kill you if you don't tell me where the safe is. Word."

Marvin let out a groan as he looked up at the wall. Lashay noticed him. She walked over, never taking her eyes of the picture on the wall. She looked closely and then pulled the picture off the wall to reveal a wall safe under it.

Shorty sat down next to Marvin. "What is the combination?"

"I don't know."

Shorty struck him in the head again. "What is the combination?"

"I told you I don't know."

Moe walked over to Nina. "I'm going to shoot your girl if you don't tell me the combination." Moe fired his gun right next to Nina's face. He slowly raised the gun to her knee cap. "Do you want her to walk with a limp?" Nina's eyes got wide. Marvin yelled out the combination.

Lashay used it to open the safe. She reached in and grabbed stacks of cash and a yellow envelope. She looked in the envelope and saw the pictures. She nodded.

Shorty turned to Marvin.

"Hey, we know who you are. We know how you spend your days, and we know where you live. It's over, the end, so no need to go to the police. If we wanted to hurt you, we would have done that already. You'd be dead. We got your money. We're taking your weed too. Have a nice day."

27

Delo walked through the side door of his club and out into the alley. He bumped against a dirty staircase. He couldn't think of a more unsavory place to be at night. Rodents scampered about freely, and the trash smelled sour. An unmarked police car had parked next to the dumpster in the middle of the alley. This was their usual meeting place: dark, inconspicuous, and quiet.

Frank stepped out of the car and walked over to the silhouetted figure. They stood shrouded in darkness, facing one another.

"What's up, Delo? This better be good," he said.

"We got fucking robbed last night. And Marvin was here. He is pissed and so am I."

"What?" Frank said. "How's that possible? Nobody would rob us."

"I don't know, man, but he says it was three people. Two guys and a girl. I can't believe it either. For one, that's an odd group. And two, how would they know?"

"How much did they get?"

"Thirty racks and some weed, and those pictures and the masters," Delo said.

"The pictures?"

"Yeah, the found the safe and took everything in it."

"Wow, must have been some dumb-ass fools. Or that's what they came for," Frank said.

"Yes, Marvin he thinks he knows who it was, and one of them for sure."

"Really?" Frank said. "This gets better and better."

"Yeah, a big guy who's always saying 'word,' and they were asking about the safe. How'd they know the safe was in my office?" Delo said, holding his hands out, palms up.

"Fucking college boy. Shit, I'll have my people snoop around," Frank said.

"I'll ask around too," Delo said.

"What's going to happen now? Have you spoken to him?" Frank said.

"Naw, not yet, but I can." Delo pulled his phone out.

"No, we don't have to bother him with this now. We can't afford to make any mistakes. We've got a big deal going down. This shit is small potatoes, but we have to go plan B now and find those crooks and send a message," Frank said.

"Wait, Frank. Marvin is hot as hell, and he wants to find out if it's an inside job," Delo warned.

"Yeah, how did they know about the safe?" Frank prompted him.

"Marvin said he didn't give up any information."

"None of this makes any sense. That was supposed to be one of our low-key spots. If Marvin isn't able to get results, then we"— Delo pointed to himself and Frank—"will step in and get to the bottom of all this."

"Clay is on a need-to-know basis," Frank said, cocking his head.

"Don't play me, Frank, and don't play ya'self. Clay has enough to worry about without this shit. You gotta keep yo' shit straight, and I have businesses to run. Let Marvin deal with the streets as he always has."

"I just wanted to be sure we were on the same page," Frank said.

"We're on the same page. That's for damn sure. I also wanted you to know that I heard some crazy stories about college boy," Delo said.

"It's all rumors. He has everything under control," Frank said.

"That's good to hear. So, once Clay's franchises are sold, we will all be rich men, right?" Delo said. "Well, richer men."

"Yes, money from the sale, and when the conglomerate goes public, our percentages we keep will be worth millions," Frank said.

"Do you ever think Clay would try to double-cross us?"

"No, we have too much dirt on him. That's why I was always willing to help him with his wife stuff. He hates her so much now."

"She must know something we don't know."

"I think it was the awards incident, in front of his mother, that sent him over the top."

Delo walked over to his car and popped the back. He pulled out a square package and raised it in the air. It was sealed with duct tape, with a big green *D* written on it with a Sharpie. He walked over and handed it to Frank.

"I was getting tired of him using our resources to fix his fucked-up personal life. But now I see the big picture," Delo said.

"We'll continue to do what we need to do until everything is in the corporation's name and we can get our hands on college boy's files. Those files have all the information on the Unit's businesses, plus all the contacts we'll need when we decide to get rid of him."

"That'll be one fine day," Delo said. They laughed.

"He wants her to suffer, and he wants to break her. It's all about him getting custody of the kids. Call our people, find our contacts inside, and tell them to get ready. She'll be joining them soon, and once she's in jail, we can get rid of her with no problem. Nobody cares when somebody is taken out in jail."

"Yes, I know," Delo said.

"College boy has one hell of an ego on him," Frank said. He grabbed the card, jammed it into his pocket and hid the package under his jacket. "See if Marvin and his crew can get some information on the sister, and I will collect some information on this 'word' guy. Once I get some info, I will contact you."

28

Clay gazed at the luxurious interior inside the limo. It was spotless and smelled of new car. The warm seat and soft carpet promised comfort, and the champagne bottles and flat-screen would provide entertainment. The limo pulled in front of the apartment complex. Clay watched as Kendra approached the long limo. She wore a nice simple dress. Clay had the soft music of Jaheim on in the background. Clay's hair was neatly faded, and he was dressed in navy-blue slacks with a sharp crease and a perfectly starched white shirt. A tan corduroy jacket and suede Oxfords completed the look. He smiled at her, folded his arms and winked. He motioned for her to come sit next to him. She made her way to his side of the limo and sat down. She carefully placed her right hand on his left knee. He gently placed his other hand over it.

Clay brushed her hair off her forehead and tried to pin it behind her ear, then he reached out and touched her cheek.

She giggled. "Be careful, you're going mess up my makeup."

The limo drove through downtown and stopped in front of Thomas Pink. Clay liked to spoil his women. It didn't matter if he'd just met them or not. He liked spending lots of money on them without worrying about expensive price tags. After Thomas

Pink, they hit Emporio Armani, then Neiman Marcus. Street performers lined the streets as if giving their own personal concert. Clay served as her personal escort, prancing her from store to store, giving fashion advice, and passing over the credit card without even paying attention to the amount.

Kendra strutted through the curtain wearing a close-fitting silk designer dress and black heels. "You like?"

"Very sexy," he murmured in a low, deep voice. "Now you need a pair of shoes."

He led her into Jimmy Choo's and picked out a pair of high heels for her.

"Kendra." She looked over her shoulder and back at him, smiling. "I want to see you in the dress and the shoes. Now."

"Now?" she asked, raising her eyebrow.

"Now." He nodded as he led her from the store and back into the waiting limo. Clay and the driver stood outside while she changed.

When she stepped out, she placed her heels on the asphalt, first revealing her slender ankles. Then she slid forward, revealing her smooth, toned legs. Clay thought he'd finally met the woman of his dreams. The silk dress hung across her every curve. The square neckline highlighted her collarbones, and her midnight-black locks bounced above them. The dress had a turquoise belt, accentuating her waistline. She looked like an American princess.

Clay held her hand the entire ride over to the restaurant.

"Reservation for two, under the name Clay Williams," he said to the concierge.

"Of course, Mr. Williams," he replied.

The host led them to a nice, dark area of the restaurant. As they sat down, a waiter handed them each a food and wine menu. "Can I start you off with something to drink while you decide?"

"Give us a bottle of your finest champagne."

"Very good, sir."

"You're drinking tonight, right?" he asked.

"Well, I didn't plan on it . . ." She scanned the room, looking at the pictures of different vineyards from all over the world. "But I suppose I can have one."

The waiter returned with the bottle on ice. He held the bottle with the label tilted toward Clay for his approval. Clay nodded, and the waiter popped the cork and poured the champagne for them. Clay raised his glass.

"A toast. May this be a special start with a special person for something that's going to be special for a very long time." They clinked glasses, and she took a sip.

A young woman with dark ringlet curls, dressed in an all-white dress, sat on a low stool, playing the harp. Kendra picked up the menu. "I don't know what to order."

"Don't worry," Clay said. "The veal here is the best in the world, and believe me, I have been everywhere."

"How?"

"I own a lucrative tax firm. I have businesses all over this region and the Caribbean islands, and we're still growing. I'm in the process of going national."

"You must be a serious businessman."

"Yes, my work keeps me busy. But enough about me. I want to know more about you. How did you get started with dancing on the pole?"

"Well, that night I met you, I had been there a few days. I just finished college and was looking for work when a friend told me I could make two thousand dollars a night dancing and giving VIP lap dances with a mask on. I needed the money and figured I had nothing to lose. I didn't think I would meet someone like you."

"So, you're looking for a job? I have a few openings at my firm."

"Really?" she said. "You would hire someone like me? Do you need something like a resume from me? And let me reassure you, I won't ever go back to dancing anymore."

"Well, maybe just private ones," he said. She blushed, feeling his heat from across the table. "What's your degree in?"

"Business administration."

"What would you like to do in the future? Not just as a job, but what do you enjoy doing?"

"I don't know. I've been so busy looking for a job, I haven't had a chance to do anything else."

"I understand. After college, I was lost for a few years."

"How did you figure out what you wanted to do?"

"You're beautiful."

She blushed. Clay liked the way her skin flushed when he asked her something personal or gave her a compliment.

"You know what I liked about you most that night at the club? That I could talk to you. My soon-to-be ex-wife and I hadn't slept with each other in a year, and we stopped talking years ago. She blamed me, of course. But it takes two. I used to think she felt that she was entitled to all the attention I gave her just because she was my wife and the mother of my children. My mother never liked her. She wanted me to marry someone else."

"My mom wanted me to grow up and meet a nice, rich young man, get married, and be happy," Kendra said. He tilted his head at her.

"She used to ride me a lot about keeping my body in shape. She told me no rich man wants a big girl."

"I can't believe that. You have a great body."

"I mean, I used to have issues with food," she said.

"It's okay. Is that why you ended up on the pole?" he said, then laughed.

She flushed again. "I told you, that was a one-time thing. Either way, I'm grown up, and it's my life."

"Yes, you are, and yes, it is. Your mom sounds like my wife, never satisfied with anything. She tried to act like she didn't want the big house or the fancy cars, but that was just an act. The bitch was greedy. She tried to say I was ashamed of my son because he has autism. Can you believe that? I wasn't ashamed. I just thought he would get better one day, so I was waiting. I was scared and didn't know what to do."

She reached across the table and rested her hand on his, with firm yet sensitive pressure.

"She just left me alone and got all involved in autism walks and wore shirts that said, 'Proud Mom of Autistic Kid.' I mean, I was happy she was doing all that, but it stressed her out. I think that's when she started sleeping with the private investigator and left me with the kids. What kind of mother would do that?" He wrapped his fingers around hers. "I'm so sorry. I'm just blurting out stuff. I just had to get that off my chest. That's why I like you. I can just talk."

"I like listening to you. It sounds like you've had a rough patch." She patted her hand over his. "Did you try to work things out?" she asked before taking a sip from her glass.

"I wanted us to go to marriage counseling and couples therapy," he continued, "but it was all wasted time and money. She was too busy getting her next fix." His phone started buzzing. "Excuse me, let me get this," he whispered.

"Of course," she murmured.

"Hello? Okay. I'll meet you at my office." He smiled at her. "Okay. Okay." He then hung up the phone. "I'm sorry about that. Business never stops. After we finish eating, I need to stop by my office. It's on the way to your place. You can see where Mr. Big Shot works," he said, winking at her.

* * *

The elevator opened to the large empty lobby outside Clay's office. Nobody sat behind the big mahogany desk. Kendra read the big bronze letters that spelled out "WILLIAMS & ASSOCIATES."

Clay led her into his office and motioned for her to have a seat. She relaxed into the chocolate-colored leather couch opposite his desk. He grabbed a black briefcase and carried it to a filing cabinet, which he had to open with a key. He took papers and a USB drive out and put them into the briefcase.

"Are you okay?" she asked.

"Yes, I'm sorry. We'll be done soon." He began pacing and glancing at his watch. While he paced, she read all the awards and honors on his wall, but she kept glancing over at him. He didn't seem nervous, but something was bothering him. Sometimes she didn't know what to make of his facial expressions. However, she did observe that when she gave him the slightest bit of attention, his eyes took on a bright, almost puppylike gleam. At other times, he would make strange faces while he was silent, which made her uncomfortable.

"Sorry about this. I'm waiting on a business associate," he said.

Frank walked into the office. His eyes fell on Kendra.

"Hey, Frank, you got everything?" asked Clay.

Frank handed him a folder. Clay placed his keys on the desk, grabbed the folder, and took out some of the contents. He put the folder in the briefcase.

"Frank, this is Kendra. Kendra, meet Frank."

They both said "hi" in unison, equally unenthusiastic. Frank looked at her closer.

"Do I know you?" he said.

"No, I don't think so," Kendra responded, winking at him. He cleared his throat and looked away.

"Clay, can I speak with you out in the lobby?" Frank said as he walked out of the room.

"Sure, I'll be there in a minute," he said. "Kendra, give me one more sec."

* * *

Frank paced in front of the big fancy sign with Clay's last name on it. When Clay approached, he said, "You may not be aware of this, but Marvin was robbed."

Clay glanced back over his shoulder to his office. "How much?"

148

Frank shook his head. "I didn't want to tell you this, but we got more information. We believe it was your sister-in-law and her friends who robbed Delo's place."

Clay rubbed his chin. "Are you serious? Are we one hundred percent sure about that?"

"We're pretty sure. There were three of them, two men and a woman, and they had to have a getaway driver, because by the time Marvin and Nina got free, they were long gone. They also got the pictures."

"How did they even know where they were kept? We must have a leak in the organization."

"We never had a problem until your wife became a problem," Frank said, but Clay didn't hear him because he was too busy gazing back toward his office. "Clay, could your wife have somebody on the inside?"

Clay whipped his head around. "Erica?" He laughed. "No, but if the pictures are gone, we need to go to plan B quick."

"Already in motion?"

Clay hadn't stopped moving since he'd left his office. Sure, he was distracted by his latest guest, but Frank began to wonder if maybe he was back on the stuff.

"Do you think I'm stupid?"

Frank shrugged.

"Look, I have all the files stashed away where nobody will ever get to them. So, you tell those thugs to calm the fuck down and stop worrying about shit that we can handle. So a little fucking money was stolen and the pictures are gone. Big deal."

"These guys can't allow their money to get stolen. No matter how little it is. You know that. It's a street thing, and they have to do something about it," Frank said.

Clay clenched his jaw. "I don't need this shit."

"This is my livelihood too, Clay, and you're being selfish." Frank had lost his patience. He didn't care how mad his words made Clay.

149

Clay straightened up. "Now, listen, this is what we need to do," Clay said in a low voice as he glanced over his shoulder to the office. "Let me walk you outside."

* * *

Kendra looked out the open door. She couldn't see Frank or Clay. However, she could hear them mumbling in the distance. She wanted to know what Clay had laid out across his desk. She walked over to the file cabinet first as she kept looking over her shoulder, then she peeked inside. She held her breath and dug into the top drawer. She grabbed a few papers and examined them, twisting her head to listen. She took her phone and took close-up snapshots. When the mumbling stopped, she returned the papers to the drawer and crept to the door. She saw the men walking down the hallway to the elevator and watched as they both stepped in.

She knew she had a few extra minutes that she hadn't anticipated. She hurried over to Clay's desk and peeked at the open briefcase with the files he'd just placed on top. She glanced at them, then snapped her head around to see if anyone was coming. She examined a few more of them. She opened the top drawer. There was copy of a boarding flight to Belize and Clay's passport, along with a wad of cash and a driver's license. She took pictures of everything in the drawer and on the desk and as much of the briefcase files as she could. When she heard the lobby door open, she quickly put the papers back and sprinted back to the couch. As soon as she sat down, Clay walked in. She felt his eyes grazing over her. She was breathing hard.

"Are you okay?" he asked, watching her chest heave up and down.

"What's a girl to do when she's all alone in Mr. Big Shot's office, in a sexy dress with even sexier shoes?" she asked as she ran a finger down the back of her calf, drawing attention to her Jimmy Choo's and her cleavage.

"That's why I like you. You're honest, smart and funny."

He walked over to the desk, making sure everything was in the briefcase. He closed it and grabbed it to take with him. "The night's still young. Maybe you'd like to go get some gelato."

"Mmm… that sounds great."

"Okay, first I need to drop something off at my mother's house. Is that okay?"

"Meet your mother already? Don't you think that's too soon?"

"No, it's eight thirty. She's already in bed," he said with a laugh.

They walked out of the office and into the hallway. He locked the main door. She saw all the lights go off in the empty lobby. The big bronze-plated Williams and Associates sign had an evening glow. Clay watched her.

Within minutes of pulling off the freeway, they entered the upper-middle-class neighborhood where Clay's mother lived. They turned left at the corner and pulled up to the security booth. A guard stepped forward where an iron gate separated them from the community within.

"Hello, Mr. Johnson," Clay said to the older guard sitting in the booth.

"Hello, Mr. Thomas," the guard said as Clay coughed loudly to drown out the guard's words.

Kendra could see in the distance the huge luxurious sign that read "Morada Estates," as the moonlight and the lights from the sign lit up the well-manicured lawns. Clay parked the Benz in front of his mother's grand estate. Clay leaned toward her to reach into the backseat and paused. He grabbed his black briefcase and got out of the car.

"Kendra, baby, I need to put some stuff away, but I'll be right back." He pointed to the floor in the backseat. "There's some water in the backseat if you get thirsty."

"Okay, take your time," she said as he finished adjusting his clothing. She reached back and grabbed one of the bottles of water.

Clay shut the door and strolled away from the car. She watched him walk up the driveway to the front door. She grabbed her cell phone and made a call. "I think there's some information in his downtown office, and I may also know where he's keeping other stuff."

29

Erica walked into the corporate lobby. Will was right behind her. Her shoes clicked against the dark tile. She moved to the elevator, head held high. They stepped into the elevator and pushed the button for the fifth floor.

"Will, thank you for meeting me here, but when we get up there, don't say much. Carmen knows you'll be with me, but she's doing me a favor, and I don't want her to get in trouble. She informed me over the phone that Clay won't be in anytime soon, but we should still hurry."

As the elevator rose, she wondered why everything was happening. Why had she lost the baby? Why had she been attacked? Why had she lost everything?

The doors opened, and she walked down the hallway into the office reception area. She approached the administrator's desk with the large Williams and Associates sign with bronze letters bolted onto the raised, mounted dark red board hung on the wall behind it. Erica thought about the day Clay had gotten his big office on the fifth floor of the corporate building. He'd wanted to put *Williams & Associates* in big brass letters on the door, and she hadn't wanted him to do it. In her opinion, it was loud and tacky. At the time, he'd agreed and told her that he would do something else, but the next time she had gone into the office, she had seen those big brass letters, *Williams & Associates*. That was the first time Clay had flat-out lied right to her face. She'd always wondered why he hadn't just told her how he'd really felt. Now, she could see that he was selfish and a habitual liar, and he would hurt anybody that got in his way.

The old curly-haired administrative assistant spoke into the phone. She pointed them toward Clay's office. Erica waved at her, then walked down the hall. As she approached his office, she admired the view of the city behind his desk. It was a sought-after high-rise building, and the firm's main office, right in the middle of downtown.

"Doesn't feel any different from any other sofa, and God only knows what he's done on it," she said. Will jumped up and brushed himself off. "I'll look in his desk, you look in the file cabinets, and we'll take pictures with our phones." She reached into Clay's desk and felt around the top of the side drawer. She grabbed a key and raised it up to show Will. "For someone so smart, he sure is predictable."

She noticed a driver license in the drawer with Clay's picture. She grabbed it and held it up for Will to see. "James Evans."

"Keep that," Will said.

She put the license in a big white plastic envelope.

About fifteen minutes later, the curly-haired assistant walked in and raised her eyebrows at Will, who was clearly digging through her boss's files. "Erica, honey, Clay called and asked me if I wanted anything to eat. He said he should be back in the next thirty minutes."

"Thanks, Carmen. We'll make sure we're out of here long before he returns," Erica said, putting a file back in the drawer.

Carmen backed out and closed the door behind her.

"You think that old broad knows something? I mean, she is his secretary," Will said.

"I'm sure Clay just has her doing the real business stuff, because if she knew something, she would have told me. I learned very early to make sure you have good relationship with your husband's secretary. I also know that during regular business hours, Clay wasn't cheating on me, at least in this office, because Carmen would have skinned him alive."

"You're right. Clay would know the secretary would be the first in line for questioning. He probably has another place he does his dirty deeds."

Erica raised an eyebrow at Will. He realized his mistake and blushed. "His dirty business deeds, I mean."

"Let's do this as fast as we can," she said, hurrying to put folders back into the desk drawers. "I'm sure he has some important paperwork here. We just need to find the hiding place."

She ran her fingers under the surface of the desk but didn't feel anything. She pulled out the main desk drawer and noticed a set of keys and a piece of paper peeking out from under a folder. The folder had Erica's name on the tab. She set the keys on the desk and slid out the piece of paper. It was a GPS map printout. The doctor's office was part of the highlighted route, and scribbled in the left-hand corner of the paper was Erica's due date. She fell back in the chair. "We got him. We got proof he was behind the GPS on my car." She pulled out her phone and started taking pictures.

Will moved the keys closer to him and started taking pictures with his phone.

"What you doing?"

"I'm using the Keyme app: you just snap pictures of keys and you can get copies made."

"Wow."

"Yeah, you never know." He picked up some papers. "We need a copy of this, but you should know, we may not be able to use this information in a court of law."

"Why?"

"The way we're getting it is illegal."

155

Erica rested her index finger on her temple while she tried to think of something. "I just want what's mine and my kids'. Maybe we use it to scare him."

"We might be able to use some of the stuff in the divorce settlement, and Clay may just give into you." Erica lifted her head in confusion. "But with what we have here, all you have to do is prove to one judge that it's in the best interest of your children to be with you."

"Right now, that's all I want. Clay's greedy. He'll cave if I don't fight him over finances. I can start over if I need to. I just need my kids." She looked at the clock on the wall. "We got what we need. I have to go pick up my kids. I'll see you at your office tomorrow."

* * *

Erica rushed her Range Rover down the street. CJ was safe in his child seat. She just needed to pick up Chloe and go celebrate. She reached the neighborhood. The houses all had decent lawns with neatly trimmed grass, concrete driveways, and mailboxes lined up along the curbs. The houses were painted pastel shades of pale blue, soft yellow, and khaki brown. There were even a few brick homes. Most had white picket fences surrounding the front yards, with dogs and kids playing behind them.

As she was stopped at the red light, a truck raced up beside her. The driver rolled down the window. "Get off the damn road." Two young white guys sat inside the white Ford F-250 pickup with Go Big tires and an American flag waving in the air off the back of the cab. The driver was bald, and the passenger had a long blond ponytail and lots of tattoos. The passenger gave her the middle finger.

She tried her best to ignore them. When the light turned green, she continued out of there, only to be stopped by the next red light. The truck stopped next to her. She waited, her heart racing so hard she thought it would pop out of her chest. She'd had more than enough stress for the day. When the light turned green, the bald guy hit his gas pedal hard enough to make his tires screech. He raced ahead of her, then swerved into her lane, cutting her off. She veered to the right side of the road and slammed on her brakes, narrowly avoiding the curb. She almost hit a parked car in the process.

"Fuck you," the driver yelled as they sped off. Erica stared at the "God Bless America" bumper sticker on the back of their truck. She was holding her breath to keep it together and finally, when she couldn't hold it any longer, she let out a slow exhale.

"Huhu, huhu," CJ chirped out.

"Okay, baby, it's okay." He stopped moving. She sat for a moment, sighing as she leaned her head back against the seat. "I'm sorry, baby," she whispered, thankful neither of them had gotten hurt. For that moment, they both sat in silence. She was slumped over the steering wheel when a man started banging on her window. She shrieked, thinking the truck had returned. When she gathered some nerve, she peeked out the window and saw a police officer standing there.

"Ma'am. Open the door." She rolled down the window.

"Do you know why I'm pulling you over?" the officer asked with his hand on his holster.

"No, I don't, officer," Erica said.

"Ma'am, I'm pulling you over because you almost hit a truck a few miles back."

"They almost ran me off the road, Officer."

"License and registration, please," he demanded.

Erica reached into her purse and pulled out her license. She handed it to the officer.

"Registration, miss," the officer barked.

"Okay, Officer, I am going to reach into my glove box now. Is that all right?"

"Okay, keep your hands where I can see them."

Erica reached over to the glove compartment and opened it. Another officer began beating on the passenger window. She couldn't move. CJ began to scream. The man on the driver's side yanked open Erica's door. The officer pointed a gun in her face.

"Freeze," he said. Her eyes opened wide.

"What's going on?" she cried out.

"Put your hands on the dashboard and don't move," he stated. She followed his orders. When she tried to say something else, he interrupted her. "Quiet, miss. Now, get out of your car and lay flat on your stomach."

Erica got out and lay on the ground. She'd been taught at an early age to do everything a police officer told her to do. She didn't want to wind up dead. "Place your hands on the back of your head."

The officer gave a "coast is clear" command to the other officer, who opened the passenger door. She could hear him rummaging around the car. She had no idea what he was looking for, but she hoped he didn't scare CJ, who had stopped screaming after the officer made her get out of the car.

"I got it," he said as he raised the package in the air. It had a big green *D* written on it. He placed the package back on the floor and used his knife to poke a little hole in the package. He tasted the contents and then spat. The officer yanked her up off the ground and handcuffed her. Another officer came over and walked her to an undercover squad car and put her in the backseat. She glanced out the window. A female officer pulled out the new box of crayons she had just bought and handed them to CJ. She watched as the woman walked her son to another squad car.

30

Lashay walked into the courtroom building. A black security man with grayish hair smiled at her, but she knew it had nothing to do with her appearance. She was unusually tired and wasn't sure she'd make it.

The court was crowded. A hush fell over the courtroom as people filed in. Once they were seated, the bailiff commanded, "All rise." His voice was so loud and powerful that Lashay jumped and had a sudden urge to go to the bathroom. She didn't know why she was so nervous; she wasn't in court for her life. She looked around the court and noticed a familiar man standing in the back the courtroom. She'd seen him a few times with Clay. She believed he was a cop.

"Nature of action: the State versus Williams, the Honorable Judge B. Edwards presiding. Court is now in session," the bailiff said.

"Good morning, ladies and gentlemen," the judge said. "Calling the case of the People of the State versus Erica Williams. Are both sides ready?"

"Ready for the people, Your Honor," said a tall man in a gray suit, who looked like he meant business.

"Ready for the defense, Your Honor," Debbie, Erica's attorney said in a firm voice.

Lashay looked sideways at Erica. Her sister was dressed in a suit, with her hair and makeup done, but she looked terrible. She was paler than Lashay, with dark circles under her eyes. She stood motionless, clutching hard at her right arm, like she was barely keeping herself together. Lashay perused the people in the courtroom. Some looked to be in their thirties, while others spanned the fifty-to-sixty age group.

"We will proceed with the case against Mrs. Williams. Mr. Schmidt, please begin," the judge said.

"I seek the maximum on the bail, your honor."

"Does you defendant have any questions?" Debbie stood. "Thank you, Your Honor. My client, Mrs. Williams, has been an upstanding citizen for her entire life. She is the mother of two children and has no prior record. We would like Mrs. Williams released on her own recognizance."

The prosecutor stood and walked over to the judge. "Does the defense have anything else further to say?" the judge asked.

"Yes, Your Honor," said Debbie. "Mrs. Williams should not have to stay another day in jail. She is no threat to society."

"She's being charged with possession of an illegal drug, also abandonment of a child and reckless child endangerment." The judge looked down at the papers in front of him. "How does the defendant wish to plead?"

Lashay watched her sister stand there, like she had nothing to say, like she had already given up.

"Not guilty, Your Honor," Debbie said.

The judge looked down at Erica with his head cocked to one side and frowned. Lashay had seen that expression before, but not since she was a kid, when she was helpless and innocent.

"Bail set at five hundred thousand dollars," the judge said.

As soon as the judge banged his gavel, the silence of the courtroom erupted into a conversation as people rushed for the door. Reporters pushed forward to take pictures of Erica.

The bailiffs had her in handcuffs and took her through a door to a back hall.

31

Officer Frank put on his sunglasses as walked out of the courtroom. He hadn't said a word to anybody. Before stepping from the curb, he waited for several cars to pass. When it was finally clear, he strolled across. He thought about all the times he'd had to play middleman between the two guys he had grown up with. He remembered when the three of them used to play together. Delo had wanted to act like a mobster and Clay had wanted to show off for the girls. Clay and Delo had once fought over a girl, and Frank had had to play cop and be the one to calm them both down.

He approached the parked Buick. Clay was sitting in the car, his head cocked to the right. A smile started to take shape in the corner of his mouth. As cars passed by, Frank stood beside the driver's side, talking to Clay. CJ was in the back, halfway asleep.

"New car, Clay? Better hide it before Erica puts you on punishment."

"Funny, you got jokes." he said as he handed him an envelope full of cash. "That's for you and the boys for a job well done. I don't think anybody is going to come up with three hundred thousand. I went to all the banks and froze the accounts of her associates."

"Delo and Marvin are getting tired of using our resources for your personal business. This is the second time this much time and effort has been put into your personal life. Do you even still talk to that woman from the Caribbean?"

Clay paused before answering. "Remember, she got deported."

"Yeah, I know we set it up." Frank said and looked in the backseat at CJ, who was sleeping. "So now you got both kids. Can you handle that?"

"We're staying with my mother…"

"At the old folks' home?"

"No, but I take the kids to visit her."

"Okay, it's your thing. Just make sure—make sure—you are good to go with everything on the sale of the firms. By this time next year, we all will be rich men."

"Yes, indeed, the deal will be finalized in a couple of months. Our guy at the big tax company said he needed that much time, and then we'll be on our way."

"Great."

"Did we make contact with our people in jail?"

"Yes, but that's more of our team being used for your personal stuff."

"Tell those thugs this is business."

"Those thugs have made us a lot of money and have handled the business quite well."

"Like I said, after these next moves, my wife will be neutered." Clay laughed, Frank didn't. Clay laughed louder. Frank stared at him. "Women, cats, pussy, neutered. Get it?" he said.

* * *

163

Lashay stood outside the courthouse behind a column, watching the man she believed to be Clay's friend as he stood next to the car chatting to the driver.

"What are you doing?" Will walked up and blocked her view.

She shushed him with her hand and moved off to the side so she could get a full view of Clay's friend and try to figure out who he was talking to. She nodded as she continued her surveillance.

"Can't we just go to bail bonds and get her release?" Lashay asked.

"Yes, if you have ten percent of the bail or some collateral."

"Erica has some money and businesses."

"She didn't tell you? Nothing is in her name."

"What?"

"It's complicated right now."

"I only have a few thousand left from the robbery."

"Maybe your friends can help with their cut."

"That will still leave us short."She said.

She took a deep breath. "Erica can't spend any more time in that place. She's losing her mind. Didn't you see her? We have to get my sister out of there."

"I know. She didn't even want any visitors."

Lashay could hear the sadness in Will's voice, but her eyes never left the person across the street. "I...I want to protect my sister and help her get out of this mess," she said. "That poor girl is at the lowest I've ever seen her. I don't know what to do, Will." Tears crawled down her face and into her already-soaked bloused.

Will glanced at her. "I feel so bad for her. I feel so helpless. What kind of man am I?"

"Will, you're a good guy."

"Okay, here's what we're going to do. I'm going see a lady with a lot of connections and find out if she's has any more information and if she can help Erica in jail."

"While you're doing that, I'm going to work on getting some money so we can bail her out."

"Will it be obtained legally?"

Lashay looked at him. "I'm getting my sister out of that cage."

"I understand. However, give me a couple of days. I may have something that can help," Will said.

32

The ride on the freeway was smooth. Will had the windows down, and the wind—that perfect, warm wind of spring—blew through the car. He barely noticed the smell of exhaust and diesel. Will exited the freeway and drove through streets until he pulled the car over and stopped in front of the building. Will looked up at the sign: "WAVES."

This was the second time he'd come to the organization site. He scanned the area, nervous, but there weren't any people out and about. After what seemed like hours, a young woman came out, a smile on her face and items in her hand. She jumped into the passenger seat. It looked like a stack of papers with addresses on them.

"Will, right? We met the other day. You can call me Francine," she said. He started the car and headed down the road. He looked in the rearview mirror a few times, then over at Francine.

"Am I in danger?"

She laughed. "No, it's just that the boss wanted to talk to you in person at the ranch. You have nothing to worry about."

"Okay, good." Will reached for the satchel and showed it to Francine.

"Now, pull over and let me drive. We have one more stop."

Will stopped the car and got out. She slid over into the driver's seat as Will got into the passenger seat. She reached inside the package she'd brought and pulled out a dark scarf. "You need to put this on," she said when he got in. He reached for it and tied it around his eyes. Everything became dark.

She drove down the freeway. Twenty-minutes later he could hear the crumpling of paper and wondered where she was taking him. He knew they were outside the city limits, and if he had to guess, they were in a construction zone, because the only rough sections of the freeway were closed to public use. But he knew WAVES had connections and power everywhere. She pulled over.

"You can remove your scarf now," Francine said.

He did as she instructed, but it didn't make a difference anyway. He still couldn't see anything in the pitch dark, although he could make out a big ranch-style house set way back. Three women wearing cowboy hats and holding rifles stood in front of the car. Francine rolled down her window. Will didn't move.

"Francine?" a gruff woman's voice said.

"Yes. I'm here to see the lady of the house."

"Follow the road up to the house."

Francine rolled up the window, and the three amigos disappeared into the darkness.

The home looked like it had once been a large boarding school. It had more windows than Will felt like counting. In the curve of the large circular driveway stood a statue of a naked man pissing water into a tub that surrounded him.

"Bring the satchel, Will," Francine said. He slung it over his shoulder.

A woman escorted them inside and asked if they wanted a drink. The house was bigger than it looked from the outside. Will's palms were clammy. He could use a drink. But before he could answer, a strong aroma filled the room, like vanilla and burning

167

leaves. From behind a cloud of smoke, a man appeared. Though muscular, he was short and wide. His muscles weren't defined, but he looked like he could do some damage. His hair, dyed jet-black, looked as though it had been slicked back with used motor oil. He wore a neat golf shirt and starched khaki pants and smoked a large cigar. When he hooked his sausage-like forefinger over the cigar to take it out of his mouth, Will noticed his pinky ring had a diamond the size of a full-grown cockroach.

"Follow me," he said.

Their female escort leaned close. "This is Big John. He'll take you from here."

Francine nodded with a head tilt of thanks, and they followed him through the house to the basement door. They descended the stairs, and Will was surprised to see that the basement had been transformed into a fully operational business office. The room's five different workstations each had their own desk, chair, and flashing telephone. The stations, separated by large portable walls, created the feeling of being in a large maze. A long electronic ticker displaying updated stock prices spanned the room.

As they walked through the maze, Will took notice of the people sitting at the workstations. One white girl with curly red hair looked up at him. She smiled and bent back over her desk, a phone to her ear. She scattered some papers and, in one quick motion, spread them out across the desk. At the next station, a girl with black hair cut into a bob and dressed in a double-breasted skirt suit also talked on the phone, and Will recognized her voice. She had been at the headquarters on his first visit. "Hey, there," she said.

They arrived at a separate office with a desk and leather chairs, but nothing on the walls.

"Take a seat," Big John said.

Will sat down in one chair and Francine sat in the other. Francine didn't appear nervous, but Will decided she owed him an explanation. Just as he opened his mouth to ask her some tough questions, Mrs. Porter walked in. Francine jumped up with excitement. They hugged each other.

"Hello, crime boss," Mrs. Porter said with a smile. Both of them laughed. Will was puzzled, not understanding their inside joke. Mrs. Porter turned to him. "Good to see you again, Will. We miss you."

Francine looked at Will, and he tried to smile. She reached into the desk and pulled out a thick folder stuffed with documents. Will nodded his head, pleased.

"That's what we need," Will said.

"You do have the money, right?" Will lifted the satchel and placed it on the desk. "Now it's time for business," she said. "Our research team has found most of the money Erica's husband hid. We came up with a list of a hundred companies."

She turned over the folder and dumped the contents. What popped out blew Will's mind. There were real estate documents and court documents. Will picked up one.

"These are his main assets. Erica's husband has many trusts, giving certain people voting shares. He wrote out a shareholder's agreement for the family corporation. It's set up through a woman named Emma Thomas," Mrs. Porter said.

"I think that's Clay's mother, but I'll ask Erica."

"Yes, this old broad is worth twenty-five million dollars. There are a total of five trusts. One for each of their kids at five million apiece, and in two other names at five million each. The house she lived in is owned by a trust."

"But on the documents I gave you earlier, the house was in Erica's name," Will said.

"Now, I think Clay created fake documents to give to her and other business associates, and nobody ever double-checked with city hall to make sure the information was legit. Her husband is such a good manipulator of numbers, the only thing she would get in a divorce settlement is a percentage of his eighty-thousand-dollar-a-year salary," Mrs. Porter said. "You know we are the ones who find stuff lawyers and investigators don't. Her husband has cars at storage facilities and has property all over the city. He has offshore accounts and owns some businesses in Belize under different names. His business partners don't know about that. However, they are waiting for a sale of his legit business to go through, which will take the business public, and Clay and his partners will be rich men."

"Really?" Will asked as he stared at Mrs. Porter.

"Yes, they're in negotiation with the lawyers. But guess what's holding it up?"

"What?"

"The sale of the original tax office. They want it, but Clay didn't include it."

"He wants to keep it for himself?"

"Yes. Not because it's some great business, but because it's the only thing in Erica's name."

"Why not forge those documents, like he did everything else?"

"He can't, because Erica has to sign it over in front of two independent notary publics."

"So does that mean what I think it means?" Will asked.

"Yes, Clay wants her dead. Or if she's a convicted felon, then it will be all his."

"So that's why he doing what he's been doing."

"So, here's the situation. There are more documents out there implicating his business associates, and our inside source believes she knows where they are. You get this information, you can use it against him." Mrs. Porter put everything back in the bag and handed it to Will. "In these bags, you'll find the rest of the instructions on what to do and the directions to where they are. Also some things your friend would want to see."

Will reached in, pulled out the papers and examined them. "I'll get this information to her sister."

"Yes, the sister. She's something special. When all this is done, you make sure she comes and sees me," Mrs. Porter said, smiling.

Will laughed. "That's why I love you. You have the best sense of humor."

"I know."

"Oh yeah, you know about Erica somehow ending up in jail for crimes she didn't commit, and she's in real danger in jail. She also has two kids she wants to see, but her ex-husband is denying her request to see them."

"I'll see what we can do to help her in jail. It can be a dangerous place for a novice," she said.

"Thank you so much, Mrs. Porter."

Someone cleared his throat behind him, and Will whirled around. Big John walked back into the room. Will shifted his eyes.

"I'll call you when it's the best time to go get that information. When we know he'll be occupied." Mrs. Porter clasped her hands in front of her.

33

Erica stepped into the gallery and followed everyone to the chow hall. She got in line with the other women and waited for her share of gray goop. She looked down to the bottom level as she walked down the corridor and saw three girls looking up at her. She was in no rush to get to the cafeteria. The guards ushered them down the long hallway. The cinder block walls were painted a dirty blue color in the eating area, as if they'd tried to spruce up the place but didn't want to make it too nice. She couldn't shake the feeling that someone was watching her. She felt eyes drilling into the back of her head. She turned around to find a short dark-haired woman staring at her. A tall slender woman stood next to her.

The short dark woman could have been a linebacker for the Green Bay Packers as she charged towards them. She stopped and planted her brawny legs wide apart. Her hands were on her hips, her face was twisted with hate, and her disheveled hair did nothing to help her appearance. She was not a pretty woman by any stretch of the imagination. It all would have been comical if she wasn't coming to start some drama.

"Look, Angela, we have fresh meat here. What you doing in here, you bougie bitch?" she said. She was more man than woman.

Even her voice sounded like she was born smoking Kool Menthols. She leaned in close to Erica. "You real cute, baby doll. I'm going to make you mine in no time." She began sniffing around Erica's breast area. Erica acted as if the woman didn't exist.

Angela, the tall friend, chimed in. "She thinks she too good for us, Hilda. A bougie bitch."

"Keep it moving," the guards yelled.

Erica made it inside the mess hall without any major drama. It was one big sterile room filled with an endless number of aluminum picnic-style tables. A sea of orange suits flooded the area, but inside the uniformity of clothing were inmates of all ethnic groups. All diverse, yet looking like one big international team of criminals. This was a place where real shit could hit the fan, because only a few guards patrolled the area. There were four seats attached to each table, and ten tables meant there were forty seats. Problem was, fifty girls lived in that particular unit. Those who had been there the longest were supposed to get first dibs on the seats.

Erica collected her meal tray and sat down in the first open seat. Before she took a bite of food, Angela was right on her, yelling. She could barely speak English. From her accent, Erica couldn't tell what country she was from. "Dat dere is my seat."

"This is my seat. I always sit here," Erica snapped back.

Angela got right in her face. Erica could smell the cigarettes on her breath. "You try to be a smartass?" she asked.

"If I was?"

Angela took a swing, and Erica ducked out of the way and swung her food tray at Angela. Angela immediately dropped to the floor, but on her way down, she bumped her head on one of the aluminum stools. She screamed out of pain and then hit the floor. Hilda took the opportunity to pull out a shank and sprinted toward Erica. Erica was watching everything in slow motion and couldn't move. Before Hilda got too close, another female grabbed a tray

173

off the table and hit Hilda across the back of the head. Hilda fell to the floor next to Angela, who was still wriggling in pain.

Erica saw that the woman who'd saved her was no more than a young freckle-faced girl.

"I got you. Name's Bella," she said.

As the guards rushed over, everybody dropped to the ground and lay on their stomachs. Erica was already down, and Bella was pushed.

Two guards lifted Angela up. "What happened?"

"Nothing. I tripped and fell and then dropped my tray," Angela said, her eyes never leaving Erica's face. The guards looked around.

"Sure, you did. Williams, you have a visitor," the guard said.

Hilda was about ten feet away. Erica was still clutching the shank. She nodded at Erica. Before Erica walked away, she read Hilda's lips—*I'm going to get you, bitch.*

* * *

The guard led Lashay into a narrow room. It was dim and quiet. Light blue concrete walls were on one side and a glass wall on the other side.

He instructed her to sit at one of the booths.

"Take number three," he said. Other visitors sat in the other booths, talking in low voices, waiting for the guards to say their time was up. Erica sat behind the glass wall that separated the visitors. She held a phone up to her ear. The phone was connected to a cord that came out of the wall.

When Erica saw her on the other side of the glass, she had a glimmer of hope in her eyes. She held the phone up to her ear. Lashay sat down directly in front of her and picked up her own phone.

"Hello," she managed.

Erica took a deep breath, closed her eyes, and tried to muster the bravest face she could. "Hi, Lashay, I'm glad you came," she said.

"My poor sister. I didn't know you were in here. How are you? Are you okay?"

"Not so good. This place is not me. I have to get out of here," Erica said, her voice catching.

"Don't worry. We'll get you out of here. I promise you that."

"Clay did his job very well," Erica said. "I'm not so optimistic."

Lashay clawed at her knee, not wanted Erica to see just how angry she was. "Clay is a lowlife. Forget him. Forget anything that keeps you from your kids."

"What about my kids, Lashay? Have you seen them?"

"That's just it, baby girl. I haven't. Clay has them holed up somewhere. They are not staying at your house in Brookside. But don't worry, I'll find him. This bogus charge has tied up every aspect of this case and your family, including custody and visitation. The good news is they can come visit you anytime. The bad news is you need Clay's permission for it to happen. Will's office put in a request, and Clay's saying the kids aren't ready to see you.

"Erica, baby, they're working on your case right now. Right as we speak. In addition, I'm still in the process of getting my finances straightened out. I am determined as ever to get you out. Will's still investigating some things, and he wants you to know that he will never stop. I'm going to get the money to bail you out. Trust me, sis."

"I need to go home," she groaned. "I miss my kids." Her voice broke. She paused as her eyes began to water. She began hyperventilating.

Lashay had always assumed Erica was the strong one between the two of them, but right now, she knew she needed to take over that role. "You'll get out of here soon. They'll drop the bogus drug charges, so you will beat that. You just hang in there."

175

"Thanks, I'll get it together," she said, her voice strained. She forced herself to calm down.

"That's it. Just relax, and try not to worry yourself."

"Lashay, that's not it. I'm at the point where sometimes you have to ask *why?* If I had been doing what I needed to do from the get-go instead of worrying about him all the time, I wouldn't be in here now. And where is he? He has the kids, and he got me out of the way. In general, that asshole got it all. He won. He stole my future."

"We'll get him, sis. We'll destroy him. I'm going to meet Will. He has information that can help."

"You know that's not in my nature. I don't want to hurt someone."

There was a long pause. Lashay didn't know what to say next. "Yeah, right. If you could run Clay over, then back up and do it again, you'd do it in a hot minute." Lashey laughed.

Erica laughed too. "You're right. But only if I was driving a Mack truck. He's not worth denting a good car."

They both broke out laughing like they were having drinks in a bar and talking about old times.

"Thank you for coming. I feel a little better now. And, Shay, you're all I got. Take care of yourself."

"Girl, don't worry about me."

"If Clay was calculated enough to pull off putting goody-two-shoes me in jail, just think what he could do to you." Erica put her hand up on the window, and Lashay did the same.

34

The afternoon sunlight beamed in from the bay window in the living room. Clay stood still as he looked around the inside of the mansion in Morada Estates. The black leather couch with the matching love seat and zebra-print throw pillows looked good next to the black-and-white dining set. It looked, on the surface, like they were living well. The ceilings in the living room rose twelve to fourteen feet above his head. With the open-space design plan, you could see the back door down the long hallway.

Aunt Mena, with a full head of wiry gray hair, stood there in her muumuu with creases in the wrong places. Clay knew she loved him. She had been trying to find some time to talk to him for the last few weeks, but he'd ignored her and her calls. Whenever he did come, he was in a hurry.

He stiffened when he heard her. She made no attempt to greet him. He knew what was coming. "This is going to be hard to hear, but I'm going to tell you anyway. Your kids need their mother. They miss their mother, I know she in jail, but why can't you take them to see her? It's been two weeks since they've seen her."

"Auntie, I know you're concerned, but I know what I'm doing," he said as he glared at her. He leaned against the wall, trying to calm his anger. Mena had proven once again that she knew just how to say the wrong thing at the wrong time, but he couldn't just let her comments slide. He spun around to face her so fast that she felt the wind in her face. His trembling finger was inches away from her nose. He narrowed his eyes. "You can't run my life now."

"I still haven't heard you say that you're going to take the kids to see their mother," she said. "Since when don't you respond to reason?"

His face burned with anger. He resented the fact that his aunt might be right.

"Let me talk to him," his mother said. The carpet crunched under her house shoes as Mena walked away. Clay didn't turn around. When he turned back, his aunt was far down the hallway, but his mother was still there.

"I understand you have a plan, but the kids have been cooped up in the house for several weeks. No school and no time with their friends. They want to go to their house. I know you love your kids, but they miss their mother." She took a deep breath. "Clay, I want you to understand that your auntie wants the best for you and the kids."

"Mom, I already took care of everything with the school. We have another month here, then we'll be moving to the Caribbean. I just know everybody will be happy there. You will too." She gave a tight smile. "Mom, you've always been there for me, and now it's important to me that you help me keep everybody relaxed. I have to finish putting the final touches on my deal."

"Baby, I'm here for you, but this is different. The kids need their mother," she insisted.

"The only thing different is that Erica embarrassed herself and endangered our kids by selling drugs, and now I have to do what's best for them. And, Mom, please trust me on this."

"Baby, I'm just worried about you. You've always been in control, and I'm just concerned that you're letting business take up all your time."

178

"You don't need to worry about me. I'm fine. I've got this," he said.

"I see that you think you have it all under control, but are you happy?" she said.

"Happy?" He looked perplexed.

"Yes, happy," she repeated. He fell silent. "I want you to think about that."

"Of course I'm happy," he exploded. "Look, Mom, I know you're concerned about me, but I have it all under control. Just like you love this place, you will love Belize."

"Clay, you just don't seem happy. You stay in that other house by yourself sometimes, you come here late some nights. Mena said you're spending a lot of time at a strip bar or club. Whatever they call those places."

"No, no, I do the taxes for that place, Mom. That's why I'm there all the time," he said. His mother was beginning to get upset. "I'm not going to let anyone take my kids to see that woman. It's not good for them to see her like that right now. Not you, not Auntie, not the state, no one."

His mother grabbed his arm and pulled him close. Her grip felt like steel. "You need to calm down."

"I'm sorry, Mother, but I got this," he said. "I'd like you to take your hands off of me." His eyes stayed fixed on his mother's as they fought a battle of wills.

"Son, I'm going to forget all this ever happened, because I know you've been going through a lot lately." She let go of his arm and surrendered the fight. "I know you'll do what's right. I'm going to lay down. I love you." She walked down the hallway.

Clay made himself a drink, then walked up stairs to his room and grabbed a bag. He went down to CJ's room and looked in. He was taking his afternoon nap and had left a toy on the floor. He walked to Chloe's room. He opened the door and stuck his head in. She turned to see him standing there, holding a bag in front of his face.

"Daddy," she shrieked and ran and jumped into his arms.

179

He felt genuine love blossom in him. He hugged her. "How is my princess?"

"Aunt Mena won't let me watch Nick Jr."

"Oh. Well, maybe Aunt Mena knows something Chloe doesn't know yet."

He put her down and handed her a little bag. She pulled out a dress that was just her size.

"I love it, Daddy, but I love you more," she said as she wrapped him in another hug.

"And I love you most, little angel," he said as he stroked her hair.

"I'll be right back, Daddy." She ran out of the room.

He arranged the dolls while Chloe put on her new dress.

"Ta-da," she yelled, jumping into the room. Together, they played dolls, and Clay's mind felt peaceful for once. Aunt Mena was wrong. The kids didn't need their mother. They needed him.

Clay stood to stretch. She came over to him and hugged his legs. "Daddy, I miss Mommy. When will we see her again? I want to go home. I want to see my Mommy, and CJ misses her too." She started to cry.

Clay put a few of her dolls on the bed. He looked at his daughter's sad face and hugged her. "Soon, baby, real soon."

"You're the best daddy ever."

His face flushed. He pulled on his ear. He squeezed Chloe. "Daddy has to go get ready for a business meeting I have this evening. I want you to know that I love you so much."

She hugged him back, then sat back down, playing with her dolls. He darted out of the room.

35

Erica fell in line with the woman in front of her. She glanced up. Hilda was mopping the floor of the cell hallway. With every step, the woman gave her an angry glare. As she passed an open cell, Bella, the reddish-blonde-haired girl with the freckles on her cheeks who'd helped her before, fell in line in front of her.

Erica kept walking toward the cafeteria, Bella right in front of her. The line stopped. She looked around but couldn't see any movement in the whole place. She could almost see the tension and sure as hell could smell it. She saw Angela walking toward her. Angela didn't say a word until she had passed her, but then Erica heard her say to someone, "Move. My place in line."

Angela pushed her way into line two ladies behind her. Erica looked further back over her shoulder. The guard was coming down the corridor. Hilda didn't even try to hide the fact that she was watching the guard.

Erica knew this place was the type of place William Shakespeare had described when he'd said, "Hell is empty, and all the devils are here."

Erica and Angela glared at each other. Erica glanced down the corridor. Hilda was moving toward her with her broom moving back and forth. She knew Angela was behind her, gearing up for something. The guard was heading back their way. The line moved into the cafeteria. She watched Hilda as her broom swept along with the flow of the line. Erica gave Bella a questioning look to see if she was ready. Bella nodded. Erica saw Hilda glance at the guard, who wasn't paying attention.

That was all Hilda needed. She came with her broom handle raised. Erica got her makeshift knife ready and raised her arms, then yelling and commotion broke out as people gathered in a crowd. She heard screams, and Angela was on the floor. Bella kneeled over her, stabbing her repeatedly with her knife, and then Hilda, bypassing Erica, smacked and pummeled Bella with the broom. The rest of the women in line jumped out of the way. No one wanted to get involved in the fight. Erica scrambled forward to help, and when she got close to Hilda, another inmate in green came out of nowhere, tackled Hilda, and wrestled her to the ground, holding her tight. As the guards ran toward them, the two in the green suits who'd helped stop the fight walked away, leaving Erica rooted to the spot.

The cluster broke, and Angela got up. She stumbled around the corridor, grimacing and holding her stomach, and the guards followed. But Erica knew the guards had seen and marked her as one of those responsible. Angela's face twisted into a hideous combination of pain, fear, and panic. Her mouth gaped open, emitting wordless sounds as she tried to breathe. She staggered down the corridor, the guards getting hold of her arms, while a crowd of people followed behind her. Some of them screamed for a doctor. As Erica walked toward them, Angela fell back to the floor.

She rolled over onto her back. Blood lay in puddles everywhere. She shook like she was having a seizure. Her body stopped moving. A medic showed up to attend to her while guards rushed in and grabbed Erica, Bella, and Hilda.

* * *

Bella paced back and forth in the cell she now shared with Erica. She had taken her socks off to feel the cool smooth paint on her feet. Bella watched Erica's strange behavior closely as she paced the floor. Erica was wrapped in her covers with only her head sticking out. She lay there motionless. Bella walked around the bed to get a better look. Erica's hair was plastered to the sides of her face, caught in her cold sweat. Tendrils of her hair lay on her cheeks, limp and lifeless like her expression.

"What's wrong with you?" Bella asked. She bumped her shoulder when Erica didn't respond right away.

"Not well."

Bella got closer and saw Erica's clinched fists twisting the edge of the blanket.

Erica got up from her bed and paced back and forth in her cell. She walked over to the small mirror hanging over the sink. Her thirty-second birthday was coming up in a few weeks, and she looked as old as she felt.

As she watched herself, her forehead broke out in a sweat, her mouth went dry, and she couldn't catch her breath. She was having another panic attack. It was the third one since the fight. She sat down so hard on the bed that it made Bella jump.

"What's really going on, Erica?" Bella said. Erica broke out of her deep daze. Bella raised one cheek in a half-smile. "Come on, Erica."

"Somebody is trying to kill me, and I could spend the rest of my life in jail," she groaned. "I may never see my kids again." Her voice broke. She paused as her eyes began to water. "Who would want to kill me?" Erica began hyperventilating.

"This is jail, nobody will talk. You'll get out of here soon. They'll drop the bogus drug charges, so you'll beat that. You just hang in there," Bella said, trying to elevate her mood.

"Thanks, I'll try to get it together," she said with a strained voice as she forced herself to calm down. Bella walked over to her and hugged her.

"You've been my angel in here. If it wasn't for you, I'd be dead.

"Things will change for the better," Bella said, putting her arms across Erica's shoulders. Erica wiped her tears. Bella looked around to make sure no one could hear her. She got close to her. "Erica, I'm going be straight with you. I was hired by some important people on the outside to look out for you. You have some friends in here. That's how we pulled some strings to get me as your roommate. You also have people working to get you out. There are people who want you dead, and there will soon be a bounty on you. Once that happens, who knows."

There was a long pause. Erica seemed unsure of what to say next. She was surprised to hear that. "Who hired you?" she mumbled beneath the cover she had just pulled over her head.

Bella reached over and yanked it off. Erica wouldn't look at her. She remained fixated on the blanket. "That's not important right now. I told you so we can work together to keep you alive. Me and you just have to stay on guard," Bella said. "You'll be out of here soon, and you're going to go straight back to the good life. Focus on that."

"All this just because I wanted to divorce my cheating husband."

"Your husband is a punk, but it's his associates now, his silent partners, who want you dead. They decided jail would be better, and if you died in here, nobody would care. Nobody would think twice about the victims in jail killings. However, the bounty is coming because of what your sister's doing."

"My sister? What does she got to do with this?"

"Your sister robbed one of them and is planning on robbing more places. They know it's her and her friends. They're planning to stop them."

Erica jumped off the bed and ran to the bars. "I've got to tell her."

"Nobody has contact with her. Will can't even get a hold of her."

Erica turned back around. "You know Will."

"Will is working with my boss, trying to get information to free you. Your sister is out of control."

Erica smiled to herself. "She's always trying to protect me."

"That's family. That's what they do."

"True, but it's just different with her. When we were little, something happened that made her the way she is. Even years of therapy didn't help."

"What was it?"

Erica paused. Bella sat down again. She grabbed Erica's hand. "You tell me when you're ready. We have all the time in the world."

36

Lashay tied the laces of her Adidas Cloudfoam running shoes and began pacing back and forward in the living room of her apartment. She couldn't get Erica out of her head. Erica wouldn't approve of what she was doing. To make matters worse, she hadn't seen her niece and nephew in a month. Nobody had any idea where Clay had taken them.

Lashay heard a knock at the door and looked out the peephole. She opened the door. Meeka walked in. "Hope I'm not late. I headed this way as soon as I got off the phone with you."

Lashay grabbed the bag. "It's okay. Let's get started on my hair, then we can talk about what's going on."

"Okay," Meeka said as she walked past Lashay to the kitchen. She looked over her shoulder. "Where's Shorty?"

"He's in the bedroom sleeping. He spent most of the evening keeping an eye on one of Marvin's spots. We're hitting one of Marvin's ghetto banks in few nights. You and Moe will go get a burner car tomorrow night. Me and Shorty will sit on the spot."

"I get to see Moe again?"

"Yes. Look at you, liking Moe."

"He's a cool dude, that's all."

"The information I got from Will has been spot-on. We just have to make sure the money is there. I don't want my sister to sit another day in that jail."

"I'm ready. I'll do anything you want."

"You've done enough," Lashay said.

Meeka pulled one of the bottles out of the bag and chucked it at Lashay, who caught it in midair. Lashay grabbed the plastic bag and started laying out the hair products on the kitchen counter. She grabbed a plastic party chair, dragged it toward the double stainless-steel sink and sat down. Meeka trailed behind her with wine and glasses.

"Girl, I don't want any wine right now, I have to concentrate on what we need to do. Look in the fridge and bring me a bottle of Mike's," Lashay said.

Meeka gave her a bottle of the cider before pouring herself a glass of wine.

"Let's get started. A different color, a different look," Lashay said, rolling her hips.

"You're all business," laughed Meeka.

"Damn straight. I need to save my sister."

"Yes, ma'am," Meeka said.

She put all the products in order before she started mixing the Dark and Lovely chemical relaxer into a glass bowl. No matter how much they craved the smooth results delivered by the creamy chemical, they'd never get used to the chemically induced smell of rotten eggs. She put the sour substance on Lashay's head.

Twenty-five minutes passed as she prepared her hair.

Lashay head was burning. The two rushed to the sink and started rinsing the chemicals out of her hair. Meeka grabbed a bottle of apple cider vinegar from the pantry and poured the entire bottle over Lashay's head. This neutralized the burning but did little else. After a thorough rinse and conditioning, Meeka wrapped a towel around Lashay's head. She blotted her hair, then removed the towel. Meeka started toward Lashay to hug her, but stopped when Lashay said, "Hey, with all that's going on, what's a little hair?"

Lashay ran to her bedroom and returned with a scarf on her head, wrapped in a classic forehead bun style.

"Wig or this?"

"You a trip," Meeka cried.

"I'm a field trip without luggage." Lashay howled with laughter.

"Okay, I'll see you later."

* * *

The next morning, Lashay made her way to the living room. Shorty greeted her with what he called his "sexy look." He had on a silk robe and slippers.

"Hello, sexy lady," he said as he hugged her.

"Hey, Shorty," she said.

"I'm glad you're up, baby." She could hear soft music playing.

"Why's that?" she said as she wrapped her arms around his neck and leaned in to kiss him. He pulled away, took her hand, and walked her into the dining room. His hands were sweating. "Whatchoo nervous about?" she asked.

"Listen, Shay. I want you more than anything in life right now. I want you to be *the* woman in my life," he said. Lashay was about to say something when he put a finger on her lips. "Listen, don't say anything." His voice was very low. "I've made a simple breakfast to show you how much I care about you." Lashay looked around the room.

On the table were two plates, two wineglasses, and red roses, Lashay's favorite flowers. Large candles flickered around the room. He walked over to the stainless-steel oven. She saw that the dishes were washed and the kitchen floor was swept. He picked up a hot pad, reached into the oven, and pulled out a plate of French toast. Three small pans simmered on the stove. Lashay watched him as he plated the food. She enjoyed watching him do what he loved. She loved the white square plates he'd bought and the professional presentation of the French toast, sausages, cherry tomatoes, cut-up fruit, and bottle of apple cider. He always bragged that he cooked better than any chef downtown, but Lashay knew it was true.

"Have a seat, baby," he said as he walked to the table with the plates in hand. "I wanted to take care of you for a change and show you how much I appreciate you for you being in my life. I see what you doin' for your sister. I know you're a loyal person, and I like that."

"Thank you, Shorty. You're so sweet. But any good sister would help her own family, right?" she said, picking up her fork.

"No, not all family is like that."

"You know, Shorty, you don't have to do all this with me."

"What kind of man would I be to let my woman do this by herself? Besides, I want the motherfuckers who did that studio shit to my woman to pay, so even if you didn't want to get them, I would be getting them myself."

"I'm so glad you're the love of my life."

"Did I tell you how special you are?"

"Yeah, baby, you did." She smiled. "Is this about you not supporting my singing?"

"Naw, baby. Look, Shay, my life has been hard, but with you, I feel I can take on the world. And once we get through this drama … I'ma go back to culinary school."

"Oh, baby, that's great. You're my Clyde. I know I'm focused on Erica and everything, and we haven't had time to spend together, but cooking is your gift, and I can't wait to see you live your dream."

"Lashay, I want you to be my wife," he blurted out. Her head jerked up. "Will you marry me?" He pulled out a diamond ring and laid it on the table. She covered her open mouth and reached over to the small box with tears welling up in her eyes.

"Oh my God, Shorty," she managed to say. "But—"

"Will you be the Bonnie to my Clyde?" he said.

189

Lashay took the ring out of the box. Her eyes bubbled over with tears as she slid the ring onto her finger.

"Yes, I will be your Bonnie, baby. Yes," she said, jumping out of her chair. Shorty hugged her.

"I love you so much."

"I love you."

She kissed him.

"I want you so bad," he whispered in her ear. She reached over and kissed him.

"I want you too, baby." She held the back of his head against her palm.

He cupped her round bottom in his hand and pulled her into him. He was always gentle with her.

"Come on, baby," he said as he led her to the bedroom. She followed him as if under his spell.

Lashay helped him pull his shirt off. She kissed the top of his head. He grabbed her and started kissing her. At that moment, she felt he loved her more than anyone else in his life. Lashay straddled his lap and began to moan. He pulled her hips closer and began to nibble the nape of her neck. She sighed and began to grind him. He carried her to the side of the king-sized bed and laid her down. He ran his hands up her thighs and then kissed her lips. He pulled off her clothes, her warm, soft skin like a magnet to his hands. He looked at her naked body while he slid off his pants, then climbed into the bed next to her and cuddled her deep in his arms. He seemed to be in no rush, savoring the experience and making her want him. Lashay rolled to her side, and he spooned her, holding her breasts in his palms. He sucked on her neck and pressed himself against her back, then he was grinding against her and she could feel his hard erection. She was trying to be patient, but he was driving her crazy. He rolled her onto her back and ran kisses down her entire body. He buried his head in her chest and softly sucked on one hard nipple and then the other. He moved back down across her stomach, placing more kisses on her thighs, and then slid her panties off. They made passionate love.

After the blaze of passion had subsided, she looked at his face, serious and full of love. This was going to work out. Neither of them had loved anyone else like this. Before she knew it, she was asleep in his arms.

37

The late-night moon shone on the wet grass. As Moe walked up to the front door, he saw that all the blinds were closed, and it was dark inside the house. His grandmother lived in a small house in the back of the Southside. Many of the houses around the neighborhood were decaying. Moe pulled out his keys to search for the right one. He inserted it into the door lock and opened it, hesitating before he moved, not wanting to wake up his grandma. He peeked inside the house. None of the lights were on, and neither was the TV. He stepped inside and closed the door behind him, moving through the living room to the kitchen. Moe was carrying his grandmother's favorite food from Lee's Bakery and BBQ.

He was about to sit down when he heard the faint sweet tone of his grandmother's voice. "Is that you, Junior?" she asked, calling from her rocking chair.

"Yes, Grandma. Why are you sitting here in the dark?"

"Huh, what you say?"

Moe walked closer to his grandmother. "I said, why are you sitting here in the dark?"

"Well, I couldn't sleep, and they cut my lights off. I won't be able to pay it until my check comes on Friday," she said.

Moe grabbed his cell phone and turned on the flashlight app. Mama Rose got up from her rocker and walked over to the kitchen table. He rummaged through the junk drawer in the kitchen and found several candles. He lit them and put them on the table. They provided a soft glow that illuminated the room. He walked over to his grandma and gave her an affectionate hug and kissed her cheeks.

"Where you been, sonny? I don't believe I've seen you in several days," she said. She was a short, slim woman with close-cropped gray hair. Her narrow face lit up at the sight of her grandson.

"We had to work three days in row, Grams. Me and Shorty found some new work, and it means we're gone sometimes." A lump formed in his throat. He hated lying to his grandma.

"Huh? What work?"

Moe got close to his grandmother again. "I said I'm working with Shorty."

"What I tell you about hanging with that boy, Maurice? If you hang out with nine criminals, sooner or later you're going to be the tenth," she said.

Moe smiled at his grandma. "Here, I brought you some Lee's," he said. "It's a good thing I did, since the lights are out."

"I appreciate that, baby. I can eat some now and save some for tomorrow. I been keeping stuff next door at Miss Jean's."

Moe began pulling out boxes from the bags and setting them on the table. They ate in silence.

"Grandma, why didn't you call me when the lights went out? I woulda come home," he said, putting his hand on her arm.

"Oh, I don't know, honey. I didn't want to worry you. I knew you would be around soon. Besides, I don't understand these new phones."

After they finished eating, Moe started cleaning up. His grandmother tried to help.

"I got it, Grams, relax."

She sat back down, calm and relaxed on the old flower-patterned couch in the living room. Her blank stare gave no indication whether she even knew what year it was.

He had been living with her his whole life. Both of his parents had died when he was a child. He'd watched them get shot at his home when he was five years old. He'd been left in the house with them for days before someone found him. When he'd gotten older, he'd been told that it was a drug deal gone bad. He didn't think the events had affected him, because in his mind, he had his dear Grandma Rose, a woman who had been there for him his entire life. He loved her more than he loved himself.

"Junior, I would have baked you a pie, but everything's off until I get my check on Friday," she said.

"Don't worry, Grandma, I'll take care of that." Moe reached in his pocket and pulled out a wad of money. As he walked toward his grandmother, he tripped on the rug and stumbled. His gun fell to the floor before he caught his balance. She leaned over to see what had fallen, but he planted his foot down in front of it.

"What was that?" she asked.

"Nothing, Grams, I just lost my balance is all. I think it coulda been a rat," he added.

"They been coming and going since Fluffy gone. That cat used to chase all the little critters away." Moe reached out and handed his grandmother the money.

"What's this, and where you get it?" she asked, sounding displeased.

"It's money, Grams. I know I owe you more than that, but it's all I got. You can get the lights turned back on, so we can watch television." Moe knew she loved her shows. She had her favorites, and she watched them religiously. A lot of nights he liked to watch them with her.

"Did you steal this? Please don't tell me you did. I told you if you go back to prison I can't go to visit you. I'm too old."

He remembered all the times she'd come to visit him in jail; every Sunday at two o'clock. He'd always looked forward to her visits. It was the thing that had gotten him through his sentence.

"No, Grams, I told you, Shorty and I got new jobs, and we get paid weekly."

She put her hand on his face. "Okay, baby. Because I don't know what I would do without you," she said as he put his hand on her face in return.

"And I don't know what I would do without you, Grandma." He leaned in to kiss her on the cheek.

Grandma Rose began to trail off. "I'm tired. I'm gonna hit the sack. I put some clean sheets on your bed, the comfortable ones you like," she said.

"Okay, Grandma, thank you. I love you so much. Make sure you get some new batteries for your hearing aid."

"Huh?"

"Nothing, Grandma. I wanted to tell you, I love you so much. I have to go to work tonight. I'ma go get ready."

She took the money and placed it in her bra, then blew out the candles and sat back down in the dark. Moe walked into the small bedroom next to the living room.

38

The evening moonlight was fading behind dark clouds as Frank sat in an unmarked car parked a few houses down and across the street from Maurice Thompson's grandmother house. He had information all about the man they called Crazy Moe and his criminal background. He'd also heard that Moe had lived with his grandmother since the age of five, after watching both of his parents get shot to death in a drug deal gone bad.

Frank watched from his car across the street as Maurice came out of his grandma's house and got into old Dodge station wagon that was in his grandmother name. Frank watched as the car backed out of the driveway, then drove down the street towards him. He ducked down until the car passed him. He started his car and made a U-turn. He kept his distance, tailing close enough to keep up with them but far enough back so he wouldn't get caught.

Following the grandma's station wagon, Frank was surprised to be driving in a neighborhood called Southfield, a place over the bridge where most people didn't go too much anymore, but still on the Southside. Open fields, train tracks, and a freeway separated the neighborhoods. He made a left and followed the station wagon over the bridge. Within five minutes, he was in a different neighborhood. He was in the original community of the Southside.

As he peered out the car window, he couldn't help but notice the scraggly lawns and the junk in front of the houses. He drove by one house that didn't even have a proper front door, just a screen door hanging from rusty hinges. The street was narrow, with cars lined up on either side. Another house had dozens of broken-down cars in the driveway and yard, while others had old, worn-out couches on the porch.

Frank kept his distance behind the old station wagon, making the same turns it made. This was the neighborhood he had grown up in. His parents had first bought a house in Southfield when he was little, when they worked at the factory. He turned to look and saw a big fat lady with two front teeth missing, standing on a porch. Her legs were so big and bright you would have thought she was standing on two Michelin Men. The bright blue veins made her legs look like a road map made out of cottage cheese.

The station wagon entered a nice working-class neighborhood. It was nothing like the original section. The houses all had nice lawns with smooth green grass and no signs of rusted-out cars or Michelin Man legs. They were painted colors like pale blue and soft brown, and some were even brick. There were chain-link fences surrounding the front yards.

The station wagon stopped in front of a house, and a woman walked out. He couldn't get a good look at her before she got in the car and it drove off again. The moon was just beginning to come out behind some clouds as the station wagon weaved through traffic, still at a steady pace. Frank drove in silence to the highway and stayed in the outside lane. He checked his mirror and didn't see anything out of the ordinary.

* * *

Moe pulled the Dodge into a shopping center and drove up and down the aisles until he pulled into a spot next to a four-door Chevy Malibu. Moe pulled his car into the empty parking space.

Maurice climbed out of the car and looked around. He pulled out a sliver of long shiny metal. Meeka slid over to the driver's side of the Dodge. Maurice opened the door and got in the Malibu, and within minutes, he pulled out of the shopping center with the Dodge not far behind.

Moe drove through neighborhood after neighborhood until he reached the business warehouse district. He pulled into an alleyway and parked next to some other cars. The Dodge pulled in behind him. Satisfied with his parking spot, he jumped out and hopped back into the passenger side of the Dodge. Meeka nodded and drove off. As they headed down the street, a flatbed truck with a small tractor on the back moved slowly. Meeka honked the horn. An arm from the passenger side stuck out to wave them on, and they sped past.

"Word, we ready for tomorrow night," Moe said.

"It's still early, and Lashay told me to meet her at her place around eleven p.m. She should be done meeting with Will by then," Meeka said.

"Yeah, Shorty will be on that punk Marvin's other spot for a while," Moe said.

"I'm starvin' like Marvin," Meeka joked.

Moe laughed. "Let's stop by Lee's, pick up some food, and take it my place while we wait for Lashay to call."

"Word," Meeka said, trying to be funny.

Moe paused. "You on a roll, huh?"

They both laughed.

39

Marvin and Nina looked at each other but didn't say anything. Marvin drove down the freeway in a flatbed diesel truck, following the directions Delo's associate had given them, which took them right outside the city on a section of the freeway that was under construction. He pulled over and turned off the headlights. They were far enough out of the city that it was dark without the car lights. She pointed to the construction site filled with Case bulldozers, John Deere loaders, earthmovers, and Caterpillar dump trucks the size of buildings.

Marvin smiled. They climbed out of the car and walked through a field until they got to the construction area. He looked up at a massive dump truck. The tires alone were taller than him. Next to it was a medium-sized tractor with a big shovel connected to the front and a long backhoe for digging on the back. It was much smaller than they'd thought it would be. It looked like a steel baseball glove with four giant tires. Marvin crawled up on the tractor. He played around with some wires and the thing started.

"Can you drive it?" she yelled.

"Yes, I've driven them before."

Nina backed the flatbed down the street and lowered the liftgate.

Marvin decided it was best to drive across the open field. He leaped back on the tractor and took the monster up the hill and onto a dirt road. He drove about twenty feet through the dark open field with a cloud of dust following behind him. He hit the concrete, then stopped and got out of the tractor.

"This thing can't get up enough speed," he said.

"Look for a button that will make it go faster."

He jumped back into the tractor and started down the empty street. The little monster was hogging most of the road. It was hard to see anything in front of it. He hit a button and grabbed a lever. Something moved in front of his wheels. He realized that it was the big shovel in the front. It hit the street, and sparks flew as it dragged along the concrete. The tractor swerved, but Marvin regained control. After a few anxious moments, the shovel rose. He drove around the corner to where the flatbed was parked. Nina lowered the flatbed's liftgate. He drove the tractor right onto it. They spent the next fifteen minutes tying it down.

They took all the back roads to the heart of their neighborhood. They passed an old business district where every building had either broken or boarded-up windows. Every now and then, Marvin would look back at Nina.

"Keep your eyes on the tractor. Make sure it's not moving," he shouted.

He kept driving down the dark street. He turned down a street that led them past the warehouse district.

Up ahead, he spotted a No Way Out sign, but he kept going. The pavement turned into gravel, and then they were in an open field that bordered one end of the docks. There were a few ships rocking along, silhouetted by the moonlight, and the pungent odor of brackish water filled the air. It was the back way into the neighborhood. He drove five more minutes and then parked the beast. They walked up on the side of an old two-story house, opened the gate, and backed the flatbed up into the driveway.

"Why's it so quiet here tonight?" Nina asked.

"We sent customers to the other spot until tomorrow night," Marvin said.

"Well, let's get to work."

* * *

Shorty pulled the stolen Malibu into a spot across the street from an old two-story house. Lashay sat quietly in the front passenger seat. Meeka and Moe were in the back. They sat in the car for hours watching the old two-story house. When he saw the flatbed truck park at the house, he watched with amazement. He got out of his car and made sure he had his Desert Eagle 9mm on him before he crossed the street. He crept up to the side of the house, peeked through the back fence, and watched as Marvin dug a hole in the ground. Shorty thought nobody would ever think about robbing the Unit. Even if they did, they'd need heavy equipment to get to the main money and drugs.

Shorty came back after getting a close look at the new location. "Okay, the money is still in the house. They haven't started burying it yet. Marvin and that Pocahontas-looking bitch just walked in the house. Two goons are downstairs and two upstairs with guns. There's a room upstairs in the back where Marvin counts and bags the money."

"Great," Lashay said.

"Let's hit them while they're getting the money ready to bury," Shorty said.

"How are we supposed to get it? We don't have any shovels," Moe asked.

"I just said they're wrapping the money in plastic, and there's a tractor in the backyard."

"I didn't hear you say anything about a tractor."

Lashay's stomach lurched as she watched the dilapidated old house with its steel door that reminded her of a prison. No one seemed to be upstairs, or at least no lights were on. The sound of shattering glass and swear words erupted occasionally from inside.

"You hear that? We need to hit them quick, while they're working," Lashay said.

"I'm ready for this party to get started," Meeka said.

Moe looked out the window and up at the sky. "What party? We're here to steal mo' money, word."

"Moe, you must be suffering from SAS," Shorty mumbled.

"SAS? What's SAS, Shorty?" Moe asked.

"Simple and stupid," Shorty whispered.

"Moe, you're okay. What counts most is what's in your heart," Meeka said.

Lashay caught Meeka's eyes in the rearview mirror and saw her smile, as if she had something up her sleeve. She was getting soft on Moe. They seemed such an unlikely combination. But, heck, they both deserved a little happiness.

Moe started to say something when Lashay interrupted him. "Okay, okay, listen. Here's what we're going to do. I'm gonna go knock on the door, and you guys will sneak up and stand by the steel door. Once they open it, bum-rush them."

Lashay got out of the car and started ripping her clothes up, then she put dirt all over her face.

"What are you doing?" Moe asked.

"Trying to look like one of them drug addicts. Once we're in, we'll subdue the two guys downstairs. Then we make our way upstairs and force Marvin to open the safe and take everything in it. Then we tie him up, and we got about twenty minutes to dig that backyard up and be rich bitches."

Lashay staggered up the front steps and knocked on the door, feeling nervous. She had never been in a drug house, but that didn't stop her. She watched her team get into position as she looked around. The front of the place was run-down, as were many of the houses around it, and the yard was nothing but dirt and weeds. An abandoned car sat in the front of the house with no rims or tires. It wasn't even on cement blocks.

Lashay knocked on the door. One of the men inside opened it, holding a gun in his hand. "There's no product here right now. Go to the house around the corner," the man said, but before he was finished, Shorty and Moe burst through the front door. Lashay snuck up behind the guard and put her gun to the back of his head.

"Don't move, motherfucker," she whispered. He threw his hands in the air. She took his gun, then patted him down.

Shorty had a gun to his head. "You say anything, I'll blow your head off." They heard a noise coming from the kitchen. Moe and Meeka ran over to the dining room door, and right when another man walked out eating a sandwich, he had a Desert Eagle to his head. He raised his hands.

"Where's Marvin?" Shorty whispered.

"Upstairs," the man said.

Meeka walked in behind the other goon with her gun pointed close to the back of his head. She forced him to the floor next to the other guard. Pulling out some plastic zip ties, she cuffed both their hands behind their backs, then she covered their mouths with duct tape.

They made their way over to the stairs and crept up slowly. When they reached the top, one goon sat in the hallway with headphones on rocking his head. Moe and Shorty pulled their guns on the goon, who raised his hands. Shorty pushed him to the floor in the hallway.

"Where's Marvin?" Shorty hissed in the guy's ear. He pointed to the bedroom in the back, straight down the hallway. Moe finished tying the guy up, and they crept down the hallway.

They reached the back room. Shorty stood on one side, Lashay on the other as Meeka watched their backs. Moe busted through the door. Marvin had a gun in his hand, Nina was holding an assault rifle, and another henchman had a gun too. Before he could react to the ambush, a shot rang out and hit Moe in the chest. He fell to the floor, and Shorty came in firing both of his 9mms. Marvin, Nina, and the other henchman took cover behind a desk while they kept shooting. Shorty helped Moe out of the room as

203

Lashay and Nina fired at the desk. Moe looked up just in time to see two men coming up the stairs. He raised one of his 9mms and hit one of the men. Nina let out a scream of rage as she fired. One of the men ducked into an open room. Lashay managed to back down the hallway without being hit. Moe picked up the tied-up henchman and used him as a shield. Shorty continued firing at the room with the henchman as they backed down the hallway. Marvin and Nina came out with their guns pointed at them. Moe fired at them, and they backed back into the room when they realized they couldn't get a clean shot. Moe backed down the hallway, holding the man in front of them as a shield.

The henchman came out of the room, pointing the gun. He saw Marvin nod his head not to shoot. Marvin didn't want his captured goon to get shot.

They reached the bottom of the stairs and walked to the back door with guns raised, Moe still using the man as a shield. Marvin and his crew stood at the door, pointing their guns at them. Marvin looked around, shocked. Moe and the gang made their way through the backyard. At the gate, Moe threw the man down, and as they ran out the back door, someone shouted, "Police." They ran faster. They jumped a few backyard fences and headed around the corner. They crouched down and waited as police cars sped down the street past them, then made their way back to the car.

40

Erica stared at the bottom of the top bunk.

"Bella, I've got a story to tell you."

"I'm listening."

"I was about twelve at the time. My mother put superglue in my father car door locks again. Somehow we always end up in the car driving around, and somehow my mother always would end up in the trunk of the car. Well this particular night, she wouldn't stop banging on the inside of the trunk, when we got home. My father told me to take my sister to her bed and go to sleep.

I did as I was told. Daddy carried my mother into the house. As I lay in my room quietly arguing broke my thoughts—first low talking, then loud talking, then low talking. I couldn't concentrate with all the shouting, so I squeezed my eyes shut real tight and before long I fell fast asleep. I was soon awakened by an urgent need to pee, but was too scared to get out of my bed.

Bella interrupted, "Your mother put glue in the car locks— awesome. My type of girl. But why did she end up in trunk of the car?"

"Please, let me finish," Erica said, then continued.

"I imagined what would come next. Then it got quiet, and quiet didn't always mean the fight was over. Quiet could mean something terrible had happened. I listened intently for the sounds of my parents in endless battle, but I didn't hear anything. The house was eerily quiet.

"After going back and forth in my head several times, I worked up enough nerve to get up and look around. When my foot hit the floor, it made a creaking sound, a little bitty creaking sound, but it was enough to wake Lashay up.

"'Where you going, Erica?' she said with sleep in her eyes. I looked at her, worried she might be affected by the fight.

"'Nowhere, go back to sleep,' I told her, and she rolled back over in her bed.

"I crept to the door and took one courageous peek into the hallway. All the lights were out in the house. No one could see me, so I stumbled into the uncharted war zone. I crept down the hallway, and I kept listening for any sounds, but heard nothing.

"Once I reached the end of the hallway, I had a view of the living room. I surveyed the aftermath of the war fought on domestic territory. The couches and chairs were turned over, sofa pillows were tossed around the room, and the TV was busted with the screen lying on the floor. Some of the pillows had made it all the way to the other side of the room, and one had even landed in the fish tank. The linoleum floors, usually clean and shiny, were littered with furniture used as weapons and smudged with drops of blood. I located the shiny object on the end table next to the couch. I moved in closer. It was a gun. I feared the worst but kept walking.

"As I made my way over to the kitchen, I passed the living room window, and for some unknown reason, I looked out. The window faced Mr. Towns's house next door. I felt drawn to it. I peeked out and pressed my face against the glass and saw Mr. Towns peering back at me.

"No doubt my family's fight woke him. He stared back at me for a moment longer, and then he frowned, shook his head, and closed the curtains.

"I heard a noise in the kitchen. I peeked through the crack in the door. My father and mother were struggling over a big cast-iron skillet. My mother frantically slapped and clawed my father's back with one hand and swung the iron skillet at him with the other. Each time, my father tried to get closer to her. I closed my eyes. I couldn't bear to see the worst, whether he deserved it or not. The next thing I heard was the loud smack of his hand hitting her across the face. Mama dropped the skillet. The sound was so loud it made me jump. I felt the need to run to my mother's defense, but I dared not move. My mother let out a painful yell, but she yelled out of anger, not agony.

"Mama didn't hesitate. Her injury didn't slow her down. With what must have been pure adrenaline, she pulled herself off the floor as if she were being counted out in the ring and leaped onto his back. She dug her long nails into the side of his head. He flung her over his shoulder like a rag doll, tossing her on her back onto the table.

"She reached back behind her and picked up the iron skillet, and before I could say anything, she hit my father on the back of his head. There was a sickening thud. He fell to the ground. My mother stood above him, breathing hard. Muffled moans came from him. My mother raised the skillet again as if to finish him off, and he swiped the skillet from her as she swung and pulled her to the ground. He sat up and raised his hand to hit her with the skillet and struck her on the head. Her skull struck the floor, bouncing against the unyielding surface. She stopped moving. He raised the skillet, waiting for her to get up.

"All of a sudden, I heard a loud bang and watched a bullet tear through my dad's chest. He grabbed his torso and fell on top of my mother. The gun blast shattered my eardrum. I couldn't hear anything, but I could see them both laying there unmoving. I turned around to see who had pulled the trigger, but hot smoke billowed from the gun's barrel into my eyes, blinding me. Then, the smell of strong, sour powder filled my nostrils. I passed out."

Bella paced around the cell. She looked from Erica to the cell door with her big eyes. "What happened when you woke up?"

"Both my parents were dead, and we went to live with our grandparents. We went to therapy for most of our childhood."

Bella sat back down on the bunk. "It explains why you stayed in that toxic relationship so long. But are you're saying Lashay…"

"I'm not saying anything. But from that day on, our hearts resolved that for as long as we lived, no man would ever put his hands on either of us. Lashay has always taken that to heart when it comes to me. She won't stop until I'm safe and out of here."

41

Lashay's heart pumped hard. The blood rushed through her veins. Shorty had driven off slowly, but they hadn't driven more than a few miles before they were spotted.

"The police," Shorty said in a fierce whisper. He snatched the gun from his hip and hid it in the door pocket. Moe and Meeka sat in the back. "Duck down, you two," he hissed.

He sat up straighter as the police car pulled up next to them. The police officer glanced over. Shorty pretended not to see him.

The cop slowed down and got behind them. The sirens began chirping. Shorty punched the pedal of the Malibu and made a screeching U-turn. A cloud of smoke hung in the air from the burning tires.

"Yeah, that's right," said Moe. "Hit it, Shorty. I got two strikes, and I'm not going back to prison alive."

"I gotchoo, Moe," Shorty said, growling. He pushed down on the accelerator. Lashay flew back in her seat as they drove off the top of a small hill. The Malibu landed front end first. There was a loud cracking noise, and she wondered how long the car would hold out. They turned onto a narrow street with the cops not far behind.

"This is it, I'm going to die. What are we going to do?" Lashay glanced over at Shorty, who seemed to be relaxed; calm, even.

"Watch it, Shorty," Moe shouted.

They hit the corner going at least fifty. The Malibu rode on two wheels. Meeka grasped the headrest of the seat in front of her but couldn't hold on. She slid to the other side of the car. Shorty held tight to the steering wheel with one hand and used the other one to hold his gun. He rolled down his window.

Lashay looked behind them. The police weren't far behind. She began to breathe hard. They turned right into an alley, but before they could get to the other end, another black-and-white came flying out, followed by another police car. Shorty sped up and split the two police cruisers, blasting out of the alleyway.

They came to an intersection. The right side was under construction. Shorty turned right. The Malibu ran over a fence and down into a drainage ditch, bouncing up on the other side.

They got to an overpass. He stopped the car beneath it and turned off the engine and lights.

"I think we lost them," Moe said.

"If we could please make it home," Meeka whispered, looking to the sky.

"Shut up," Shorty exploded. "You just committed crimes. God not thinking about us."

Shorty looked down the street. The traffic had started to get thick. But just as he restarted the engine, police cars came out of nowhere. There was even a police helicopter shining a big spotlight down on the Malibu. He threw the car into gear and drove straight up the service entrance of the drainage ditch. Once they were back on the city streets, he began weaving through traffic, helicopter in tow. Every time he dipped and dodged, Lashay felt a chill ride through her body. Moe looked out the back window.

The police were gaining on them. They bounced over a big bump. Shorty drove the car down the street with one police car behind them. He made a quick turn, then headed up another street.

He was flying. He entered a park with a lot of tree cover. Some people were already out jogging, but Shorty's car was so loud, they got out of the way fast.

"Where we going?" Lashay asked.

"I'm going to the tunnel on the other side the park. Once we there, we can park and get away in the drains," he said.

Shorty pulled the car into the tunnel and stopped. They grabbed all their bags and the suitcase. He lifted the drain cover up and dropped the bags down the drain. He helped Lashay down and then Meeka.

"Let's get out of here, man. We made it." He began to lower himself down and saw Moe walking back toward the car. "No, man. Come on."

"I'll buy you guys some time. Just go," Moe said, looking back at Shorty. "Make sure you take care of my grandmother if I get locked up. Word?" He didn't wait for an answer before he ran off.

Shorty heard cop cars in the distance. He knew he couldn't change Moe's mind. Meeka stuck her head out. "Moe, come on. We can get away."

"All of us won't make it. They'll know we're in the tunnel," he shouted from the side of the car.

"Please come, Maurice." Meeka started crying. "Please, Maurice."

He turned to go back toward the manhole, but the sirens were getting louder, and three cop cars came into view.

Shorty forced her head down into the manhole. He looked down at Lashay. "You girls go. We'll buy some time, everything will be okay. Go, go, run." He pulled the cover back over the manhole and started firing his gun at the cops.

Moe raised the 9mm and started firing too. They sprinted towards the car, but before they got there, Shorty was shot in the back of his leg. He fell to the ground. Moe reached down to help him.

"Go, Moe. You can get away. I'll be okay. Go, go."

Moe paused and looked at his buddy. He then ran fast and jumped back into the car and sped out of the park. The cops were behind him. Two cop cars pulled up on Shorty with guns out. He raised his hands.

* * *

Moe sped back into the community, then down a long street. He pushed the pedal all the way to the floor, and as he zoomed, he turned his head to see where the police were. As he turned back, he realized he was headed straight for a utility pole. He braced himself. The car slammed into the pole. He hit his head on the windshield. Blood gushed from his forehead and poured into his eyes. He squinted and could barely see as he yelled, then groaned in pain. A short, slim man in running shorts and a mop of jaw-length brown hair witnessed the accident and jogged up to the car to help.

"Hello, sir, I'm a nurse. Are you okay?" Moe shook his head in a daze, but he grabbed his gun and jumped out of the car. Moe yanked the nurse by the hair and started limping down the street, holding on to him and waving the gun.

A police officer came out of nowhere, pointing his gun at him. "Freeze."

Moe held the man in front of him, using him as a human shield. He backed down the street, and then he lifted the gun and fired at the cop.

POP! POP! POP!

The police officers took cover behind some parked cars. A round of bullets shattered a store window beside him, and Moe realized that the police were shooting back. The nurse twisted, trying to get away. Moe jammed the gun in his ear and the man stopped moving. Moe fired again at the police. The man screamed. People on the street ducked for cover.

"That's right, hide, chump-change chumps," Moe shouted at the police and bystanders alike. He laughed.

212

The nurse's legs began to give. "Let me go, you bastard," he shouted.

"Shut the hell up," Moe sprayed back. The man tried to wipe the spit off the side of his face. Moe tried to drag him around a corner.

"You're going to get us both killed. Let me go," the nurse pleaded.

Moe had a serious grip on him. He fired the gun again. This time he was so close to the man's ear that the sound likely ruptured his eardrum. The man doubled over with the pain. Moe's face contorted like an angry gorilla's as he felt his control slipping. What seemed like a thousand police cars screeched to a halt in a semicircle around them. They all took firing stances behind their open car doors.

Moe fired again at the police. *POP! POP! POP!*

They fired back.

RAT-TAT-TAT.

"Please keep my kids safe," the nurse prayed out loud.

Moe backed them around the corner. A woman walked out of a building, and when she realized the danger she'd walked into, she ran toward her car. The nurse looked at Moe and then at the woman. Moe made a quick decision and backed closer to her.

"Give me those fucking keys. Word."

He grabbed her keys and fired at the officers.

POP! POP! POP!

The nurse put his hands to his ears. Moe pushed the woman out of the way and threw the nurse inside the car. The back of his head slammed against the console. With his back lying on the car's seat, he kicked Moe in the midsection as hard as he could. He closed his eyes and continued throwing wild kicks. Moe stumbled away from the car. An explosion of gunshots followed.

A shocked look came over Moe's face. Blood from multiple holes drenched his shirt. He stumbled toward the car, the dangling gun dropping from his fingers. Before the nurse could react, Moe fell on top of him. The man screamed again. There was nowhere for him to go. Moe's eyes closed as he lost control of his bodily functions. He took his last breath.

42

The crowd packed the high school gym. The sound of basketball shoes squeaked as they made contact with the hardwood floor. Marvin sat in the bleachers off to the side, away from the crowd. He didn't watch the plays or the hundreds of cheering fans at Delo's son's high school basketball game. Sweat dripped from his forehead. He knew what was weighing so heavy on his mind. He wanted to kill his business associate, Clay.

Delo sat above center court, yelping and hollering for his son, with those crazy fat sideburns and that loud pink shirt. He couldn't understand why anyone would wear a pink-flowered shirt to a high school basketball game, but that was Delo. He'd always had questionable taste when it came to fashion. Marvin got up and moved to where Delo sat.

"Bro, we came close to getting them, but the sister-in-law got away. They got the word guy, and the one they call Shorty took a bullet in the leg," Marvin said.

Marvin paused. "You talked to Frank?"

Delo turned away from the game to look at Marvin. "No, but he got his people at the hospital waiting to talk to Shorty, and some others are looking everywhere for the sister-in-law.

"His cops came late. I thought they were supposed to have a tail on them, but they were late and almost got me killed," he said. "I think Frank's up to something."

"What would Frank do if he found out you suspected something like that?" Delo shot back.

"Fuck him. He's a cop. What can he do?" Marvin said.

"Well, Mr. Scarface, it's just not about growing up with them. Where you think we be without police protection? And while we're talking about it, where you think we be without Clay washing the money and his business connections? Listen," Delo continued, "Frank has covered for Clay from day one, not because of friendship, but because college boy has enough on all of us to send us up the river. We need to find out where he keeps the files he has on the Unit. Then we can get rid of him."

"That punk could be keeping that shit at his fancy place in the Caribbean," Marvin said.

Cheers erupted from the crowd, distracting Delo. His son Tyson had the ball and was dribbling up the court. The kid had game. Delo whooped and hollered for Tyson as he went in for another layup. "That's my boy out there," he said in his proud papa voice.

"We got info on where the sister-in-law is hiding. Someone spotted her on the Westside, so she has to be in one of the hole-in-the-wall hotels in the area. It's a matter of time before we find out which one. I'll get her, then I'll get my money back, then I'll get those files, and then I'll get Clay," Marvin said.

"Okay," Delo said. "Don't forget we're having issues with the wife. Those hitters in jail are running into a lot of problems. She might have help in there." Delo grabbed Marvin by the shoulders. The move took him off guard.

"Now you're talking." Marvin smiled at Delo. This was the brother he had gotten into the street game with, trying to play the businessman role with his other boys. They were growing without the other two. Delo had brought them in because of business, but now Marvin was ready to move on without his business partners.

216

"I am serious, little bro. Business comes first."

Marvin got up and moved to the bottom of the bleachers. He turned and looked up at his brother, then back to the court, where Tyson had the ball again. He watched as the boy scored a basket. Marvin looked back at Delo, who jumped up with joy, the tough-ass businessman gone.

He walked out to his SUV, and Nina was waiting in the passenger side. "What did your brother say?" she asked as she took a sip of her Monster energy drink.

"Fuck this business shit. We going to get the sister, Clay, Frank, and even Delo will be asked to step down if he doesn't act right. It's time for a real boss to run things."

Nina rubbed her hands on the back of his neck. "That's right, baby, you the true boss in this shit."

"Frank's men got all the airports and buses covered, so we know she is still in the city. I believe she is in that area. There's around twelve run-down motels on the Westside. Get all the boys together. We need to get eyes on all those motels."

43

The room at the Ivy Motel on Thornton Road was old, small, and cramped. The carpet had dirty spots. The bedding had bigger spots. Lashay walked out of the bathroom. Meeka stood at the window peeking out, holding her gun.

"Will's here."

Will rushed in the door, breathing hard. He was shocked by how much Lashay had changed in mere days. She didn't have that cute little innocent look anymore. Her face was still pretty; however, with her lime-green terry-cloth sweat suit that glowed like a fluorescent light, flip-flops, and big thick cornrows, and chomping on gum, she looked like a patchwork quilt of hard times.

She grabbed Will. "How is Shorty?"

He tried calming her down and sat her down in the chair and paced around. "He's okay. They took the bullet out of his leg. He'll be fine. He's recovering, but he's surrounded by police."

"I want to go see him."

"Maybe you hadn't noticed, but you're wanted, and your pictures are all over the news. They're trying to link you to Moe's death, those fuckers," Will said.

They all paused for few seconds. Finally, Lashay spoke." Moe's grandmother will be look out for, trust me."

Meeka walked over and patted her on the back. "Moe was a good dude," Meeka said. "I didn't want to say anything, but the night we got the burner car, after we picked it up, I went on a mini-date with Moe. It was the most romantic date I have ever been on in my life. We picked up some food at Lee's and then went to his grandmother's house and watched television the whole night. I've had guys wine and dine me before. I've been to fancy restaurants, but I never felt it was all sincere, and those guys always ended up assholes. With Moe, it was just so real, and it was so honest. His grandmother went to bed, and we watched all these shows I never heard of. *Gunsmoke*, *The Big Valley*, he knew all the episodes and characters. It was so cute the way his grandma kept calling him Maurice," Meeka said. Tears rolled down her face, and she put her hand over her heart. "H-he knew those shows were made of fictional characters. When he said that crazy stuff, he was just talking about when he was a kid. Bless his heart."

"You really did like him. He did have a big heart," Lashay said.

"He didn't even try anything the whole night, even when his grandma went to sleep. He was like, 'I can't do that in my grandma's house while she's home.'"

"Now that's a good guy, right there," Lashay said.

"I told him when this was all over, I was going to help him find a job. He said he already tried, but no one would hire him because he had a criminal record." Meeka wiped her tears off her face.

Lashay's eyes teared up. "He was a good dude. It's my fault he's dead. I'd rather switch places with him."

Meeka hugged Lashay. "Baby girl, I love you. This'll all be over soon. Moe's in a better place now." She hugged her back, wiping the tears from her eyes. "When we're done, I'ma get those bitches, all of them."

"Meeka, they have no idea who you are or that you're involved in this," Will said. He poured the contents of the bags onto the table, including a newspaper, two burner phones, and five prepaid credit cards. "Here's everything."

"That's great," Lashay said, wiping her tears. "If we have to hit the road, we'll have everything we need."

"Meeka, are you ready?" Will said.

"Yes. I set up everything for tomorrow night, but I don't know where," Meeka answered.

"Okay, that's fine. Here's the plan. The numbers for all our burners are on the back of the phones under our code names. Meeka is M, Lashay is L, and I'm W. Meeka, when the time is right, you call Lashay. She'll come pick you up wherever you are."

"Where did you park the car?" Lashay said.

"It's around the corner in front of an old white two-story house. It's a silver Ford Taurus. When you get it, you call me, and I'll meet you guys at the spot. And we'll go to that house and hopefully find something in there that will free your sister."

Will hugged them both before he left.

Lashay began stuffing the items into a pillowcase. Meeka watched her as she stared at the day's newspaper lying beside her. On the front page was a picture of Lashay and Shorty side by side. She was wanted in connection with the murder of their friend, Maurice "Moe" Thompson.

"This is bullshit," she said. She balled it up and threw it against the wall.

"Everything will be fine soon, sweetie," Meeka said.

"One more day. We got one last shot. If we find information we can use, we're set. If not, I'll be on the run a long time," Lashay said.

"Let's get some rest." Meeka pulled her away from the window. "We have a long day tomorrow. I know the police will be all over, and they won't even know it's you with your disguise."

Lashay looked at Meeka like she didn't know how she could be so optimistic right now. But it made her smile.

"Okay, let's get some rest and get ready for tomorrow."

44

Marvin's vehicle stuck out like a sore thumb. All of his men's cars stuck out like sore thumbs, but it didn't matter, because no one was going to mess with them. He sat on a park bench on the Westside which had become a makeshift command center. He barked orders to twenty of his best men, and they took off to the streets.

The neighborhood had once been nice. The homes had been built back in the forties for the factory workers, but now many had become dilapidated. Some even had been bulldozed down and left as empty fields. The only ones left in the neighborhood were people who couldn't afford to move or just didn't move because everyone they knew still lived in the area. There were only two stores, one at each end of the hood. However, there were about twenty small run-down hotels in the area, mostly used by drug addicts or for prostitution.

Nina sat with Marvin. One of Marvin's men approached them. "Boss, we hit most of those small hotels, but we didn't find nothing. Some of the owners wouldn't even cooperate."

"I know she's around here somewhere. I can feel it," Nina said.

"Frank's men set up roadblocks out of the city quick. And this is the only area where they would come. She can't go anywhere else because we have people everywhere," Marvin said.

"Maybe she got out. There are ways out besides the main roads," said another henchman.

Marvin jumped up from his seat. "Go to the far west side of this neighborhood and talk to anybody on the street. Knock on doors and look for things out of the ordinary. Me and Nina will drive around."

They drove around until they reached a store around the corner from the Ivy Motel. It had a glowing sign in the window advertising the prices of cigarette cartons, and a sleazy cardboard cutout of a girl swilling beer. There wasn't much light in the parking lot. Young men were loitering outside the store. Marvin strolled into the store and came out with a brown bag in his hand. He stopped to talk to a slender black man. Marvin reached into his pocket, pulled out a five-dollar bill, and gave it to him. The man started talking.

Nina sat in the car. She couldn't make out what the conversation was about, but she hoped it was about that bitch's location.

A woman stepped up to Nina. "Hey." Nina looked at her. Her jeans were stained, and her shirt was too big for her. Nina knew right away she was a crackhead. She reached for her 9mm under his seat, but before she could get it, she felt a warm pistol on her temple.

"Don't move, motherfucker. Let me see your hands."

Nina put her hands on the steering wheel. She saw Marvin begin to move, but the slim brother he had given the money to put a gun to his head. Nina could make out his words clearly. "Give it up, brother. Ya'll on the Westside now."

"You don't want to do this. We work for some powerful people," Nina said.

"Give me your money, bitch. I don't care who you work for." She grabbed the keys. Nina grabbed the gun with her left hand and with the other hand smashed the woman in face. She fell to the ground.

Marvin went into action and elbowed the gunman in the face, snatching the gun out of his hand and pivoting at him.

"Please don't kill me."

Marvin kicked him in the gut, and the man curled up on the ground. He hit him with the butt of the gun.

"What else you know?" Marvin said to him.

"Nothing!" the man screamed.

Marvin struck him again with the gun, and the man cried out in pain. Marvin stuck the barrel of the gun to the man's head. "What do you know?"

"I told you everything already."

Marvin poked the gun into his rib cage and dug in real hard. "You do know if you don't tell us, we will kill you."

The man's eyes got big, and Marvin jammed the gun deeper. "We seen a man that's not from around here park a silver Taurus a few blocks away. We was going to see what was up, so we waited for him," he said.

"Fuck that. You guys were going to rob him. Tell us the truth, motherfucker."

"Like I said, we waited and he never returned to the car."

"Where did he walk to?" Marvin asked.

"I don't know. We followed until he was out of sight, then went back to the car to wait. He never returned."

"So, you guys broke into the car, huh, mu'fucker?" Marvin said and grabbed the man by the throat.

The man nodded. "Yeah, I used my metal rod, but all we got was some change. We didn't mess up anything."

Marvin snatched the man by the collar. "Where's this car?"

45

Clay drove down the street in his shiny Benz with Kendra, on their way to the movies. She turned and nestled her arm under Clay's outstretched arm. He rubbed his hand around her smooth hand, but she didn't seem to respond to his touch. He tried reaching for her again, but she still didn't react to him the way he wanted.

"You okay, baby?"

She raised his right hand and kissed it. "Yes, but it's six o'clock, and we haven't decided what movie we're going to watch."

He rubbed her face. "It doesn't matter. I'm just elated to be here with you, by ourselves."

She laughed, and in her best Scarlett O'Hara voice, she said, "Darling, nothing would make me happier than listening to the drone of pasty-faced banking moguls." They both laughed.

"I'm so glad you called me back and wanted to spend time with me tonight." Clay stared at her longingly.

He pulled into the movie theater parking lot and found a parking space. As he opened his door, he glanced up.

"What the fuck?" he whispered to himself.

He saw two of Frank's men about fifty feet away, sitting in an unmarked police car, staring at him. His heart started racing. He grabbed Kendra's arm.

"Is everything okay?" she asked.

He pulled her close. "Yes, I just don't want anything or anybody to ruin our night. Something's been going on. I've seen police all over the city."

They started walking toward the theater entrance. He couldn't stop looking back, even though he was constantly talking and moving Kendra toward the theater.

"Nothing like hot, buttered popcorn to take your mind off real life," he said as he paid for their tickets.

Right before they went inside, he looked back over his shoulder and saw one of the men speaking into a cell phone. Inside the movie theater, the previews were just beginning. Kendra sat down in a seat one away from the aisle. Clay sat beside her, holding their drinks and a big box of popcorn. She settled her head on Clay's shoulder.

"It's chilly in here. I should have brought my sweater in."

"You want me to get your sweater?"

"I don't want you to miss any of the movie."

"It's cool. It's a two-and-a-half-hour movie that hasn't even started," he said, setting his drink in the cupholder.

When he went out to the lobby, he didn't see Frank's men anywhere. He didn't see them in the parking lot either. Within minutes, he was back with Kendra's sweater. She thanked him with a long kiss on his cheek. His body filled with that hot lava sensation again, just like it had on that day at the strip club.

Clay held her hand as the movie started. He couldn't wait for it to end. Then he could take her back to the condo and make her his. Her phone started vibrating in her purse. She grabbed it. "I have to take this call. I'll be right back."

"No, go ahead. I'll fill you in on anything you miss," he said as he loosened his shirt up. She rushed to the entrance and looked frantically at the phone until she went out the double doors.

226

* * *

Lashay drove through light traffic. She was supposed to meet Meeka in two hours. She'd been driving for twenty minutes without incident, deep in thought over her next move, and lost the edge of alertness. She failed to notice the white 2006 Cadillac Escalade ESV with dark-tinted windows tailing her. When she saw it, she realized that when she stopped, the Caddy stopped. When she made a left, the Caddy made a left. She pulled up to a red light, and the Caddy pulled up next to her. She dared not make eye contact.

Pulling her car out into traffic, she made an illegal turn. Just before she gunned it, a black sedan pulled up out of nowhere and parked right in front of her. She shifted into reverse. The Caddy slammed into the back of her car, and she was pinned in place. Two men dressed in black and wearing ski masks got out of the sedan. One pointed a gun at her. Too scared to move, she felt paralyzed.

"If you move, I'll shoot," one said. She almost laughed. That sounded so much like a line from a movie.

"What do you want me to do?"

"Shut up. Don't say anything. We're not going to hurt you," the other said. "Get out of the car and get your ass down on the ground."

One of the men snatched the door open and yanked her from the car. She pressed down on the accelerator in a futile effort to get away from the crazed man, but he pinned her against the open door and slid inside the car, jamming his foot on the brake, managing to get the car into park. She looked around as she tried to wiggle from his grasp. He held on and smiled.

Her muscles came back under her control, and she swung at him, catching him completely off guard. While dodging the blows, he hit the gearshift and the car started rolling. She kept slapping at him. He got control of the car and pulled it to the side of the road, all the while holding her against him. Before she could cause more trouble, he snatched the keys from the ignition. She managed to get free and leapt back into her car, scrambling over to the passenger's seat. He reached in and grabbed her by the neck, yanking her out of the car while her feet kicked the air.

She screamed, not stopping until the other man came and grabbed her. He dragged her to the back of the Escalade and opened the hatch. She saw a huge black box. Inside there was a long cage the size of a large dog kennel. She screamed, trying to swipe her nails across their faces, but they kept her at a distance. With their brute strength, they shoved her inside the cage, keeping clear of her kicking feet. Once she was completely inside, they snapped the padlocks, and then close the box.

"We have the files," she said. "Listen to me, we have Clay's files. Tell your bosses we want to make a deal." She kept screaming even after he slammed the box closed.

The car shifted as someone climbed in, then rumbled as it drove off with her in it. She kept screaming and screaming, knowing that the driver had to hear her.

Another car pulled close. A deep voice said, "I'll follow you."

She stopped screaming and panted, trying to breathe. She was scared to death.

"What do we do with her?" her attacker said.

"First, we're gonna torture her, and then we're gonna kill her," the other said. They started laughing.

She banged on the cage but tired of it after a while and got quiet. Something was digging into her side, and she remembered she had the burner. She could barely move her arms, the cage was so tight, but she managed to reach into her pocket with her left hand and grab the phone. She brought her right arm up to her body and rested it on her chest.

The next time the car stopped, she flicked the phone up on her chest and grabbed it with her right hand. She punched numbers with her thumb. When she heard a voice, she whispered, "Listen, don't say anything. I've been kidnapped. No, no, just listen. You and Will need to go and get the information. Then call me back. Just do it, Meeka, and hurry." She hung up, put the phone on silent and shoved it in her other pocket.

46

Delo sat in his brand-new Escalade. His eyes never left the road as he watched the headlights of cars passing him by. He was at Lloyd's Market, the neighborhood grocery store in the small section on the Southside. There were a group of young men hanging out in front of the store, talking trash to each other without paying any attention to Delo or his Escalade.

He looked up in time to see the unmarked police car.

Frank parked next to Delo's car. "What's the emergency?"

Delo bit his lip as he clenched the steering wheels before looking over.

"Marvin has the sister-in-law."

Frank straighten in his seat. "When?"

"Tonight. It got ugly, but she's still alive. I told him not to do anything until I checked in with you. You know he's itching to get revenge for the robberies, but she said something about having Clay's files, and I don't want to miss out on a chance to find out what Clay has on us."

Delo kept his eye on the young men, who were now staring at them.

"Could be a bluff. Clay has never let anyone know where he was keeping those files. I don't think he confided in his sister-in-law," Frank said.

"We can't take a chance. He has too much documentation on us that could be very damaging. Where is he at, anyway?"

"Right now, he's on a date. I have eyes on him," Frank said.

Delo shook his head. "What the fuck. We need to sit down and have a serious talk about getting a new accountant, if you know what I mean. We grew up with the guy, but he'll never change. We clean up his shit and he gets the pussy. I don't want to take this shit anymore."

"We'll talk later. Right now, we need to find out if they really have the files. We have to make sure they don't get in the wrong hands."

"I'll work on Marvin, but I don't know how long I can hold him off."

"Make sure he waits. This is business. Better yet, let me go talk to the sister-in-law. Tell Marvin I'm on my way," Frank said, shifting the car into gear and driving off.

Delo watched him, then punched the pedal, and the Escalade burned rubber out of the parking lot. The young men stopped what they were doing and watched as they choked on the smoke.

* * *

The back of Escalade ESV opened, and the thugs carried Lashay into a house. She was led blindly around until they stopped at a room. Someone laid a hand on her shoulder and pushed her down. "Sit," he ordered, as if she had a choice.

"Hello, sir. I don't know why I'm here. I didn't do anything."

"You think I give a shit? Don't you know why you're here?"

"I'm here because you brought me here."

"Jesus, this girl must be the prize idiot," he said, irritation edging the words.

"That's not what I meant."

"I'm sorry. What did you mean?" Sarcasm this time.

The phone rang in another room.

"Go answer that," the man said to someone. "Now, back to you."

He was interrupted again. "It's the boss."

231

"Dammit, give me that." He spoke into the phone. "But— okay, okay."

He hung up.

"He's comin'. After he leaves, we'll deal with this dumb chick."

She heard footsteps leave, and she knew this was her chance. She started bucking, trying to get loose. Her wild flailing made the chair fall over, and her blindfold slid off.

"Fuck, now we *really* going to have to kill this bitch. She's seen our faces," one of the goons said.

Marvin handed him a wad of cash wrapped in thick rubber bands. "No, we're going to wait to get those files, then we're going to kill this bitch, and her sister, and whoever else." The thug's eyes gleamed with excitement.

Lashay wondered whether he was excited about his wad or the prospect of the killing part. She shivered as he left the room.

"Back to you, bitch. I know who you are."

Lashay's eyes widened as Marvin moved closer. "Listen, the reason I was hitting your spots was because I needed the money to get my sister out of jail, because your fucking punk-ass business partner, Clay, isn't worth shit."

He stopped when she said Clay's name. "I think you're working with the police. You came into one of my businesses, slapped me around and robbed me, and a few minutes later the police raided it. Luckily, I had left already. And then there's the fact that you still have over fifty thousand dollars of my money."

"Uh, no, I don't," she said. "We divided it, but I was only using it to bail out my sister."

He turned to someone behind him. "She's getting smart-mouthed with me. Once I get word, I'll personally take her to the tub and kill her."

"Please don't. Please. I was just trying to find information on my brother-in-law to get my sister out of jail. We have it. We have all his information."

Marvin left but was replaced by Nina. She stalked over, picked the blindfold up off the floor, wrapped it around Lashay's mouth and tugged tight. Lashay tried to talk around the cloth but gagged instead. She was having a hard time breathing.

"Breathe out of your nose," Nina said.

Lashay didn't know why the bitch was giving her advice on how to survive when the last time they'd seen each other, Lashay had kicked her ass, but she did as she had instructed. She managed to breathe, but she knew she was in big trouble.

Nina walked over to the closet and pulled out a big piece of plastic. She folded it and placed it on the floor. Then she walked over to the dresser and pulled out three towels. She placed them on top of the plastic. In the corner of the room, she pulled up part of the floor, reached in, and pulled out a gun. She set the gun on the floor and then reached in again and pulled out a little piece of steel. She picked up the gun and started twisting the piece of steel on the end of the gun. She looked at Lashay.

"Don't be scared," she said. "It will all be over soon. I'm going to kill you myself, because I don't want my baby involved in my revenge business." She sat back down.

Lashay managed to untie the rope behind her back. Nina saw her moving. "Don't move, bitch," Nina said as she walked over to her.

Nina turned back to finish her killing station just as Lashay tackled her. She wrestled her to the floor, but Nina wasn't going down without a fight.

Frank and Marvin walked into the room.

"What the fuck?" Marvin ran over and held Lashay down while Frank pushed Nina out of the way. When the women were far enough apart, Marvin tied Lashay's hands behind her back and then tied her legs together. He sat her back up in the chair.

"We're not going to hurt you, Lashay Parker. I want the files," Frank said. Lashay looked at Nina and kept quiet.

"Nina, go and check on the others, will you?" Marvin said. Nina glared at Lashay, then walked out of the room, gripping her gun.

Marvin walked over to the closet and opened it.

"Is this all worth it for your sister? I mean, isn't she already in jail? How is getting yourself locked up with her gonna help?" Marvin said.

"Shut the fuck up," Lashay yelled back. Marvin hit her hard across the face.

Frank caught his arm midair as he tried to hit her again. "We need her alive, and we need her to talk, so knock that shit off."

Marvin squinted at Frank. Lashay knew he didn't want to listen to Frank, but Frank must rank higher in the chain of command.

"Do you have the files?" Frank asked.

"Yes, and if you want them, you need to let me go and get my sister out of jail," she said.

"Oh?" Marvin said.

"Yes, we have them in a very secure place."

"So how do we get them?" Frank said.

"We wait for my partners to call me," she said. "But they're only going to hand them over if you let me go and get my sister out of jail."

"Call you! How will they do that?"

"I have a phone in my pocket."

Marvin reached into Lashay's pocket and pulled out the phone. "What the hell? Those motherfuckers didn't even search her."

"Now, I have a question for you, Mr. Marvin. Tell me what happened to me and my sister at the studio that evening. Is that where you guys made the pictures of us naked with young-looking boys, you little pervert motherfucker?"

Marvin didn't say anything, but he knew that shit at the studio had been Clay and Delo's doing. He didn't like that they'd sunk to violating the women that way, but it was all part of Clay's stupid-ass plan.

"Ask your brother-in-law," Frank said.

"I don't have a brother-in-law. Not anymore," she said.

Marvin stood over her. "I had nothing to do with that shit."

"We're giving you until morning to get the phone call. If you don't get the call, then that's that," Frank said.

"And if I do get the call?" she asked.

He didn't even glance at Marvin before answering her. "Then we make a deal, and I'll tell you everything you need to know."

"We know the Unit has a lot of political power in this city. You clear me and my fiancé of all charges. You can get Erica out and have one of your flunkies take the drug rap and get those wannabe hit women in jail to catch amnesia and leave her alone. And I want her to get her kids back."

Frank looked at Marvin. He hesitated but nodded in agreement. "Well, we can deal with the first three, but the last one is between Erica and Clay."

He took his phone from his pocket and called someone. "Go in there and find him. I don't care about the damn movie."

He patted Lashay on the shoulder and headed out the door.

47

Clay walked out of the theater with the rest of the moviegoers, looking around. His head hurt, and he felt dizzy. He looked around for Kendra, but she was nowhere in sight.

As people piled into their cars and drove off, Clay stood in front of his car. He pulled out his keys to open the door, but he dropped them. His head began to shake from side to side with every movement. The movie theater, the parking lot, the moving cars…all seemed to fade into the background. But before he could move, he saw a man take his big hand and slap him so hard he crashed to the ground.

"Frank wants to talk to you. He's on his way," the man said.

Clay pushed the man away. "Leave me alone," he shouted. He grabbed his keys and tried to stab the man with the longest key. The man threw him up against the car. He fell to the ground but jumped up and started attacking the man. The other man rushed over. He grabbed Clay and slammed him hard to the ground. Clay grunted and tried to get up, but the man elbowed Clay in the head and he fell back to the ground.

"Clay, get your ass up and stop fighting my men," Frank growled.

Clay glared out him. "Tell your men to back off. Why are they attacking me?"

"They're trying to keep you from leaving. Now, does your sister-in-law know where you keep your files?"

Clay was speechless. He felt something in his throat again, but this time it was fear. He couldn't say a word. Frank gave him a dirty look. His face, long and pinched, stared at him.

Clay glanced at Frank and his men. "Can I have a little space, please?" They nodded and backed up.

"Listen, Frank, I need to hurry and see what's going on."

"You need me to come?"

"Not right now. I'll call you." Clay reached in his car, pulled out a device and scanned his car for GPS trackers. "I'll call you, Frank."

Clay hopped in his car and flew out of the parking lot. He reached into the glove department, pulled out some white powder and put a pile on the middle armrest. He grabbed a handful and snorted it up his nose. He'd stopped using it for a few weeks, but shit if he didn't need it now.

48

Will exited the freeway and followed the directions Meeka gave him. Turn after turn, he began to wonder if she knew where she was going. He didn't take his eyes off the road. Meeka was slumped down in the passenger seat, staring out the window. Will watched how the neighborhoods changed as he drove through several suburbs.

She reached for the bag and pulled out a wig, putting it on, along with some makeup. "You think you're ready?"

"Yes, I have to be," he said. He gripped the steering wheel, his muscles tense.

"Clay keeps his files locked up in this big house."

He looked at her in the dim light. All traces of her hair were tucked up into a sleek blonde bobbed wig.

They drove into another section of royal suburbia. This neighborhood was nestled between rolling hills, shielded from all the lights of the city. Will couldn't help wondering why these people bought these huge houses and put them in places that no one could see. The whole atmosphere screamed money. He thought for just an instant that he could smell it. The houses were bigger than his whole neighborhood.

"You're going to park here, and then we'll walk."

Meeka grabbed the bag and ran up the hill. Will followed close behind. When they came to a wire fence, Meeka pulled out wire cutters from under her loose top and cut the fence enough for them to get through.

"Why are we going this way?" he hissed.

"Because they have a guard gate in front."

They hurried across a grassy area, wet with dew, and made rapid progress in the dark by the dim light of the waxing moon. Meeka scrutinized each house. When they neared a two-story stucco with pillars out front, she said, "That's it."

Golden light shone from the house. People's silhouettes moved around inside, doing the types of things that people did in their own homes when they felt safe. A little girl danced. A woman cupped her hands around her mouth and called for someone. A boy bounded down a staircase, vaulting over the last few steps.

"Okay," Will said, his low voice on the verge of a stutter. "Fuck, I thought you said the coast would be clear and nobody would be home?"

"That's good someone is in there, because if nobody was home, the alarm system would be on. Damn, for a private investigator, you're awfully slow, and a chicken. This is our only chance. Now listen, those are Erica's kids in there. Clay's mother and auntie live there, too."

"What the fuck?" Will looked up at the house, and all he could think of was how many things could go wrong.

The whites of Meeka's eyes glowed in his direction. She watched him, assessing his level of readiness. "Okay, fuck it," he said. "Let's go." They bumped fists.

Meeka took off her shoes.

They crept alongside the house and through the backyard, navigating around bushes and kids' play equipment, doing their best to stay low and in the shadows. On their tiptoes, they attempted to peek in the back window and caught a glimpse of a petite older black woman watching TV with two kids in the other room. They were sharing popcorn, bursting into laughter in unison.

Will headed for his post next to the tall bushes by the patio, but a hand grabbed his shirt and pulled him back.

"Slap me," Meeka whispered. She ripped her shirt, part of the front hanging in a tattered shred over her skirt.

"What the hell?"

"Listen, I know what works, Will. Now, do as I say."

"I don't hit women."

"Shut up and slap me in the face."

"I'm not slapping you."

"We don't have time for this shit." Her hands were on her hips, nostrils flaring. "Pimp-slap me, punch me, just fucking do it."

He pulled back his hand and slapped her across the cheek.

"Harder."

He slapped her one more time, knocking the wig crooked. Tears ran down her face. Lipstick was smeared from her mouth to her ear, and already, a dark hue colored the areas where the skin had bruised on her cheek. He stopped, feeling lousy. He figured she might go ape-shit on him. Instead, she took off running around to the front of the house, her back straight, arms at her sides. She broke the heel off one shoe and threw it into the bushes, just before she turned around and waved him to his post. He was sure he saw a little smile creep onto her face.

He crept forward and waited by the back door. The only light came from the lamps around the swimming pool. He scanned the whole back area, looking into the darkness of the open, manicured lawns that lay between the houses, about five hundred feet apart. Quiet. Nothing moving out there.

He turned back around to look inside the house. He could see all the way to the living room and could hear noises from the television. The three of them hadn't moved. He thought about how all of their money made them feel so safe in their bubble that they didn't even think to pull the curtains closed. He looked at his watch. Eight thirty-seven. No activity from the front door yet.

240

Then it came: a frantic simultaneous door banging and doorbell ringing.

The noise startled the people watching TV. The woman rushed to the door and looked through the peephole. From where Will stood, he could hear Meeka hysterically telling the woman that she had been attacked, that she'd escaped the attacker, and that she thought that maybe he was following her.

"Please," she shouted. "Can I use your phone?"

The older woman let her in the house.

The woman said something to her, but Meeka shook her head no and snatched the phone away. Her face looked worse than Will thought. Blood ran down the left side of her neck, and the sight of it made him feel sick.

She pretended to call 911. She pretended to tell them what happened. She even asked the lady the location of the house before she yelled, "Hurry."

Will could see the kids staring at her in disbelief. He recognized little CJ. No doubt they were wondering why this young woman, with her face the color of ground beef, was in their house.

She asked the woman for something, as she wiped her eyes. The woman rushed out of the room. As soon as she was gone, Meeka asked the kids something, and the girl pointed to the kitchen. Meeka hurried down the hall and into the kitchen. She looked back over her shoulder to make sure the coast was clear and then unlocked the door. She pointed toward the stairs and ran back into the living room.

Will tiptoed through the back of the house. He reached the stairs undetected, just like Meeka had planned.

"Hey, where's your water?" the girl asked her.

"My hands were shaking too much. I didn't want to spill it on your carpet," Meeka answered. "You guys been so nice to me."

"Here, sweetie. This will keep you warm until the police come."

241

The lady's voice faded as Will began his climb to the second story. Will turned right at the top of the carpeted stairs and walked straight through the open door of the master bedroom, just where Meeka had said it would be. In the closet, there was a filing cabinet. He moved the shoes and boxes and lifted the clothes off it. With a trembling finger, he tried the three small keys on the lock. The first didn't fit, but the second worked. The top drawer swung open to reveal four stacks of cash and jewelry, three CD cases, two flash drives and some documents. He pulled a bag from his pocket and stuffed the money and everything but the jewelry into it. He cinched the bag closed, and then he heard the doorbell ring. He leaned up against the edge of the window.

Through the open bedroom window, he heard a man's voice. "Police."

Will set the bag down. His attempts to replace the boxes and shoes in their original positions were hindered by his trembling hands. He couldn't believe the cops had shown up so fast. In his neighborhood, most people bled out before the police or ambulance got there. He hurried down the stairs.

"You guys got here fast," the little girl said. "My auntie and the girl went to the kitchen."

"What girl?" the cop said.

"The one who called you. The one who was attacked," she said.

Will knew he'd never make it to the door without the cop seeing him, so he sprinted back up the steps and into the bedroom.

"Young lady, I'm here because your neighbors said they saw a strange person at your back door."

"Auntie," the girl shouted. "You better get in here."

Will could no longer hear words, just the woman's muted voice. He popped the bedroom screen out and, with one leg over the sill, surveyed his options. There were none. He'd have to jump. He saw movement in the yard and thought he was already busted, but it was Meeka hobbling across the yard, looking around for him. He tossed the bag over the edge of the roof, lowered himself down, hung from the sill to cut the drop in half, and then dropped into a flower bed. Meeka grabbed the bag and started running. He chased after her. The rhythmic squishing of his shoes got faster and faster. He was a freaking cheetah. No way was he going to get caged up. He lost traction on the wet grass and fell flat on his face. Sand gritted in his mouth. He knocked it off his wet face.

"Get up." Meeka's hand was under his arm. "They're coming."

They ran again, traversing the golf course, weaving around sand traps and poles, grunting up slopes and stumbling back down. A glance over his shoulder revealed the flickering of flashlights in the distance.

"There's the car," she whispered urgently. She took a hard left and he followed. Will's thighs burned. His lungs grappled for air. "Get moving."

She opened the passenger door, and Will dove in. In a flash, he'd scooted into the driver's seat. She launched the bag of money and documents toward him and it hit him in the stomach.

"That's for fucking up my face," she said, laughing.

The engine turned over.

"We did it," he shouted. Adrenaline surged through his veins and, combined with the success of their mission, gave him a high unlike anything he'd had in a long time.

A silver Mercedes flew by them. Meeka recognized the car, but Clay was too late. They had beaten him at their own game. They waited until the car passed, then shot out like a rocket in the opposite direction.

49

The light shining through the bars didn't make Erica's cell bright. Bella lay in darkness, curled up in a fetal position, her hands tucked between her legs. Her arms were bruised from all the fighting. She did everything she could to keep Erica safe, and her body felt every last punch and kick of it.

Erica was going through her workout routine. She started with pushups, then ran in place, and when she couldn't breathe anymore, then she hit the floor and did pushups again. She knew that she might spend the rest of her life in jail, and working out gave her focus. Because other times, she tried desperately to have positive thoughts about her kids, playing in the yard, thoughts of when she was little and playing with Lashay. Those times brought a smile to her face.

But these thoughts were constantly interrupted by the ones where she rotted in jail the rest of her life. She collapsed on her bed in exhaustion. Clay had won. He had defeated her.

No, Erica, you can't think that way, you can't think that, she told herself. *Please, God, help me out of here. I will be a better person. I will try to live my life better.*

When the bad thoughts came back, Erica began doubting if there was a God. How could there be? She, who was innocent, was in jail, while Clay, the worst person she'd ever known, was out, living in a big house and more than likely doing a horrible job taking care of her children. If there was a God, why would Clay be living so joyfully, and getting away with it?

I hate him so much right now. She crawled back to the floor and did another twenty pushups, but her frustration consumed her. She tried to keep silent but couldn't. She cried so hard that the tears soaked her jail top. She didn't care who heard her. She thought about ending it all. She could take the wet top, hang it from the side of the toilet and wrap it around her neck and all her problems would be over.

Shaky and exhausted, she stopped, wiped her face with the thin sheet, and sat on the end of the bed. There must be a good reason for all that had happened to her.

She heard the footsteps of a guard and the rattling of keys coming toward her. The big metal key grated in the lock of her cell door, and it opened. Light burst in from the corridor and shone right in Erica's face. She had to put her arm up to block it. She backed up then, thinking maybe they had come to harm her.

"Williams, get up. You're going home."

50

Delo sat behind his desk in his office in the strip mall. It was quiet. Delo looked at Marvin. "You know, we've made a lot of money for the Unit."

"I know, bro, we were very loyal, and we controlled our businesses very well. We were like a family. No one has ever been better than us," Marvin said.

"No, we were great," Delo said, peering out the window overlooking the city.

Marvin looked around the big office, wondering why his brother was having this moment of nostalgia when there was still a lot of shit going down. "Where do we stand now?"

Delo glanced at his wristwatch. "You're right. Clay has become a major liability. Last night somebody hit his mother's house. I don't know how they found it, because we didn't even know where that place was." Marvin smiled, realizing that his older brother had just given him an apology. "So, it's good you and the boys got the sister-in-law when you did," Delo finished.

"Well, let's do what we have to do," Marvin said. "So now someone close to his wife has the files with all our information. Can you believe it? We never knew where this punk had it stashed away, and now they may be going to the feds." He wiped the sweat from his forehead.

"Now we have to hold on to the sister-in-law in exchange for those files before she gets them to the alphabet boys," Delo said. "I know you wanted to kill her after you get your money back, but hold her until we know the next move. Once we get those files, I'll give you the say-so, then we'll take care of everybody."

Marvin raised one eyebrow but didn't say a word. He didn't have to. He sat back. "That's what I'm talking about. It's time to get rid of all this dead weight." He smiled. "We did all the street work anyway. We practically spoon-fed them applesauce and tied a money binky around their necks. I need to take care of us now."

"Marvin, you got greatness in you. I know it." Delo scattered a line of white powder on the coffee table and snorted it up.

"I don't know how you function on that stuff," Marvin said.

Delo laughed. "It's normal. As Clay would say, it's what all us great businessmen do. Follow me."

Marvin followed him through the back of the club to another office. Delo sat down behind the desk. Marvin sat down in a leather chair. "Now listen," he said. "I've gathered all of my clientele and a few of the ones Frank brought in. Also, some of Clay's businesses." He pulled a small drawstring gym bag out of the desk drawer and dumped out the contents. Two bundles of cash sat in front of Marvin. "Frank is going to make a deal for the files. Once he gets the files, you can get rid of the sister-in-law. Then you guys can go get Clay. He'll be at his main house. When you're done with him, we will have a sit-down with Frank, and if he doesn't act right, it's lights out for him."

"What about Clay's wife?"

"She's going to be part of the deal. She'll be free."

"All this shit for nothing." Marvin grabbed his gun off his back hip, raised it, then cocked it. "I'm going to make Clay suffer."

* * *

247

Frank ran up and down the long hallway, losing count of the number of rooms. He looked in Chloe's room, he looked in CJ's room, and still no one. From behind locked doors, he heard hysterical laughter. "Clay. Let me in." He backed up against the opposite wall and launched himself toward the door, kicking it just below the knob.

Clay didn't even look up at him when he came crashing into the room. He was too busy staring at himself in the mirror, laughing. His nose was covered with powder, like he'd just had his face up the Pillsbury Doughboy's ass.

Frank ran to him and started shaking him, but Clay wouldn't stop laughing. He rubbed his hand across the counter and ran his fingers down his face. Frank pushed him away in disgust.

On Clay's lap was a tray with powder, a dollar bill, and a bottle of clear liquor on it. He took the rolled dollar bill, bent forward and used it to snort a line of cocaine.

"Damn, Clay. Like that? You smarter than this, man."

Clay pulled himself up off the floor. "Don't worry, I got it together. I got money everywhere. Fuck Erica. I got women all over the world." He pulled out his cell phone and dialed Kendra's number. No answer. "That bitch never answers the phone when I call."

"I need you to get it together, Clay," Frank said. "I know it's over, but you have get on your toes. Marvin's pissed at you, and there's no telling what he's going to do. You need to get your shit together and get out of here."

"Fuck, Marvin, I have security guards at the gate and more on the way, and if he wants some, tell him to come get some," he slurred out.

"That's the alcohol and drugs talking, Clay, because you know if Marvin and Delo want you dead, you're going to wind up dead."

"I have the wall up, and the security booth set up. Nobody can get in here unless I want them to."

"Are the kids still at the Morada house?"

"Why would I have my kids there after it was robbed? My kids are somewhere nobody will find."

"I think you should just let Erica have the kids and you can start over, bro."

"Fuck that—she will never beat me. I'm the king."

"Clay, if something happens to you, she'll get the kids. I know they're somewhere with your mother, and she'll bring them back if something happens to you."

"Nothing is going to happen to me. I have twenty heavily armed men on the way, and in two days, I'll be long gone, my friend."

"Where you going?"

"One of them islands, bro."

Frank turned to Clay. "When?"

"When I'm ready and I'm finished with all my business here."

"So, until then, you going to stay cooped up in this house?"

"Yes, until I know everything's safe."

Frank glared at him. College boy was going to make a run for it and leave everyone to clean up his shit like always.

"So she's really going free?"

"Yes, bro, she's won. You lost."

"She hasn't won anything. She will never get the kids, or this house. I found me a new lady, and I'm going to be with her. Erica can't have me back."

"Yeah, I'm sure Erica doesn't want you back, Clay."

Clay missed half of what Frank was telling him. He kept dialing and hanging up, then dialing again. "I can't reach Kendra. I want to tell her how much I love her. I called her a million times, and she's nowhere to be found. Do you think you can put out an APB on her? You're a cop."

"All this shit going on and you thinking about pussy?"

"It's not like that. I want to be with her."

"You've never changed." He shook his head and walked out the door.

51

Lashay sat like a lump in the chair, staring at the ceiling and praying to God. She tried to make noise, but nothing came out. Marvin entered the room. She glared at him, and he walked over and shoved her chair around, nearly toppling her back to the floor. The door burst open behind him, and he spun around and stood right in front of Lashay with his back to her, blocking her from view.

"Where's Lashay?" a woman's voice demanded.

"Not yet, bitch. Do you have the package for me?"

The strong female voice was familiar to Lashay, but she could see the legs charging toward her, and then Marvin was pushed to the side. Meeka stood there.

"Are you okay?" Meeka said.

Will ran over to her and hugged her.

"Look what we have here, boys. Shaft and his helper," Marvin said, looking from one stranger to the other. They ignored him.

Meeka's cell phone rang. She answered. "Right. Okay, we're good." She hung up and looked at Will, giving him the okay.

"Untie her right now."

"Give me the files first."

Will threw the envelope over to Marvin, who caught it and began examining the papers.

Meeka untied Lashay.

Marvin looked up from the documents, a grin on his face. "This is what we want. Thank you very much."

Meeka took Lashay's hand. "Let's get out of here."

They headed for the door, but Marvin and his goons stepped in front of them. "You're not going anywhere until I get the rest of my money."

Will tossed him a bag. "Courtesy of Clay Williams."

Marvin pulled out the cash. He shook his head. He looked at the goon and walked out. Twenty seconds later, he came back in with the guns and silencers.

Meeka, Will, and Lashay all backed up against the wall as Marvin and the two of his goons started twisting on the silencers.

"Nobody gets away with stealing from me," Marvin said as he raised the gun and pointed it at the three of them.

Meeka spoke up. "Are you sure you want to do this?"

"Yes, I am sure." Marvin smiled. "I've been waiting for this for a long time."

"I don't think you want to do that, because I bet you want to make it out of here alive," Will said.

Marvin and his goons looked at each other. "Oh, what, you got some guns or bombs in them titties?"

"No, but if I was you, I'd take a look out that window."

One of the goons walked over and peered out. "Oh, shit, boss, you won't believe this shit."

Marvin walked over and looked out. He shook his head and nodded for the goons to move away from the door.

Will and Meeka cradled Lashay as they walked toward the door. Meeka looked back over her shoulder. "We're not the ones you want. Who you want is barricaded up in his big house in Brookside Estates."

Outside, Lashay couldn't believe her eyes. All over the yard, lying on the ground military-style, were women dressed in army fatigues, pointing rifles at the house. She looked on the roofs of the buildings across the street and saw women lined up in sniper positions. Another thirty women, dressed all in black and wearing purple berets, walked toward the house. In the middle of the street stood Big John. Next to him was Mrs. Porter, wearing a scarf on her head and dark shades, with a thin cigar protruding from her mouth.

52

Lashay took a deep breath to quell her nervousness. This was it. The first time she would be able to hug Erica in several months. She watched the front door open and Erica walked in, holding a brown paper bag. Lashay ran up to her and hugged her hard. The bag fell to the floor. They jumped up and down in excitement, then hugged again. The sisters grinned at each other, barely able to contain their emotions. Tears streamed down their faces. "I love you," they said in unison, then squeezed each other tighter. Erica flung her arms around Will. Lashay had told her everything he'd done to help her. He was a man of his word, and she was so happy he was back in her life.

Shorty came into the room on crutches and cleared his throat. She broke off her hug from Will.

"Shorty," she said, hugging him.

"Girl, you better have more to go around," Meeka said.

"Thank you," she cried, grabbing Meeka. Tears welled up in her eyes. "I'm just so happy. I can't believe I'm free, and I'm here with you guys."

The friends smiled, happy that Erica and Lashay were safe and together again. They walked over to the sofas.

"Are you hungry?" Meeka asked.

"I just want to see my kids."

The friends looked at each other.

Will spoke. "Right now, Clay's guards have the whole house under watch."

"He's finally putting that empty guardhouse to use," Lashay said. "The kids aren't in the house. We don't know where they are, but we know they're with Clay's mother or Auntie Mena. They were at that big mansion in Morada Estates. He moved them somewhere, but no one knows where."

"I want to see my kids."

"Let me make a few phone calls and find out if anything's come up," Will said and ducked out of the room.

Twenty minutes later, he walked in with a bag and handed Erica a manila envelope.

"What's this?" she asked. She ripped it open. As soon as she saw what was in it, she dropped it and clamped her hand over her mouth. She slid the pictures toward Lashay.

"Those are the masters," Will said.

"That motherfucker." Lashay stood up and paced around the room. She couldn't believe what was in the photos. "Does anyone have any matches?"

"I have a lighter." Meeka pulled a lighter out of her inner pocket and handed it to Lashay, who took it and all ten of the pictures to the sink. She proceeded to burn each photo, one by one. When she finished, she ran the cold water and the remains disappeared down the drain. She walked back to the table, wiping her hands together in a gesture of good riddance.

Shorty, Meeka, and Will stood silent. Erica slid out the documents and examined them.

"Frank didn't directly say it, but Clay was behind you losing your baby," Will said.

Her forehead bunched. "Does anybody know what mifepristone is?"

Meeka googled the name. When she finished, she stared at Erica.

"What?"

She paused for a second. "It's medication to induce an abortion."

Meeka sighed and looked at Erica. Will shook his head and sat down on the couch. Lashay, furious, didn't say a word. She grabbed the other envelope and pulled out the contents.

"Clay is a ruthless, gutless lowlife," Will said.

"Tell me something I don't know," Lashay said.

"We need to find my kids," Erica whispered. "I need my kids. They need their mother."

"Our best bet is to put a gun to Clay's head," Shorty said.

Lashay's eyebrows shot up. "You think so?"

Will shook his head. "That could be dangerous. The house is surrounded by guards."

Lashay put her hand on her hip. "You're the private eye. Come up with something."

Will laughed. "I'm a private eye, but that doesn't mean I have special powers that allow me to walk past armed guards."

"Well, then, where the hell are my niece and nephew, Shaft?"

Erica gave her a look.

Will's phone rang again. He looked at it. "That's Frank." Will walked over to a quieter area and spoke into the phone.

Shorty stood by Erica. "Everything's going to be okay. You'll see your kids, even if I have to take out this whole city." Erica patted him on the cheeks.

"That was Frank. He said Clay is out of the Unit. They're just waiting for Marvin to make a move on Clay's house."

"How does that get my kids back? They can't do anything to him until I know where my kids are," Erica screamed. She put her hands over her face and started crying. Lashay patted her on her back.

"Clay's staying inside, finishing up whatever he needs to do. Frank said even if he gets by Marvin's men, they'll track him down," Will said.

Erica glanced at Will. "He's a cop. They can just go and arrest him."

"They have to wait and see if Clay has anything else on the Blafia. They're working on it now, that's all I can say."

"All this time, Clay was working for organized crime. I had no idea." She looked at everybody in the room and shook her head. Silence prevailed for a brief moment.

Lashay stood up. "Well, at least that no-good punk is out, and they will get him soon."

Someone's phone rang again. Meeka pulled hers out and looked at it. "Oops, wrong one." She then reached and pulled out another phone, saw who was calling, and smiled. "I've got an idea."

53

Clay grabbed another bottle from the office bar, twisted off the top, and took a swig. It tasted harsh and burned going down, but as soon as the liquid hit his stomach, he felt warm all over. He could barely stand, he was so dizzy. He set the bottle back down in front of the family photo, the one of him, Erica, and the kids. She'd framed it and given it to him soon after it was taken. He picked up the photo and held it in his hand, remembering the happy vacation they'd taken just two years earlier. It was the last time he'd been happy as a family man.

He sat in his desk chair with a drink in his left hand. His hair stuck out in random spikes, and he hadn't changed his clothes in two days. A bottle of whisky sat on the desk. He stared out the window, unmoving, watching his hired guns walk around the yard. He guzzled from the bottle, then picked up the phone, dialed a number, and held the phone to his ear.

"Please, Kendra, call me back. I haven't heard from you in days," he said, then hung up. Thirty seconds later, it was back in his hand. "Kendra, I need to see you. Please call me back." He slammed it down.

Clay paused, and then the phone rang. He lifted the phone

and spoke into the receiver. "Hello? Oh my, I haven't heard from you in awhile. Don't worry about what happen at the movies other night."

"I'm good, when can I see you again?

"Okay, fine, yes I would love that. Come over after you get off work. Yes, I can't wait to see you. I miss you so much." Clay smiled and hung up the phone. His despondency lifted like magic by the thought of his favorite pastime.

Clay staggered down the hallway, unbuttoning his shirt to take a shower. He wanted to be fresh and clean. He had a pretty, hot young thing coming to visit him. He hoped the shower would sober him up a little. He needed Kendra to take his mind off the mess that was happening in his world. He didn't care what anybody thought or what was going on. This was his time to get his nut. He hadn't had a good one in a while. He would profess his love to Kendra and ask her to leave with him and his kids.

* * *

Marvin and Nina sat in the Mercedes SUV with one of his men in the backseat. They'd parked down from Clay's house on Maple Street. The top of the house rose behind the high gate, and the unfinished guardhouse stood before them, blocking their way. Two armed guards stood in front of it.

Money picked up his burner. "Huh? Huh? … Okay, I got it … Uh-huh." He hung up. "There are about twenty armed men all around the house, with three on each side and a few at the guard gate. College boy is inside by himself."

Marvin never took his eyes off the guard gate. "When the time is right, have the boys get into position. I think we can have twenty guys come from the back and ten from each side while we go right through that front gate."

His fists curled in tight balls. He had allowed Clay to use him in his escapades. He and Delo had orchestrated the naked pictures of Clay's women. He was the one who'd helped plant drugs on his wife. He was the one who had gotten the drugs for the pregnant women on the orders of Delo, but it had all come from Clay. Marvin controlled the street soldiers, Delo had the connection to the drugs, and Frank had the protection from the police. But Clay's vices outweighed his talent. He was no longer needed. Now that Delo and Frank had made a deal with a new associate who could get the business part of it done, they'd given him the okay to get rid of Clay. They said whoever was left standing today would run with it. Marvin was going to make sure he was the last man standing. No way would he let a weak college boy, a fucking taxman, beat him in some street shit. Hell, he'd even heard Clay wasn't a real CPA; he'd just passed a little tax preparer test years ago.

The more Marvin thought about Clay, the angrier he got. Clay couldn't control his habits. He had the worst kind of habits a man could have. A man that couldn't control his dick always ended up in trouble in this kind of business. Using drugs and women was what had brought down many big outfits. Marvin had seen it with his own eyes. He'd seen it when Big Willy had snitched on his whole outfit just because his second-in-command, his right-hand man, was sleeping with his wife. Even old man Gary had lost his crew back in the day because he'd started using his own supply. A man with a habit, any habit, couldn't be trusted. Marvin had no time for men like that.

A car driving by broke his thoughts. He watched the car pull up to Clay's guard gate.

"Did you see that, boss?" Bull said.

"Yes. We'll wait."

They watched a beautiful woman speak to the guards at the gate from her car window. The woman got out as two other guards came over to check the inside of the car. One had a mirror on a long stick with which he could look under the car. The woman, dressed in a double-breasted suit with high heels, was patted down by the guard, who ran his hands all over her body. When they finished, the woman got back in her car. The gate opened, and she drove through.

"Did you see that?" Nina said.

Marvin shook his head. "This motherfucker is in the middle of endless drama, and all he's thinking about is pussy?"

54

The woman took a deep breath and drove up to Clay's gate. The brick fence around the house was massive, surrounded by a tall black stone wall with torches instead of lamps, like a castle. She drove through the main gate, which opened by itself, and into the compound. As she got nearer, the real magnificence of the house struck her. It was a two-story L-shaped structure that had a four-car garage on one side and a perfectly manicured lawn with a marble fountain that reeked of the money and opulent lifestyle of its owner. She started feeling nervous. At first, she didn't know why. She'd been to the place many times before.

She rang the doorbell but realized the door was open. She looked around, remembering the place. The walls reflected the light in a way that made them look more like cashmere than drywall. The wall-to-wall hardwood floors, crown molding, and white marble accents made the huge house seem to unfold like the arms of a powerful yet kindly emperor. She couldn't believe she had fallen for him. How could she ever have looked forward to seeing this man? She remembered how her heart would flutter whenever he smiled at her. She sat down on the couch.

Clay came from down the hallway. "Hello Kendra, you sexy lady," he said as he walked in front of the couch and looked at her. "What the fuck." He dropped the drink in his hand and alcohol splattered on his smoking jacket and black slippers that looked more like Delo's Ferragamo shoes. He was obviously ready for some love action.

"Hello, Clay," Erica said.

"Erica?" Clay's mouth barely moved as he choked on his words. He was trembling as he tried not to step on the broken glass.

"So why are you here all by yourself with guards and shit? You piss off some woman?" She laughed.

"What the fuck are you doing here, bitch?"

"Relax, Clay. Anger is a bad emotion. You can't think right when you're mad. Where are the kids?"

"They're where they're supposed to be, not with you."

She spread her hands across her skirt. "Wrong answer. Now I asked you a question nicely. Next time, I won't be so nice."

Clay jumped up and ran into the kitchen. He reached for the biggest knife he could find. When he looked up, Erica was standing next to him. He fumbled with the knife. She slammed the bottom of the shoe heel into the side of his rib cage. Clay grabbed his side as blood squirted all over him.

"I'm going to ask you again. Where are my kids?"

He stumbled down the hallway, screaming. She ran behind him and tripped him. It was too easy to mess with him, in his high and drunken state. He hit the floor and moaned. She rushed over to him and knelt on the floor. She reached for him, but he pushed her back, knocking the heel out of her hand. His face was twisted in an expression she'd never seen on him before, a combination of pain, fear, and panic. His open mouth produced nothing but staccato gasps. Struggling to breathe, his hazel eyes no longer sparkled. She tried to hold him still, but he kept pushing her off, his arms flailing one minute and grabbing his neck the next. She grabbed him again, and this time he didn't fight her; instead, she looked into his eyes and pulled him close to her. He was getting weak. His lips moved, but still there was no sound. She pulled him closer.

"You killed my baby in me, motherfucker. Fuck you."

Clay said nothing, although he tried. His eyes held panic. She held him down against the plush sculptured carpet and watched the bright red blood soak into the bone-white fibers. His nose was running. He sniffled, and the leftover cocaine gave him a quick adrenaline rush.

He flipped her over and held her down. "I'm going to fucking kill you," he sputtered out. He choked her as she frantically reached around for the other heel. His fingers were inches away from choking her.

She got the heel and plunged it into his other side. He rolled over like a ragged doll. She pressed the end of the heel into his neck. He tried to raise one hand in the air. Erica pressed the heel harder.

"Don't move."

He didn't move. "Erica. Come on, love. You know I never meant to hurt you. You and my children, man, you guys are my world. All the stuff I was going through, shit, it was hard. But guess what? It's made me be a better man. And that's what I'm going to be: a better husband, provider, and protector for you and the kids. Come on, Erica." Clay used words like a counterfeiter used ink.

"You have lied to me, cheated on me for years. I believed you every time you said you would stop. I have no reason to believe you now. I have every reason to kill you. Every time I confronted you, you threatened you were going to take my kids. And then you set me up and take my kids. Nigga, please. Shut the fuck up. I'm going to ask you one last time, Clay, where are my kids?"

He pinched his mouth shut.

"You stubborn motherfucker." She stuck him in the thigh with the heel.

He screamed as he fell to the floor, clutching his thigh. "Doctor, I need a doctor. Please, please, get me to the hospital."

"Tell me where the kids are, or you'll die on this cold, hard tile."

"Get my phone."

"I can stab your other leg. Tell me where the kids are."

"No," he moaned. "My mother has them. I'll call her. It's in my office on my desk."

She ran and grabbed his phone. "Call her and tell her to bring them to the hospital. We'll make a trade."

He nodded. "Okay, okay." He dialed and then heard a voice. "My mom is going to meet us at the hospital with the kids." He called the guard booth. "My Beamer will be leaving. Let it go through."

Erica wiped the blood off her with the soft knitted throw on the back of the sofa. She glanced at her house one last time before she helped walk him out to the car. He didn't even try to fight her. She pulled out of the garage, drove through the open gate, and gunned it when she hit the street. Erica, glanced over at the Mercedes SUV parked on Maple Street. The squealing tires made the people in the Benz look at her. She noticed the man mumble, *What the fuck is going on?* She didn't care who was in the car. She couldn't wait to see her kids.

55

Erica sat in the waiting room watching TV. She hoped she looked as good as she felt.

A man in a crisp white shirt and tie came out. "Mrs. Williams?"

"Yes?"

His face showed some relief. "Your husband is recovering from surgery. They were able to stop the bleeding, and it looks like they were successful. There should be no major damage to the nerves." Erica's heart felt like it had stopped beating. Her knees buckled. The doctor caught her before she hit the floor. "Maybe you should rest for a while in the waiting room."

She nodded. Erica needed to see her husband for herself.

Her phone rang. She answered it. "This is Erica. Where are you guys? Okay, I'm on the second floor. I'll see you in a few."

The nurses wheeled Clay's stretcher down the hallway. An oxygen mask covered his mouth, but his wide-open eyes fixed on her. She followed the stretcher into the room. She looked over him for a few minutes, letting the moment rest on her while she gathered her thoughts. When the nurses left the room, she rose and stood over him. His eyes were big, and she guessed he might be thinking his luck with women wasn't going so well anymore. He closed his eyes and turned his head away from her.

Erica bent closer and whispered in his ear. She spoke the words that had been growing in her since her stay in jail. "Right now, you have people who want to kill you. They have no need for you anymore. However, I can save you. Me and my new friends have set up a deal for you. You get out of any business you were in, give all your business to your associates, and you can keep your accounting business. You can even keep the house we lived in Brookside. I don't want anything to do with that house. However, I do want the one your mother lives in. That's my new home with my kids, since they already have rooms there. Your mother can move in with you."

Clay's eyes opened, and he looked at Erica like she'd lost her mind. He could only shake his head the slightest bit, but his eyes shot daggers at her.

"Let me explain it to you another way, then. It's either that, or you die."

Erica pressed the button on the side of his bed, raising his head just enough. She moved out of the way. Clay could see out the door and down the hallway where Mrs. Porter, Frank, Delo, Will, and Lashay all stood, talking and laughing. Clay saw the woman in a full-length black coat. Beauty oozed from her pores. His eyes grew round as he watched her walk up to Lashay and give her a hug. She winked at him. Erica waved her into the room.

"Hey, Meeka, can you give these papers to Will?"

Meeka smiled at Clay. "Have we met?"

"Do we have a deal?" Erica asked.

Clay nodded, defeat evident on his face. Erica knew the site of Meeka, he realized he had been played.

"One more thing," Erica continued. "I need to say this to you, Clay. I now realize that in order to get forgiveness, I have to forgive all those who have wronged me. Even the one who wronged me the most. So, I forgive you. May you live a long, happy life."

She left the room and shook hands with everybody in the hallway. She went to the front of the hospital, where reporters swarmed her. With Lashay and Will at her side, she made it outside and saw Clay's mother and Aunt Mena holding Chloe and CJ's small hands.

"Mommy, Mommy," Chloe yelled as she ran up to her with tears in her eyes. "Where you been? I missed you so much."

Little CJ was behind Chloe, clapping and jumping. He had a big smile on his face. "Mommy."

Erica wiped the tears from Chloe's face. Erica pulled her two children close to her, and with tears of joy running down her face, she picked up CJ and pushed through all the reporters, holding tight to Chloe's hand. Her kids would never leave her sight again.

She lifted her head in a pure scream of joy. She had no time for broken men. They'd done it.

www.ingramcontent.com/pod-product-compliance
Lightning Source LLC
Chambersburg PA
CBHW070902180626
46817CB00003B/886